best friends

LAZARUS AND JESUS

best friends

LAZARUS AND JESUS

JAMES "JERRY" JOHN

VOLUME 2

TATE PUBLISHING
AND ENTERPRISES, LLC

Published by Tate Publishing & Enterprises, LLC
127 E. Trade Center Terrace | Mustang, Oklahoma 73064 USA
1.888.361.9473 | www.tatepublishing.com

Tate Publishing is committed to excellence in the publishing industry. The company reflects the philosophy established by the founders, based on Psalm 68:11,
"The Lord gave the word and great was the company of those who published it."

Book design copyright © 2014 by Tate Publishing, LLC. All rights reserved.
Cover design by Joseph Emnace
Interior design by Joana Quilantang

Published in the United States of America

ISBN: 978-1-63268-964-1
1. Fiction / Religious
2. Fiction / Christian / General
14.10.23

Contents

Introduction

The story goes on of the Christian faith and bold service in the name of Jesus Christ. And after this book is completed it will continue to march forward through the ages in the lives of all those who are believers and followers of the Son of God and the Son of man.

I hope you will read this volume with a new openness in your mind and spirit to the words of Jesus as seen through the eyes of Lazarus, best friend, believer, and follower. Generally, the words of Jesus are from the Gospel according to Matthew. It was this book that served as a witness to the Jew of the first by fulfilling prophecies. For Lazarus, a faithful Israelite and follower of Jehovah, the Creator and King of the Universe, this would have been very important.

Jesus, Son of God and Son of man, challenged the believer and the non-believer. He still does.

I hope you will be challenged in a new way by the setting in which I have cast Jesus. If you disagree with me, that is wonderful. Follow your own story line and be a witness for your faith with others around you. If you doubt that Jesus is the Son of God and the Son of man, that is an opportunity for you to do some serious study and evaluation beyond this book. Always remember, "doubt" is meant to be a pathway leading toward discovery and not a jail in which you hide or are locked away from life. It is in the shadow of doubt that you will make life's most exciting and affirmative discoveries.

So, read with an open mind, and in your own mind, with the strength of your faith, be the editor that puts new meaning and direction to the words of this book. Become a "story-teller" carrying the good news to family and friends.

—James M. John

A Call for Decision
and Action

Jesus delighted in his visits to his home in Nazareth. He seldom went and he never remained very long. He preferred to stay hidden so that crowds would not be seeking him out. He would almost always arrive in Nazareth soon after dark. He would walk the little back alleys and slip in the front door by himself.

I always made an effort to stay with him and if any of the disciples were with him, they would go to homes outside of town or Nathaniel would go on to Cana with John or another of the disciples.

Jesus would remain almost a week with his family in Nazareth. He would stay in the house and visit with his mother. Other family members would join them from time to time but in a very nonintrusive way. Jesus and his mother would spend much time in long conversations and prayer while the twins busied themselves with laundry and preparing meals for the family. At this particular time when Nathaniel returned from Cana; Jesus, John, and Nathaniel left immediately for Capernaum.

When he returned to Peter's house, there was a surprise for some of his followers. A considerable number of people, both men and women had been circulating with Jesus since the time of his baptism at the Jordan. Most of them spoke of themselves as Jesus's disciples, but when he returned from Nazareth Jesus designated twelve official disciples: *Simon, who is called Peter, and Andrew his brother; James the son of Zebedee, and John his brother; Philip and Nathaniel; Thomas and Matthew the tax collector; James the son of Alphaeus, and Thaddeus; Simon the Cananaean and Judas Iscariot.*

It was a very exciting moment for those chosen. However, perhaps, sadly, there were some followers who decided to leave and return to their homes and jobs, but there were others who remained saying they still considered themselves disciples, to be learners sitting at the feet of Jesus. They would remain faithful to Jesus and hope one day to be included in the inner circle.

I learned all of this when Philip and Nathaniel appeared at our house in Bethany. They told us the specific call Jesus gave to them and his challenge. *Jesus called his disciples to him and gave them authority over unclean spirits, to cast them out, and to heal all manner of sickness and all manner of disease.* Jesus specifically told them not to go to any Gentile areas or Samaria. This outreach mission was to be a ministry to *the lost sheep of the house of Israel.*

They were to go anywhere they decided in teams of two, preach the good news, and proclaim that the Kingdom of God is at hand. They were to take *no gold or silver or copper* for their support, but they were to depend upon the support of the people they touched.

Their ministries were to be offered in the name of the living Lord of Life. Jesus also warned them that it was possible *they would be hated for his name's sake,* so it was important that they be *as wise as serpents yet as innocent as doves.* They must *endure and always remember they will be saved* and the Spirit would give them the words they needed.

Philip and Nathaniel decided to come to the area of Bethany, and they moved in and out of homes, preached in the open air, and discovered an amazing power at their command. To both individuals and families, they brought peace, comfort, forgiveness, healing, hope, power, and even judgment to all those they touched in the name of God our Eternal Father and King.

Mama, Martha, Mary, and I often accompanied them wherever they went, and were thrilled by the special spiritual gifts they exhibited. At times, I thought we were in the presence of Jesus himself.

Jesus had warned them that they might be rejected by some, perhaps, thrown into prison by local authorities, but they must bear what the world thrusts upon them, and Jesus reminded them that he would have to do the same. There are those who would kill the body, but Jesus had promised them that the spirit would prevail.

We listened to Philip and Nathaniel and marveled at their challenge to those around them. They called people to claim the righteousness of the Kingdom of God and to become a follower of Jesus, God's Son. The opportunities for ministry kept coming to them. There were always enough people to fill our house and Mama was patient and receptive. They would preface anything they said with "And Jesus says to you…" It reminded me of Jesus as they healed and taught; and during the evening hours, at our home, they often talked about what Jesus had told them:

> He that taketh not his cross, and
> Followeth after me, is not worthy of me.
> He that findeth his life sall lose it: and
> he that loseth his life for my sake shall
> find it. He that receiveth you receiveth
> me, and he that receiveth me receiveth
> him that sent me.
> He that receiveth a prophet in the name
> of the prophet shall receive a prophet's

> reward; and he that receiveth a
> righteous man in the name of a righteous
> man-shall receive a rrighteous man's
> reward. And whosoever shall give to
> drink unto one of these little ones a cup of
> cold water only in the name of a disciple,
> verily I say unto you, he shall in no wise
> lose his reward. (Matt.10:40-42 KJV)

Jesus had told them that while they were out preaching he would also be preaching among the cities of Galilee.

Philip then told us that the morning they were to leave on this mission of proclamation, the disciples of John the Baptizer appeared as a group before Jesus. They had been in the area watching and listening to him for days and John who was still in prison, wanted to know:

> Art thou he that should come, or do we look
> for another. (Matthew 11:3 KJV)

Jesus did not debate or challenge them. He walked over to them, and in his own quiet way, he simply smiled and said,

> Go and shew John again those things
> which ye do hear and see: The blind
> receive their sight, and the lame walk,
> lepers are cleansed, and the deaf hear,
> the dead are raised up, and the poor have
> The gospel preached to them. And blessed
> is he, whosoever shall not be offended in
> Me. (Matt. 11:4b-6 KJV)

Philip and Nathaniel, both, said they knew several of John's disciples quite well, and they openly mingled with those that came to hear Jesus. There was some dissension among them, but the majority agreed that they would report what Jesus had asked. All of them were both amazed and pleased that Jesus had openly said that *there hath not risen one greater than John (Matt. 11:11b KJV).*

Most of them decided to leave and make their report to John, a few decided to stay and listen further to what Jesus was saying. Both Philip and Nathaniel agreed it would be interesting to return to Galilee and see exactly who of John's disciples were still there watching and listening to Jesus.

They continued their mission with marvelous success. Soon, it became time for them to return to Capernaum and give their report. Every day they had become more and more excited about the power and authority they commanded, and they boldly used it to minister to many people and share the blessing of God in Jesus's name.

When the day came for them to leave, I told Mama that I would join them on their return. She agreed. I suggested that I might bring Jonathan back with me and this excited both Martha and Mary.

The three of us left and decided to go right through Jerusalem and stop at the Temple. The city was packed with people. We were almost to the Temple itself when we came upon a young man crawling on the street on his hands and knees. Philip reached in his purse for a coin to give him, but Nathaniel stopped, kneeled, and asked him where he was going. "To the Temple," he responded, "in hopes that my prayers will be heard and the use of my legs will return."

Nathaniel asked him, "Have you ever heard of Jesus of Nazareth?"

"Yes, where is he? He can help me. I know he can help me," he was almost yelling. A few curious people gathered around us. "Please, take me to Jesus."

"He is in the city of Capernaum in Galilee; but we are his disciples, and he has given us the gift of his healing power. Are you willing to believe and receive?" asked Nathaniel.

"Yes, yes, please," tears started flowing in the man's face.

Nathaniel stood and took one hand of the lame man, and Philip reached down for the other. Nathaniel was praying and I seemed to see that same quiet glow that Jesus had in just such a moment of great spiritual intensity. The young man slowly raised one leg and put his foot on the ground as they steadied him. Nathaniel was still praying quietly, and the young man seemed to join him. Then with an unsteady effort he stood. He continued to hold tightly to Philip and Nathaniel.

"What is your name?" asked Philip.

"Saul," the young man answered.

People began pushing in, and they gathered around him in amazement. We quickly gathered that he was a familiar figure at the Temple, and always praying loudly for strength for his legs.

"Saul, you will be in our prayers that you will use your new strength to God's Glory," said Nathaniel.

They released his hands as Philip said, "Go now into the Temple, and give thanks to God for your new wholeness, and may God's peace and power go with you."

The three of us backed off a little ways and listened as some began questioning Saul about what had happened. He seemed a little confused, but then he turned and marched toward the Temple. We turned and walked away.

"Lazarus, how do we get out of the city and on the road north?" asked Philip.

We moved quickly and were soon beyond Jerusalem. Nathaniel stopped and turned facing that city, and Philip joined him in leaving a blessing of peace on that great city of David. Then we were off and on our way toward Sebaste. We had walked for about an hour and were getting a little tired. Both, Nathaniel and Philip, wanted to stop for a rest time.

There to my left was the same path that led toward the area we had intended to use for camping years ago. I suggested that this was a good place and we walked through the olive grove to the camp. Nathaniel and Philip quickly found a place to sit and I walked back to the low cliff and found that same cool spring with fresh water and filled my small urn and took some to Philip and Nathaniel. Then I looked for the path that had mysteriously appeared and had saved the three of us from those Roman soldiers when Jesus and I had returned to search for Aaron. I offered a prayer of gratitude for that path, and promised to never look for it again. It had been a special door opened by God to protect three desperate boys and my heart was filled with humble gratitude.

After a brief rest, I suggested that we move on a little further up the road, and that I knew a family, who might let us stay for the night. When we got there I knocked on the door and Daniel was pleased to see me. I introduced Nathaniel and Philip as followers and disciples of Jesus. We were invited in and I told Daniel and Rachael that we were in need of a place to spend the night.

Rachael said, "All of our children are grown and gone, and we have plenty of room. This delighted Philip and Nathaniel. While Rachael prepared something to eat, Daniel began recalling our stay years ago. This interested both of the disciples because it was a part of the history of Jesus when he was very young.

Daniel asked me, "Do you remember that I bought that donkey and cart that belonged to Jesus?"

"Yes," I said, "That was very hard for Jesus because Methuselah was a special friend and family pet to him."

"Wait just a moment," said Philip, "Who or what are we talking about, a donkey or a person?" The three of us laughed and then Daniel explained.

"It was Jesus's pet donkey named Methuselah," said Daniel, 'and after they left I was sorry I had made the deal. That donkey brayed all night for weeks and refused to work for me. It was one of our children that finally made friends with him and he settled in at home with us."

"Well, Jesus said he was a funny donkey," I said.

"Both funny and very stubborn and a little crazy, but he became a helpful friend through our children," Daniel said.

Nathaniel laughed, "That is a great story which I will always cherish, but why did Jesus feel it necessary to sell him if he was such a pet."

"Now, that is a much longer story," I said. The day before, we had a frightening experience with some Roman soldiers who tried to kidnap the small children. Our parents' felt they would have sold them as slaves. The men and older boys actually fought them off and the soldiers fled.

We were able to release their horses and we frightened those animals with fire sticks which we had dragged out of our campfire. Those horses bolted down the road carrying with them all of the weapons and gear of those soldiers. The soldiers ended up running down the road to get their horses back. We were afraid that if they did round up those mounts, they would return and take out their vengeance on all of us.

We left that campsite very quickly and came north on the same road we traveled today. We stopped here and Daniel and Rachael made a place for us to stay in a little shed behind the house. Uncle Joseph, Jesus's father, was afraid that the soldiers would still be looking for us the next day and might identify us by the donkey and cart. Daniel and had expressed an interest in buying both the donkey and cart, so they sold both, and they made their way home carrying their personal things on their back. My father and I returned to Bethany. Those events are well imprinted in my mind, and sometimes I even dream about that experience in my life."

"I cannot imagine Jesus fighting, even as a young boy," said Philip.

"He didn't," I said, "He was walking some distance in the woods looking for some special bird that he had seen. He missed the whole thing. You can imagine his surprise when he returned to camp and we were furiously packing to leave when we should have been getting ready to spend the night resting."

Those memories so warmed my heart that when Rachael called us to eat, I did not want to be bothered with food.

Nathaniel raised his hands and Philip joined him as Nathaniel prayed:

"God of peace and hope, bless our fellowship and this food that has been prepared. Teach us how we can be peacemakers in a world filled with fear and violence. May we be your radiant lights of hope bringing joy and kindness in this world of sin. Pour out your blessing upon all those who are fearful and bring quiet to their spirits and strength to their minds. May the gift of your peace rest upon this home. To your glory we pray. Amen.

We had an evening of rich fellowship and both disciples shared with Daniel, Rachael, and myself some of the teachings of Jesus.

Nathaniel said, "It was interesting to me when Jesus warned us:

> Beware of false prophets, which come to
> you in sheep's clothing, but inwardly they
> are ravening wolves. Ye shall know them
> by their fruits. Do men gather grapes of
> Thorns, or figs of thistles?
> Even so every good tree brings forth good
> fruit; but a corrupt tree bringeth forth evil
> fruit.
> A good tree cannot bring forth evil fruit,
> neither can a corrupt tree bring forth good
> fruit.
> Every tree that bringeth not forth good
> fruit is hewn down, and cast into the fire.
> Wherefore by their fruits ye shall know them.
> (Matthew 7:15-20)

When he stopped we all sat and thought about what he had shared. Daniel asked, "Is he telling us that some teachers of the Torah cannot be trusted? That would be very-scary and disturbing."

Nathaniel said, "There is much more to it than that. Many things make us sick, and there are teachers whose message is so distorted that it can make us sick spiritually and emotionally. So Jesus is clearly saying to us, beware, stay away from those leaders."

"Nathaniel, I remember when Jesus talked with us about that," said Philip, "and I kept thinking about some teachers who dress fancy to be seen and only make friends with people of influence."

"I know a Rabbi that fits that picture," said Daniel, "I have always been a little suspicious and afraid of him."

"Then be alert," said Nathaniel. "There are always a lot of choices in teachers and we are responsible for making the right choices."

"Life is all about choices, every day, every hour, choices. Jesus has talked about this from the very beginning. Daniel, I wish you could have heard some of his teaching sessions. Jesus always admonishes and urges us to be better, and do just a little more than is ever expected of us. Nathaniel do you remember Jesus saying,

> Whosoever heareth these sayings of
> mine, I will liken unto a wise man,
> which built his house upon a rock.
> The rain descended, and the floods
> came, and the winds blew, and beat
> upon that house; and it fell not; for
> it was founded upon a rock.
> and every one that heareth these
> sayings of mine, and doeth them not,
> shall be likened unto a foolish man,
> which built his house upon the sand,
> And the rain descebded, and the floods
> came, and the winds blew, and beat upon
> that house; and it fell: and great was the
> fall of it

"And that is what we are doing, Daniel. He has sent us to apply his teachings to real life in the world around us," Philip said.

"I wish I could have been there to hear him," said Daniel.

"But," Nathaniel said, "Always remember you can hear the words of Jesus ringing and speaking through the voices and love of true teachers. That is what we are doing, sharing both the words and compassion of Jesus with others just like you. All of his followers must pass along his message of peace and hope."

"Thank you," said Daniel. "I will look forward to other times of your sharing the words of Jesus.

When I lay down for the night I felt I had been in the presence of Jesus because his disciples, Nathaniel and Philip, had made him so real through their teachings.

Early the next morning we were on our way with a plan to make a very brief stop in Nazareth before going on to Capernaum. When we arrived at Aunt Mary's home, she was surprised and delighted to see us.

Our brief visit grew in length as she questioned Nathaniel and Philip about their mission to the area of Jerusalem—*to teach, heal, raise the dead, cleanse the lepers, cast out demons, and call people to a personal commitment to the Kingdom of God and his righteousness.*

Aunt Mary was so excited to hear their stories and especially about our overnight stay with Daniel and Rachael.

Aunt Mary filled in some of the details as she remembered them about the Roman soldiers that surprised them at the campsite years ago. It really sounded like more of a fearful experience for the adults and was almost a game for the younger children.

The next morning we pulled away and moved on toward Capernaum with a stop at Jonathan's for a little rest and some much needed water. Jonathan had just come from Capernaum and told us that the disciples were gathering at John's house.

It was helpful to know that we should go to John's house. We arrived and were caught up in the swirling excitement of what had happened. Just about the time that things would settle down, two more disciples would arrive and it would start all over again. The disciples gathered around Jesus and talked about their experiences which were all very different but most exciting. They all were talking at one time and they kept repeating what Jesus had taught as though it was all new material. Matthew suddenly captured the attention of all of us when he started quoting:

Behold, I send you forth as sheep in the
midst of wolves: be ye therefore wise as
serpents, and harmless as doves.
But beware of men; for they will deliver
up to the councils, and they will scourge
you in their synagogues; And ye
shall be brought before governors
and kings for my sake, for a
Testimony against them and the Gentiles.
But when they deliver you up, take no
thought how or what ye shall speak: for
it shall be given you in that same hour
what ye shall speak.
For it is not ye that speak, but the Spirit
of your Father which speaketh in you.
(Matthew 10:16-20 KJV)

Everyone stood there nodding and mouthing the words of
Jesus with slight variations. There were times when Jesus would
seem amused and at other times he might inject his own wording.

Jesus emphasized that it was most important for them to
always, always remember, "Your ministry and strength come
from the Lord of Heaven and earth. It is he that will sustain and
keep you." Then, it was hard for them to know if they were more
excited about the blessings they poured out on those in need; or,
the blessings they felt were returned to them from those they
blest through their variety of ministries; plus, God's Spirit moved
mightily within them.

It was Peter that now spoke the words of Jesus as he remembered them. Again, it became very quiet and many were mouthing the words with him in a slightly different way. Jesus sat and
listened and seemed very pleased.

The disciple is not above his master, nor the
servant above his lord. It is enough for the
disciple that he be as his master, and the
servant as his lord....there is nothing covered

that will not be revealed…and fear not them
which kill the body, but are not able to kill the
soul: but rather fear him which is able to
destroy both sould and body in hell….
He that loveth father and mother more than me
is not worthy of me: and he that loveth son or
daughter more than me is not worthy of me.
(Matthew 10:24-37 KJV)

Then you have what I consider a very hard expectation, but he keeps bringing it up in many of his teaching sessions. And often he will ask those present, "Are you listening?"

If you do not take up your cross
and follow me, you are
not worthy to be one of my disciples.
Those who seek and find
just a good life are not worthy of me,
but if you lose your life in service
to others for my sake
you will find it… (Matthew10:38-39 FI)

"Jesus is always concerned about others and their needs," said Andrew. "It is a living faith in our present day society to all the people who live there."

"Well said," Philip said, "I must remember that."

I suddenly felt it necessary to enter the conversation and share what impressed me so much.

"Jesus is always surrounded by children of all ages. They listen carefully and love him dearly. So I am always impressed when he mentions "children" in his teaching. Do you remember:

Look at these beautiful children,
always cherish them.
Whoever gives to one
of the little ones even a cup
of cold water

...are you listening?
...they are my disciples,
truly, I say to you that person
is my disciple
and they shall not lose
their reward
in my Father's Kingdom.
(Matthew 10:42 F I)

The disciples and friends kept asking each other what meaning these sayings have to their life. Then the disciples would try and explain to one another and to others how they understood Jesus's message.

On the other hand, they would keep asking themselves if they were measuring up to Jesus's expectations of them. Some felt he was too easy and others felt he was too hard. All knew that they must pay close attention to what he was saying and work toward living up to his kingdom goals.

They were all talking at once among themselves and it was as though Jesus wasn't there. And some began to compare themselves to others; but, I felt, that each of us must measure ourselves against the meaning that Jesus brought to life. Then we must serve him and the kingdom of God as best we can.

Jonathan and I stuck together. We felt like outsiders, but we longed to get closer to Jesus and his disciples. Some of the disciples we could relate to more than others but we tried hard to share equally with all of them.

Jesus was delighted with their enthusiasm, their reports, and even their disagreements.

"You are growing in your commitment to God's Kingdom issues, and that is never easy. The disagreements you have with each other is nothing compared to the inner struggles you will have with yourself. Never be so wrapped up in your disagreements with others that you fail to deal with the larger conflict within your own mind and soul," Jesus said.

The disciples became very quiet and a few withdrew to places where they could be alone in prayer and reflection.

Judas asked Jesus, "But, Lord, what about our disagreements with the world? Is that not the hardest battle we will face?"

"Judas, the battles with worldly issues are small compared with the inner battles in your heart and mind; plus, until you win the battles within, you will never be able to understand what the world is saying," said Jesus.

"That is the reason daily prayer is so important. A day without prayer becomes a picture of a child of God snared by the whims and conflicts of this world. Those persons become engulfed in attitudes that rage with anger, destruction, and violence. O my children, you are to be ambassadors of peace and goodwill. Pray! Pray! Pray! You are to live by justice and mercy and be ambassadors of forgiveness and love."

Jesus then rose, walked out of the city. A number of us followed him as he returned to the hillside where he had taught some weeks before. Those of us who followed gathered around in hopes that he would again pour forth some of his spiritual insights.

But he immediately began to pray, arms raised, his face toward the heavens and that wonderful picture of peace and joy on his face. Some sat on the ground, others knelt, most stood, and lifted their arms to receive the glory of God.

People seemed to come from every direction. I kept wondering how all of those people knew where Jesus was at this moment, young and old and many children. The children very quietly kept pushing into the front where they would be close to Jesus. They made no disturbance and were very respectful of those already sitting around Jesus. Immediately upon sitting or standing the children would raise their arms and turn their sweet faces into the heavens.

When Jesus lowered his arms and opened his eyes, he did seem a little startled by the number of people surrounding him. He spoke to several that he knew. One of the children walked slowly up beside Jesus and stood as though he was a personal guard.

"Let me warn you my children.
God's judgment is terrible
and it is sure,
No person escapes,
no city escapes,
no priest escapes,
no family escapes,
all the prophets must face
the judgment of God,
Elijah does not escape,
King David will face the
withering judgment of God.
Woe to those cities that are reckless
in their living and flaunt God's
call for purity and kindness,
they will bear a harder burden
and tragedy than Sodom and Gomorrah.
O Jerusalem, Jerusalem
take God into your heart
and be a true city of peace."

Then Jesus faced some of the children, he reached out to them, and some got up and drew near to him as he spoke, "Little ones, always remember, God is a loving father whose judgment is meant to help you know right from wrong, the difference between good and evil. His discipline washes us clean and makes us a new and beautiful person. Long for his cleansing, receive his correcting love."

Jesus looked into the faces of those children and his eyes embraced them all as he reached out to touch some, speak to others, and in a simple move he again raised his arms and prayed with them.

"I praise thee, O Father, Lord of the heaven and the earth. You hid some things from the wise and intelligent, but you planted the seed and quietly revealed it to these children ,of the babes of earth, and this was pleasing to you.

"Father, no one really knows the Son except the Father, nor does anyone fully understand the Father except the Son, except those the Son chooses to completely reveal the glory and majesty of the Father."

Jesus seemed to remain frozen for a considerable time and the children did not move. Then, slowly they all brought their arms down and at the same time bowed their heads and remained quiet and then together they said "Amen."

Jesus looked about him and then almost shouted, "Again, I say unto you, come to me all who labor and are heavy laden, and I will give you rest."

He rose and started walking through the multitude as they began to draw closer to him. He reached out and touched many and they reached out and touched him. There was a sudden surge of joy and happiness. A wave of quiet laughter swept across the crowd as a few of the children began to dance, laugh, and sing as they circled around Jesus. There was that quiet smile on Jesus's face as he swayed with their dancing. He then raised his hand for quiet and his face became serious.

> *I tell you take my yoke upon you,*
> and learn of me;
> for I am meek and lowly of heart
> and ye shall find rest
> unto your souls
> and strength for your daily living.
> (Matthew 11:29 KJV)

"You must learn that my yoke is not a burden. It is the glorious, perfect tool that the Father has given me to live life at its fullest. A yoke is what you use with oxen to pull heavy loads, and you are destined to pull many hard loads on the path of daily life. So, I want to share with you the very equipment God made for me. It will enable you to walk gracefully in paths of righteousness to the glory of our Father in heaven and to find fulfillment in all that you do on earth. Claim it for yourself, claim it because you love the Father, claim it because together we have many heavy loads to carry and hard experiences to pull along our way. Again, I say:

Take my yoke upon you,
and learn of me;
for I am meek and lowly of heart
and ye shall find rest
for your souls
and strength for your daily living.

When you learn that, absorb it, and wrap it around you as a shield of defense and encouragement, then your strength will be that ever flowing spring of God's love, filling your life for mission and peace.

People started coming from everywhere, and they kept coming to Jesus as he healed many. He lifted them up to his Father and his Father heard and restored the blind, healed those with leprosy, drove out demons, and all manner of other illnesses and afflictions. Then Jesus would charge them not to tell others that it was he who had healed them but to give God the glory. He even healed on the Sabbath and this greatly distressed the Pharisees; plus, they found out that his disciples had gathered grain on the Sabbath and that was not allowed.

There were some that openly challenged him, "Why do your disciples break the Sabbath and set a poor example by gathering grain on our holy day and eating it."

Jesus immediately responded,

Have ye not read what David did when
he was hungered, and they that were
with him;
How he entered into the house of God,
and did eat the showbread, which was not
lawful for him to eat,
nether for them which were with him, but
only for the priests
Or have ye not read in the law, how that

on the Sabbath days the priests in the temple
profane the Sabbath, and are blameless.
But, I say unto you, That in this place is one
greater than the temple.
And he has given the Sabbath to us for our
benefit.
(Matthew 12:3b-6 ᴋᴊᴠ)

Those Pharisees slipped away and we heard that they were plotting how they might destroy Jesus. When the disciples mentioned something about this to Jesus, he would not listen or dwell on it.

Day by day the people kept coming and Jesus kept teaching and healing.

In the evening we would return to either John or Peter's house, where we would share a meal and Jesus would answer questions raised by his disciples. All of us were struggling hard with his instructions, but it was all so exciting. Then we would discuss among ourselves long after most people had gone to sleep.

I decided that I just could not return home as yet. Everyday was more exciting than the last, and I did not want to miss a thing. Plus, think about how much I would have to share with Mama, Martha, and Mary when I did get home.

Believe, Believe, Believe

If ever there was a word that was important to Jesus, it was "Believe." It accounts for our purpose and gives direction to our life. It is the source of our hope and happiness. It is the star that shines in our mind and heart and leads us to God's path of righteousness. It is the spiritual tie that binds us to both Father and Son.

One morning before any light had come into the sky, some of us were at Peter's house and were getting some things ready to eat. Nathaniel went to get Jesus and returned to inform us that he was not in his room.

Immediately that began a search. Where had he gone? Had he been kidnapped? Some of the disciples were very concerned and even frightened by the threats being made against his life.

Nathaniel said, "Come on Lazarus, let's see if we can find him?"

As we walked away from the house Nathaniel spoke, "Where would you think he might go so early in the morning?"

I responded, "He loves the water, so, perhaps, he has gone down to the seashore to be inspired by the rising sun. His favorite selection in the Torah since his childhood is the wonderful account of Creation."

"I sure didn't know that," Nathaniel said.

"If you want to hear something exciting get Jesus to recite the story of creation. My sisters think that is the greatest blessing they have ever received," I said. "Thank you for sharing it with me. I will get him to recite it someday. Now, let's go this way," said Nathaniel as he made a turn onto a street with a steep grade down to the seashore.

In just a few minutes, we came out on the shore of the Sea of Galilee and looked both ways along the beach, but there was no Jesus.

"Let's walk south and get away from these houses," suggested Nathaniel.

He almost broke into a run and I followed.

"I wish the sun would come up so that we could see better," I said.

We were soon outside of town where there were no houses along the shore. We slowed to a walk and kept looking. Suddenly, an unexpected voice startled us, "Are you looking for someone?"

We turned and there was Jesus sitting on a small sandy knoll. He had a gleeful look on his face and was laughing quietly.

"Yes," said Nathaniel, "we have been searching for you. They are fixing breakfast, and we thought you might need some food to give you strength for this day."

"Thank you Nathaniel," said Jesus, "but my food comes from the Word of God that feeds me everyday. Isn't it beautiful out here? Turn and look at the sea. Take a deep breath. Soak up the sweet odor of the morning's newest flowers and breathe the fresh breeze flowing up from Egypt. Come and sit here with me and watch the glory of God's Creation come to life in a great display of wonder and beauty."

We joined him as he suggested and immediately he folded his hands; and we knew that he would be praying, so we folded ours and became very still. This time Jesus did not close his eyes or lift his face toward the heavens. He was engrossed in watching the view across the lake. In a very brief time, there were ribbons of light cutting across the morning sky, highlighting the fluffy clouds. Then came the sun splashing gold mixed with vivid pinks across the east. It was a magnificent sight with the sea rippling ever so slightly and reflecting the colors in the sky.

Then came the birds singing their morning song. Jesus continued to pray a prayer of joy and gladness. From time to time we would catch a word or two, but never a full sentence. His prayers were quiet and private.

It is amazing how when he prays he seems to radiate strength and joy that flows into those around him. I soaked up every bit of that spiritual gift that I could and cherished the opportunity.

Jesus stood and said, "Let's go to Peter's house. After we eat, there will be much to do; and it may be a long day."

He set a slow pace and every now and again he would stop to take in the view of that beautiful lake.

Here came several others looking for him; and we all went back to Peter's house where people were already eating; and their laugher was like a great song being raised to heaven. After we had shared our common meal, Jesus said, "Let's go down by the sea and see if anyone will join us this morning?"

Jesus and Peter led the way and immediately people began to fall in behind us. Jesus returned to the same place where we had found him and sat down. He watched as more and more people came. The lame were being helped, the blind were led, and a few were even carried on stretchers. A voice came from behind a tree behind us, "Unclean, Unclean!"

Many people quickly moved away from that area, but John slowly walked toward the voice and found a man crouching behind a large old, gnarled olive tree. John began talking quietly with him when Jesus appeared by his side.

Jesus looked at the leper who was shaking, almost violently. In a very compassionate voice, Jesus said, "Are you afraid?"

"Yes, Lord, but I am also very cold, my garment is old and thin, and it is all that I have," said the leper as he kept his head down looking at the ground.

Jesus's quiet voice said, "Look at me."

He was very slow in responding, but finally, with great hesitation, he looked up and began shaking even harder.

Jesus took off his outer cloak and put it over the man's shoulders as he said, "Let the warm glory of God's love fill you and cleanse your body and bless your spirit. Go in peace with new strength. Remember always, God loves you and will keep you."

The man looked down and saw the blemishes on his arms and hands fading and new flesh was beginning to appear. He dropped to his knees and began weeping as he said, "I am unworthy, Lord, but you have made me whole. Praise be to God for your mercy."

Jesus took his hands and raised him to his feet.

"Go to the priest and show him your new flesh and make your sacrifice in honor of God."

The man turned to leave, but kept turning back to look at Jesus. His smile was as bright as the morning sunrise and his cheeks were awash with tears of joy.

Jesus walked back to the gathering crowd and when he stopped he said, "Behold the glory of God," and he made a grand gesture toward the sea and sky. Then very slowly he began:

In the beginning God created
the heaven and the earth.
(Genesis 1:1 KJV)

Nathaniel looked at me with a bright smile and walked closer to Jesus.

And the earth was without form, and void;
and darkness was upon the face of the deep.
(Matthew 1:2b KJV)

Listen, listen, he said and believe. He paused and then raised his voice:

> The spirit of God moved
> upon the face of the waters.
> (Genesis 2:2b KJV)

His voice shook with an unusual show of emotion and then he made another grand gesture toward the sea before him, and with a great, clear voice that was full of emotion and power, he cried out,

> *And God said, Let there be light:*
> And there was light, and God saw the light,
> that it was good an God divided the light
> from the darkness. And God called the light
> Day, and the darkness he called Night.
> (Genesis 1:3-5 KJV)

He stopped. There was something different. It almost seemed like he was tired from physical exertion or perhaps the press of the crowds. He looked around as if he wanted to sit down, but it would have been difficult with the crowd pressing so close upon him.

Philip worked his way to him with a small urn of water. Jesus took it with a deep expression of gratitude. Then he began almost in a whisper and kept building until it was almost like he was giving a command.

> And God said, Let there be a
> firmament in the midst of the waters,
> and let it divide the waters from the
> waters. And God made the firmament,
> and divided the waters from the
> waters which were under the
> firmament from the waters which

were above the firmament: and it was
so. And Gad called the firmament
heaven.
(Genesis 1:6-8a KJV)

Then he called out like he wanted to inform the whole world.

Let the waters under the heavens be
gathered together unto one place, and
let the dry land appear: and it was so. And God
called the dry land Earth; and the gathering
together of the water called he Seas.
(Genesis 1:9-10a KJV)

"Children of God, behold the work of the Lord and affirm his glorious creation in your life every day you live. Sing unto him a song for his glory".

"The earth is the Lord's and the fullness thereof;
the world, and they that dwell therein.
For he hath founded it upon the seas
and established it upon the floods.
(Psalm 24:1-2)

"Praise be to God who is our Creator and Redeemer. Always… always lift the glory of his name and let him be your inspiration and strength. Lift his name in your heart and speak his name upon your lips. Thank him for the glory of what he has made and for ordaining it to be our gift and inheritance."

"Draw near friends and children of God. Let's walk a little farther down the beach where there is an open field"

Arriving at the field we came upon what seemed to be a woman crumpled on the ground with a small child huddled against her. Jesus stopped and said, "Are you sick?" There was no response whatsoever. The child stood and Jesus asked, "Is your mother sick?"

The child nodded his head "No" and finally he said "Hurt."

Jesus asked, "Can you tell me what happened?"

The child hesitated and than said "Rocks" and then quickly he picked up a stone and threw it just missing his mother.

Jesus knelt down and carefully pulled up the sleeve covering her arm, so he could see her arm and then pushed her head scarf very gently back from her face. Those close by gasped when they saw her cut and bruised flesh.

"This child has been stoned, who would do this and why?" asked Jesus.

The young woman stirred and looked up through a swollen face, "They left me for dead, but I managed during the night to get to here. My son found me some water, but I am in too much pain to move. Please, don't hurt me, please; just leave me alone," she begged.

Jesus continued to kneel beside her, "No one is going to hurt you, child. We wish to help you."

The little boy, with tears starting to flow, repeated to Jesus, "Help, help Mama." By this time, the young woman had struggled, trying to raise up a little to see Jesus.

Jesus took the little boy in his arms and held him in his embrace as the child cried. "Yes, child, we will help your mother."

Jesus kept the little boy close in front of him. Then he put one hand on his mother's shoulder. She flinched from the pain of being touched and some from nervousness.

Jesus said to the child, "Put your hand on top of my hand," which he did. Then Jesus raised his face and prayed. That glorious glow appeared on his face and then moved from his face to include the child's face and then engulfed those little arms on to Jesus's hand, and on to his mother. Jesus continued to pray as the little boy glowed in his love for his mother.

The young woman was trying to sit up. Jesus looked around and motioned for Jonathan, Matthias and Thaddeus to come and assist her. She moved ever so slowly and then as she slowly stood the swelling and bruises began to disappear.

The little boy was clasping her knees and calling, "O Mama, Mama, please, get well, Mama, please, Mama, I love you Mama, please get well."

Jesus looked at her and in a quiet voice said, "You are healed and now you can take your little boy and go home."

"I have no home," she said quietly almost as if she was ashamed of the fact. "I have no place to go."

That is the first time I have ever seen Jesus look like he was mystified about a problem and what to do about it. He stood looking at her and then at the child. He didn't speak and he looked nowhere else.

Jonathan had been standing very close to Jesus. He reached out, put his hand on Jesus's arm, leaned over, and spoke to him so quietly that no one could hear what he said.

Jesus turned to face Jonathan and said, "Thank you, friend of God."

Then he ever so quietly whispered to the young woman and it was evident that he was introducing her to Jonathan. There was a quiet inaudible discussion, which seemed to please everyone who was close enough to hear.

Jesus suddenly said, "Child we do not know your name or the name of your handsome son."

"My name is Bernice and my son's name is Zechariah," she said.

"Beautiful names," said Jesus, "now, you go with Jonathan."

But there were so many people crowding in on the scene that it looked impossible for Jonathan to go anywhere. Suddenly, a broad shouldered man with a large physical frame stepped up and said, "Jesus, may I take them where they need to go."

He was covered from head to toe with a Galilean robe and head scarf. Jesus looked a little puzzled. Quietly the man spoke, "Lord, I am Julian, and I can get them away from here."

"Julian? I am so glad to see you again, and at a most appropriate time. Thank you for your help at a most appropriate time.

Here, you carry Zechariah so that he won't get lost or stepped on," said Jesus.

Julian swept the boy up into his arms and motioned for Jonathan and Bernice to follow him as I heard him say, "Stay close." I followed right behind them.

Julian held the boy with one arm and with the other pushed and shoved his way through the crowd with Jonathan, Bernice, and I following close behind.

When we cleared the crowd Jonathan said, "Julian, let Lazarus lead us to John's house and we will be able to plan some line of action from there." I interrupted, "Jonathan, wait just a minute. We need to coordinate our plans now. Where do you plan to go? We have mules and merchandise to care for."

"Lazarus, I am sorry I have forgotten all of these things under the urgency of getting this young girl and her son cared for. So, do you have any suggestions?"

"In the first place, how are you going to manage to get her to your home? She was severely hurt and you have some distance to go."

Julian jumped in, "I will help him get the woman and boy to wherever we are going."

"But do you have time for that?" I asked.

"I am like her, I have no place to go," said Julian.

Jonathan and I stopped and looked at him and each other.

"What donkeys and merchandise are you talking about?" asked Julian.

"Lazarus," said Jonathan, "let us pick up the donkeys and merchandise, and we will leave you one donkey to bring. That will give us transportation for Bernice to ride if she needs too. Then you stay and tell Jesus what we are doing and come on to the house this evening."

"That sounds good to me," I said, "and I hope you can work through some of the problems we have learned about."

They turned and moved toward Capernaum, but I went back toward the meadow. The crowd surrounding Jesus looked larger than ever. When I got there, I slowly worked my way toward Jesus and that was not easy.

That day Jesus spoke many things in parables. At one of the break times Thomas, one of his disciples, asked him, "Why do you tell stories to the people?"

Jesus replied, "Many people cannot understand the great issues of God's word without clear examples on how it applies to their life."

Jesus started speaking to the crowd again and many drew even closer to him.

> *Behold, a sower went forth to sow; And*
> when he sowed, some seed fell by the way
> side and the fowls came and devoured them
> Up: Some fell upon stony places, where they
> had not much earth: and forthwith they
> sprung up, because they had no deepness of
> earth:
> And when the sun was up, they were
> scorched; and because they had no root
> they withered away.
> And some fell among thorns; and the
> thorns sprung up and choked them:
> But other fell into good ground, and
> brought forth fruit, some an hundredfold,
> some thirtyfold.
> Who hath ears to hear, let him hear.
> (Matthew 13:3b-9)

Jesus stopped and took another drink of water. A child came to Jesus, stopped, and looked at him. Jesus knelt down and gave him a drink of water. The child stayed by his side; and as Jesus went into a time of prayer, the child folded his hands and watched Jesus very carefully. After a little while, Jesus stood up to be able to see more of the people who continued to assemble. His voice rose:

The kingdom of heaven is like a grain
of mustard seed, which a man took,
and sowed in his field,
Which indeed is the least of all seeds,
but when it is grown, it is the greatest
among herbs, and becometh a tree, so
so that the birds of the air come and
lodge in the branches thereof.
(Matthew 31:b-32)

"Those who have ears—hear and believe. I challenge you to grow into what you have learned about the kingdom of God and his righteousness."

Someone called out from the crowd, "How important is that kingdom you talk about? Is it greater than Rome?"

"Are you listening?" asked Jesus.

They are two different kingdoms. One is physical, of this earth, while the other is a spiritual kingdom of heaven. One will eventually perish and disappear, but the kingdom of heaven will live forever:

The kingdom of heaven is like unto a
treasure hid in a field; the which when
a man hath found. He hideth, and for joy
thereof goeth and selleth all that he
hath, and buyeth that field.
(Matthew 13:44 KJV)

Jesus stopped and looked toward the area from which the question had come. There was no response or further question. "Are you understanding what I am telling you?" There was a quiet scattering of "yes." After a few minutes he began again:

Again, the kingdom of heaven
is like a merchant
in search of fine pearls,
who on finding one pearl

of great value,
went and sold all
that he had and bought it.
Again, the kingdom of heaven
is like a net,
which was thrown into the sea
and gathered fish of every kind;
when it was full,
men drew it ashore and sat down
and sorted the good into vessels
but threw away the bad.
And so it will be at the close
of the age.
The angels will come out
and separate the evil
from the righteous,
and throw the evil ones
into the furnace of fire;
where all that are there
will weep and gnash their teeth.

There was a long pause as he looked into the eyes of one person and then another. He did not look at the children. Then he finally continued:

Have you understood all of this?
They said to him, "Yes."
And then he said to them.
Every leader of the faith
who has been trained
to teach about the kingdom of heaven
is like a student in a rich storehouse
who reveals priceless treasures
that are both new and old.
Let those who have ears, hear and take heed.

He bowed his head, folded his hands in a quiet prayer. The children quickly modeled him in everything that he did. They were never noisy or irreverent.

Suddenly, Peter was pushing his way through the crowd with a young man in tow. He kept moving until he was right in front of Jesus.

"Jesus, this is Caleb a disciple of John the Baptizer, he says he has some very special news for you."

The young man seemed totally shaken and ill at ease. He couldn't seem to speak, and he kept looking around at the crowd. Finally, Jesus said, "Caleb, Peter says you have very important news, and when you have caught your breath I would appreciate your sharing it."

"Here, sit beside me. Someone bring Caleb a flask of water. I am always interested in John's life and ministry. He is a prophet of the most high," Jesus said.

Caleb started but had to stop because of a flood of tears and sobbing. "Here, Caleb, take this little flask of water that has been brought for you, and take your time," said Jesus.

Caleb suddenly stopped and through his sobs he said, "The disciples of John have sent me to tell you that John is dead."

He began weeping again; and Jesus reached out and placed his hand on his arm.

"We must all pray," said Jesus.

He raised his hands and face toward heaven as the children joined him.

"God of power and might, you have called the prophets and inspired them to bring your message to those on earth. John was your dedicated servant and prophet. He was faithful and brave beyond all expectations. Creator of life, you drew John from the womb of his mother, Elizabeth, and now you draw him into the Kingdom of heaven that he may sit in the council of those who divide and proclaim your Word. Thank you for sending him to us, calling all people to repentance. Thank you for freeing his voice to speak your truth and to tell us of your love. Embrace him and may his voice continue to ring out through those who follow him as his disciples."

Jesus got very quiet. You could hear weeping in the multitude, and a few began to move out to possibly go home. This was a holy moment; everyone was drawn into the power of this special time. Jesus called out, "Amen." It rang across the field and a sea of voices swept back from the multitude as they responded, "Amen."

"Caleb can you tell us what happened to the prophet?" asked Jesus.

Jonah in a clear, strong voice for all to hear said, "King Herod Antipas had him beheaded, and his head was presented to his stepdaughter on a platter after she danced for him at his birthday party. It was Salome's mother who requested such a punishment for John. Then Salome presented John's head to her mother, Herodias."

There was a gasp across that crowd; and Jesus fell to his knees and raised his voice in an outcry of sorrow, disbelief, and distress.

"Loving God in heaven, forgive Herod…"

There was a rumbling of No's across the multitude. With an even louder voice Jesus called forth, "Loving God in heaven, forgive Herod, Herodias, and Salome."

He stopped and listened, "God of justice and forgiveness, you know the truth of what has happened, and your judgment will be proclaimed in heaven. Forgive us when we in our life are as angry as Herod and as vindictive as Herodias. Forgive all who cultivate hate rather than love. Open the door of our mind and soul to the indwelling of your grace and love. Make us instruments of your divine will on earth, and keep us ever humble. We pray in your heavenly, forgiving and loving name, Amen." Again, there was a firm rumbling of "Amen" from the crowd.

Finally, when Jesus opened his eyes, he discovered that all the multitude were on their knees. Jesus stood and started walking toward the beach. When he got there, a small boat was beached on the sand, and Jesus got in.

Peter and John joined by Andrew pushed the boat into the water. The sail was set and they traveled parallel to the beach as the whole multitude flowed with him along the beach. Jesus would dip his hand in the water and was talking quietly with John. Jesus pointed to an open meadow beside the Sea of Galilee, and Andrew brought the boat to the beach, and Jesus got out and walked into the meadow. It was a rather lonely place being removed from any town. The children were pleased that Jesus was again walking with them. They surrounded him, and the adults were right there behind him.

There was a sad expression on the face of Jesus. He sat on a rock and immediately a little boy came up and embraced him. A quiet smile broke across the face of Jesus. It was his way of saying "Thank you" for a sweet touch of comfort.

The sun was getting low in the sky, and a full moon was rising on the horizon. Several of the disciples became concerned because they were away from Capernaum, and the people needed food for their evening meal.

Andrew asked, "Good Master, what will we do? These people need to be fed."

Judas answered, "Send them home, now!"

"But they are hungry, now; and we have drawn them away from their homes and the town," said Philip.

"Send these people away to the towns and villages; and let them buy food for themselves," insisted Judas.

Jesus quickly responded:

> "They need not go away;
> you give them something to eat."
> But Philip said, "We only have five loaves and two fish.
> And Jesus said, "bring the loaves and fish here to me."
> And then, he suggested that the people sit on the grass;
> and taking the five loaves and the two fish,
> he looked up to heaven, blest, and broke the loaves
> and gave them

and the fish to his disciples.
The disciples distributed the
bread to the people.
They all ate and were filled:
and the disciples picked
up that which was left over
and there were twelve
baskets full.
There must have been about
five thousand men, plus, women,
and children.

Then Jesus rose and directed the disciples to get in the boat and go across the lake. He told them he would join them a little later.

I had overstayed my visit and quickly I ran to Jesus. I told him that I needed to leave and follow Jonathan and Julian. It was almost dark, and I needed to get to Jonathan's house before it was terribly late.

"Thank you for coming and being here with the people," said Jesus. "Also, express my deep gratitude to Jonathan and Julian for helping with Bernice and Zechariah.

"Her homeless condition was a surprise problem, and we might have had some additional problems if Jonathan had not offered to help. So, tell Abigail that I thank her for any problems we may have created for her in providing a home for Bernice."

"It has been my joy and inspiration to share with you and the disciples," I told Jesus.

"Be sure to give Abigail a big hug for me," said Jesus as he reached out and blessed me before I left.

I had to then return to Capernaum to get the donkey and merchandise before I could start home to Jonathan's house. It was quite late when I got there, and they seemed to be getting worried about me. I was too tired to ask about Bernice, so we quickly unloaded my donkey; and we all went to bed.

The next morning when I got up, they had fed the donkeys and given them water. Julian startled me by announcing that he was going home with me to help me on the trip. I looked at him and he held up his hand for me to be quiet. There was the touch of a command in Julian's hand.

Bernice was up helping Abigail as best she could to prepare a morning meal. Zechariah was already outside and had made friends with a baby goat; and they were romping all around the house.

The meal was ready and Jonathan offered a blessing: "Holy and loving Father, thank you for the ministry of Jesus. Thank you for the love he shares with us, thank you for the healing power of his spirit, thank you for his gift of kindness to children. Keep us safe, but use us grandly and to your glory. Bless the guests in our house: Julian, Bernice, Zechariah, and Lazarus. Touch them with the power of your spirit. Bless the food we share, and the day before us when we can serve others to the glory of your Name. Amen"

During the meal we talked about John the Baptizer and his death. Abigail was shocked and started asking questions, but we had to tell her we knew very little, and her answers would have to come at a later time.

That day we worked at sorting all of the merchandise, and some would be left at Jonathan's. Bernice helped Abigail clean the house and prepare a room for her and Zechariah. After the evening meal, they all sat around outside enjoying the beauty of the place. It was then that Jonathan and Abigail invited Bernice, Zechariah, and Julian to make a home with them. The three were shocked and overwhelmed.

"Bernice," said Abigail, "I have always wanted a sister and children. I have neither, but you bring me both into our home. You will be given tasks to do and be paid for the work you perform."

Abigail then continued, "Julian, we could use another supervisor in the fields helping with the flocks; plus, someone to assist in getting products to the markets. We have a little shed that you can work toward having as a very nice little room. It will give you privacy and perhaps some independence.

"You will be free to come and go; and we will pay you for your work. We would treat both of you as family and not as hired hands. Now what questions might you have," Abigail said.

Julian and Bernice sat there stunned and could not say a word.

Finally, Bernice simply said, "Thank you."

Julian looked down at his hands and when he looked up he simply said, "I will try not to disappoint you."

Little Zechariah looked at his Mama and then at Abigail. Then very slowly, he walked over to Abigail and gave her a big hug and kiss. Abigail embraced him and shed a few tears of happiness.

The next day Julian and I left and went to Nazareth to spend a night with Aunt Mary and James. They were so glad to see me, and I introduced them to Julian with few details about who he was. I told them all about Jesus feeding the five thousand. There were a lot of questions about that and about John the Baptizer.

Since I had so little information, I could tell them no more than I had heard from Caleb, the disciple of John. That was sufficient to make all of our hearts very sad. Aunt Mary said very little for the rest of that day and would sit in prayer with tears flowing over her cheeks.

After a night's rest, Julian and I finished packing my things; and we left for Bethany. I had a long time to think about all that I had seen and heard. I must admit that the experience was amazing; the issues were challenging, and some of those things I tried to share with Julian. I must say he was a good listener and every now and then he would ask a question.

I shared with him that Jesus had said, "You are a light in this world."

He listened as I talked about how I was beginning to understand that as a candle burns, it gives of itself. And as we live in the midst of the powers of darkness we are asked to give brightness and warmth. That is exactly what Jesus brings and gives every day for all people.

So on our way to Bethany I tried to be a light, a brightness in the middle of dull routines. I spoke to people; we helped a few with simple tasks; I offered a few some of my cheese and bread; I patted children on the shoulder and tried to encourage them. It took me a little longer to get home, but I was happier when I got there.

"Thank you, Jesus, teacher, and most of all my best friend."

When we arrived in Bethany, I introduced Julian; and he was a curiosity and a joy. He stayed two days before leaving to return to Jonathan's.

Growing Challenges

It was amazing how quickly the merchandise that I had collected moved. Now, I was getting very low on what I had available to sell, and even Mama commented that my customers were going to begin to be disappointed with me.

Mary kept reminding me that she wanted to go on the next trip north, but Mama kept suggesting that the trip was not proper for a young woman. Mary would laugh and say, "But I don't want to wait until I am a proper old lady and not be able to make it." We would all laugh and go on with our tasks.

One afternoon, I was approaching home after making a long circular trip visiting some of my customers that I furnished with products. I was almost home when I saw a man seemingly asking directions from a stranger. The man was pointing and trying to get his point across when I realized that he was talking with Jonathan.

I walked up behind Jonathan and said, "Why don't I take you where you want to go." There was an explosion of happiness and I thanked the stranger for the help he had offered. Then we were off to our house. When I took Jonathan in the house Mama was thrilled to see him, gave him some water, and insisted on washing his feet.

"Where are Martha and Mary?" I asked.

"They have gone to the well and will be back in just a little while," Mama said.

Jonathan and I went outside. He had three donkeys loaded with a wide variety of merchandise. I was amazed. We quickly removed the loads, put the donkeys in a shed, and returned to the house just before Martha and Mary came home.

Mama said, "Lazarus, here come your sisters."

I asked Jonathan to keep his back to them as we talked in quiet voices to see how long it would take them to realize who he was. They brought their water jars in and were talking with Mama. Mary kept looking toward us, but I stayed very intense in my conversation with Jonathan, and he had his back turned their way.

Eventually, Mary turned and walked toward us with a sly smile and in a questioning voice simply asked, "Jonathan?"

He turned and faced her and there was the biggest squeal you had ever heard as she embraced him and laughed and laughed. Martha joined her in greeting Jonathan, but she was considerably more reserved. Mama fixed all of us some tea. We sat down, visited, and got caught up on all the news about Abigail, Tamar, and Samson. Then we began to question Jonathan about the activities of Jesus.

He knew very little about the whereabouts or activities of Jesus because he had been very busy at home. It was the time of year to prune the grapevines and work in the olive tree groves. He had been absorbed in farmwork; and no visitors had come to his house, whom he could ask about Jesus.

Jonathan suddenly stopped talking and then said, "Julian, let me tell you about Julian. He is one wonderful worker; and if it had not been for him, I could not have come on this trip. And Abigail is the happiest person in this world with Bernice and Zechariah."

Then we started asking Jonathan about what he would like to do while he was staying with us. He immediately mentioned the Temple. Because of his old physical handicap, before Jesus healed him, he had traveled very little and had never been to Jerusalem.

He also said that he would like to go with me to visit my clients and see how they respond to the merchandise that he had just brought with him.

Since the next day would be the start of the Sabbath, we decided to spend all day resting and by mid-afternoon go into Jerusalem and a good part of it at the Temple.

Mama and Martha began fixing our dinner while Mary and I asked Jonathan questions until Mama called us for dinner. Mama suggested that I pray, "Father of us all. How grateful we are for good friends, who never forget us and whose interests in life challenge us. We rejoice in the gift of happy surprises. Bless the food we now share that has been prepared for us by faithful and loving hands. Give us rest during the night and may we serve you through our spiritual worship on the Sabbath. Amen."Our conversation around the table was lively and filled with many questions. Soon after that gracious meal, we were in bed and, especially Jonathan, got some much needed sleep.

The next morning I slipped out of the room very quietly; and left Jonathan sleeping while I went to water and feed his donkeys. When I came back in the house, everyone was up and chattering, Jonathan was telling them about his trip to Bethany.

After eating a light breakfast, we went to the shed and started sorting the merchandise Jonathan had brought with him. After a light lunch, we changed into a little better Sabbath Day robe and started making our way toward Jerusalem to visit the Temple as the sun was setting and the beginning of a new Sabbath.

"Jonathan, have you heard Jesus say anything about coming to Jerusalem, possibly for the Passover?" I asked.

"I have not heard him say a word," responded Jonathan.

"Each year I watched, even before he began his ministry, but there is never any sign of him. The Passover is next week; and, again, I find myself hoping that he and the disciples will appear for the high holy days," Lazarus said.

"One of the reasons that I have come now," said Jonathan, "I was hoping we could spend some time during the Passover in Jerusalem."

"We will do exactly that," I said.

As we drew near to Jerusalem, Jonathan became very quiet. I suddenly realized how important this was for him and kept reminding myself that I should make his visit even more meaningful.

When the Temple came into view Jonathan stopped and caught his breath. His eyes were locked on the Temple. I wasn't sure if I should tell him we needed to move on or not; finally, I suggested that we step out of the way of all the people who were moving toward the Temple area.

Jonathan said, "I'm sorry but I feel overwhelmed. The Temple is so very beautiful and far different than what I had imagined. Let's keep moving."

"It's great for me to see such joyful excitement in your eyes," I said. "I have seen the Temple all my life and it seems quite routine."

"Routine!" Jonathan almost shouted, "This is the most exciting experience of my life. Oh, I wish I'd had the opportunities you had to visit this holy place. So, do you come here often?"

"Yes, almost every week. Whenever I come to Jerusalem I usually take the time to stop at the Temple." I responded. "Come let's go into Court of Israel in the heart of the Temple."

"Oh, no, no, no. I am not sure I am worthy," said Jonathan as he started backing up. I was watching him carefully and he was genuinely nervous and uncomfortable.

"Come Jonathan, you are welcome in God's house."

I realized this was going to be perhaps the greatest day of his life. His eyes were moist and his breathing was rapid, but he kept up with me as we climbed the few steps and went through the great gate and into the courtyard. I took his arm and pulled him off to the side, or he would have stopped right in the middle of that grand passageway. I stopped and gave him the time to soak up all that was there. He marveled at the building and was intrigued with the people.

"This is far enough," he said.

"But Jonathan, we are only in the Court of the Gentiles. Stay with me and we will watch and listen to the worship time in the Court of Israel. You can stop there and watch and listen as long as you wish."

Suddenly, I heard my name spoken; and when I turned, there was Rabbi Levi hurrying toward me. "My son, I am so glad to see you; what is all this I hear about Jesus; the elders at the gate stay in a constant level of alarm when someone mentions his name. Every time someone comes and tells us what he is doing and saying, it creates near panic and a few elders go nearly into a rage, but they soon forget it.

"Also, what can you tell me about John, Zechariah's son; did you know that Zechariah had died? We have not seen John since his father's death. How are you? What have you been doing? You look prosperous enough; how is your family? Your father's name is Amos, right?" Rabbi Levi suddenly froze and looked very embarrassed, "Oh, I am so sorry, I have talked so fast and you have not been able to answer a single one of my questions.

All those questions were a puzzle to Jonathan; so, I began by saying, "Jonathan, Rabbi Levi was my teacher who prepared both Jesus and me for our Bar Mitzvah. We both studied under him for several months. That is the reason for all his personal questions."

"Now, Rabbi Levi, all my family is fine, but my father died six years ago and Jesus' father, Joseph, also died perhaps ten years ago. Jesus is teaching in Galilee, and both of us see him from time to time and listen to his message. Some time I would like to talk with you about it and get your opinion, but now is not the time," I told the rabbi.

Rabbi Levi's eyes were dancing over the crowd, "Lazarus, I'm sorry but I must go. They will be looking for me. I have another young man, who will have his Bar Mitzvah this afternoon, and I just saw his family go by. It was good to meet you Jonathan, perhaps, we will meet again. Peace!"

"Thank you, rabbi," stammered Jonathan. He was still very puzzled by this fast-talking rabbi who had been my teacher.

"Come, let us go into the sanctuary and watch and listen to the proceedings," Rabbi Levi told Jonathan.

Jonathan froze, so I took his arm, and both the Rabbi and I led and pulled him the rest of the way.

They were getting ready for a Bar Mitzvah and Jonathan stood engrossed in the ceremony. After a while he turned to me and whispered, "I have never been to Jerusalem and I have never celebrated the Bar Mitzvah.

I must confess I was very surprised and simply said, "We will have to take care of that some day." During the whole of the ceremony, all I could think about was—now, how am I going to see to his Bar Mitzvah? That stayed on my mind for many days.

Jonathan watched and soaked up all that took place in that glorious sanctuary. Finally, I nudged him and motioned for him to follow me. We walked all over the facility, and he was more and more impressed. Later we stopped at the Gate Beautiful of Jerusalem, and there were all those rabbis out there debating issues of theology. At times, it got very vocal with harsh accusations.

Jonathan became upset with the display of anger and dissension between the scribes and Pharisees. One time he turned to me and asked, "Where is the openness and tolerance that we see in Jesus? Do they have any feelings of respect for one another? There is anger, dissension and open ill will among these men."

Someone on the outer circle of the crowd unexpectedly called out, "Have you heard of Jesus of Nazareth? Where does he fit into the line of the prophets?"

There was an immediate explosion of almost uncontrolled emotion. There was no discussion, it was all yelling in the direction from which the question came.

I suggested to Jonathan that we slip away and he was ready to run. We went out the gate and into the Garden of Gethsemane. He was so upset that I thought it would ruin his day of wonder and joy. I began talking about the Temple, and he added his reflections and asked questions. I felt we had put that scene at the gate behind us.

We made our way home after a brief circuit through the Garden of Gethsemane where the pilgrims from Galilee usually camp. We stood there while I told some of the stories about Jesus when he was a young boy and how he and his family camped in this area. Then we walked the path to our house as we talked about some of Jesus's teachings and stories.

It had been a rich and glorious day, and it took Jonathan a long time to stop talking to Mama, Martha, and Mary. He never once mentioned the elders at the gate.

After a good night's rest, we loaded the donkeys and began the rounds of those merchants that I serviced. Jonathan worked harder at making sales than I did. He became engrossed in the process and almost immediately mastered the art of negotiating a reasonable price for those things we were selling. I was most impressed.

When we returned to the house, I told my family how Jonathan had worked for my benefit all day. We sold an amazing amount of the goods that he had brought from Galilee, plus, much of the old stock that I had been working so hard to sell.

After a good night's sleep, we left again with the merchandise I now had and worked a wider circle around Jerusalem, visiting many small communities. Again, it was a very successful day and Jonathan was impressed with his own sales ability. He became very excited. So, when we came back toward Jerusalem, he was ready to make another visit to the Temple.

We went into the city and I decided to visit several of the dealers there and suggested that Jonathan go and visit the Temple by himself. He was exceedingly hesitant, but I kept encouraging him, and he finally agreed. I promised to come back by the Temple and pick him up, so I said, "Stay around the main door of the Temple or I will never find you."

I began stopping at dealers who were very close to the Temple area. They were delighted to see me as they were trying to find new stock for the pilgrims, who would come for Passover. Before I returned to the Temple, I had sold absolutely all the stock I had. When I stopped to pick up Jonathan, he was waiting outside; and he looked at the donkeys and their bare backs and asked, "What happened? Were you robbed?"

I laughed and told him how all the merchants were buying for the Passover and he had selected well because it was all gone except for a few things that had been left at the house.

"Mama will be amazed that I have sold everything," I said.

"Well," said Jonathan, "You must go back home with me, and we will get a new supply." All the way back to the house, we began to lay plans for a trip back to Galilee after the Passover.

When we got to our house Mama met us outside, looked at the donkeys, and looked at us. "What happened?" she asked.

"I sold it all; every last piece, and now my stock is diminished," I said.

"Well, it is time for you to go back and restock your supply."

Jonathan said, "We have been talking about him returning with me after the Passover to do some more buying. But I would like to go home by Jericho and up the Jordan River, and see the place where John the Baptizer used to preach."

"Now that is a novel idea," I said, "and it would take us an extra three or four days."

"Do you have the time to do that?" I asked.

"I will take the time," responded Jonathan.

The next week was filled with excitement and the joy of the Passover meal at our house. We had spent considerable time at the camp of the Galileans and in the Garden of Gethsemane asking for any information about Jesus. Many of those there had recently listened to him speak and watched him heal. Their stories made us eager to leave for Galilee in search of Jesus.

We left on the first day of the week after Passover to go to Jericho. We made a brief visit into the city. I stopped and found Daniel, who used to be one of my buyers as well as a supplier. We were delighted to see each other. He asked when I wanted to pick up some merchandise, and I had to inform him that we could not take anything at the moment because we were on our way to Galilee.

I introduced Daniel to Jonathan and told him that Jonathan wanted to see the Jordan River where Jesus was baptized by John the Baptizer. Once again he offered his little hut close to the River where we might stay.

"Oh, and by the way, Joshua is still living there, so you can talk with him and his wife about any needs you may have," said Daniel. "My wife is at home here, so she is not there this time."

"Daniel, I will return for some new merchandise in a couple of months," I said.

"Great, I will be looking for you."

I found my way easily to that little hut just before it got dark. Joshua happened to
be outside and recognized me, "Lazarus, what brings you back to the River?"

"My friend Jonathan wants to see the River where Jesus was baptized. Then we will be on our way up the River to Galilee. Daniel told us that we could spend the night in the hut."

"Wait just a minute," Joshua said and disappeared into his house.

Shortly he returned with his wife and informed us, "Our daughters are not here and we would be glad to have you stay in our house tonight. It would be more comfortable and after breakfast you are free to leave."

"You are generous and kind," I said.

Joshua led the way and showed us a small room where we could stay. Then his wife served us some goat's milk, cheese, and bread, which was greatly appreciated. We talked briefly and decided to turn in for a good night's sleep. The next morning we were soon on our way to the River.

I had forgotten how close we were to the River. Almost immediately, we could smell the fresh water and then there it was. No major difference could be seen except the grasses were not trampled down by the crowd, who had come to hear John the Baptizer.

I still remembered that time when John baptized Jesus.

"Jonathan, you cannot imagine how crowded this place was with all kinds of people. It was much like the crowds that now come to hear Jesus, except, there were more scribes and elders from Jerusalem in their fine clothes, and those wonderful head scarves.

"John was right over there baptizing and Jesus was watching him from about where we are. One day, when there was no on else in the water with John, Jesus slowly walked into the water. When he came to where John was standing, he just stood there facing John. You could tell that John was shocked and not sure what to do. In fact, Jesus told me later that John said he should not baptize by Jesus; but Jesus said, 'No, you are to baptize me and that will open my mission in this world.'

"John stood motionless for a long time before he decided to baptize Jesus. Eventually, John slowly scooped water into a large shell; and after a rather long time of–prayer, he poured it over Jesus's head. They both stood there in the River looking at each other for a long time. Jesus came out of the water, spoke briefly to Peter and John, and walked off by himself.

"We were told later that's when he entered the desert for meditation and prayer. I believe he was gone for forty days. When he returned, he immediately began to teach and heal the sick with an enthusiasm and power that attracted huge crowds wherever he went."

"Thank you, Lazarus for bringing me here and sharing with me what happened," Jonathan said.

With that he sank to his knees and went into a very intensive time of prayer. This was a holy place for all of us, who knew and loved Jesus.

I walked down to the River's edge and stooped over to touch the water. I was startled by a sudden explosion of screaming and wailing that came from the wooded area just across the River. About a dozen men burst out of the woods into the water. They were screaming, crying, yelling, throwing water everywhere, dropping into the deeper areas, and submerging themselves under water. Jonathan came running to me and asked what was going on.

"I have no idea, but let's back up away from the River and watch to see what happens. We may need to be ready to run," I said.

This crazy routine kept going on. A few more came and joined the men that were already there. There was not a word being said that was understandable.

Daniel appeared by our side, "What is this scene all about?" he asked.

"We have no idea," I said, "Everything was quiet, and these men suddenly appeared from the woods over there."

Well," said Daniel, "There is a small camp of John the Baptizer's followers who live over in those woods, but they are usually very quiet. I heard these men shouting all the way to the house."

"Perhaps this is some kind of ritual that John has taught them," I said.

"I have never heard anything like this from any of them," said Daniel. "Come let's walk down to the River and see if one of them will speak to us, but be very alert and careful."

Slowly Daniel and I walked to the River. We hardly got there when one of those in the river came out and confronted us. He yelled in our face and beat his chest. He was like some mad man.

"Why are you here? Are you one of Herod's people who have come to spy on us? Come on. Here we are. We won't stop you. Kill us all. We will be glad to die with and for our prophet. Kill us! Go on. Kill us." He kept screaming as he re-entered the River; and he began wildly slapping at the water and throwing it randomly.

I turned around to see where Jonathan was, and looked at Daniel and asked, "What do you think that meant?"

"I do not know, but you better turn around because here comes another one."

The next man stopped and looked directly at us, "Are you followers of John the Baptizer? Have you come to pay tribute to him? If so, join us in the water."

I asked, "Then you are disciples of John?"

He stopped and stared at us. By that time Jonathan had joined us. This strange fellow was suspiciously frustrated with us, "Why are you here? Don't you know that John has been beheaded by Herod, and his head presented to the witch, Salome, as she danced before him?"

Daniel gasped and said, "Are you sure?"

I turned and told Daniel, "We heard it when a disciple named Jonah delivered the message to Jesus, and we just had not thought to tell you."

"If you knew, why then are you not mourning. Come join us in the River," he then ran back into the water.

We watched them for a few minutes and then turned to go back to the hut for a time of prayer and reflection. It was far more than a sad moment. It was frightening and adding to the fear was the constant noise we could hear from the River.

What if Herod decided to do the same thing or something similar to Jesus? It was time to move quickly to Galilee, so we packed our few things said "good-bye" to Daniel and were on our way up the River. We walked for a long time without saying a word. I really don't think that either Jonathan or I knew what to say after that display of sorrow by John's disciples.

Even the donkeys seemed to sense our sadness and plodded quickly but quietly along the river bank toward Galilee.

Our stop for the night was in a quiet grove of trees. We had little to say to each other. We prayed and prayed some more and were praying when we fell asleep for the night.

The next morning we were awakened by the sound of galloping hooves of two horses with their riders racing down the opposite side of the River. We watched them disappear and remained quiet pondering what was the urgency of their journey. We were not able to identify them. Were they Roman soldiers or special security officers in Herod's military guard?

We were immediately on our way up the River and by nightfall we were within a day and a half of the southern shore of the Sea of Galilee. We were pushing hard to get to Capernaum to see Jesus. Our hurry nearly created a disaster, one of the donkeys stumbled and became slightly lame. Both of us decided we must slow down a little, so we stopped right then for the night when it was only the middle of the afternoon.

We bathed in the river and then gathered fruits for a much needed meal. We even began to talk and raise questions about the death of John and express our deep concern for Jesus's safety. I also realized that Jonathan was eager to get home to check the conditions at his farm and see his sister.

That evening I asked him, "Has your sister ever considered marriage?"

"Well, yes. In fact, there was a man who asked for her hand, but that was when I had major physical problems, and she felt she could not leave me," Jonathan said.

"Those were hard days after our parents died and she wanted me to succeed with the farm even though I was very limited in what I could do. She became an excellent manager of the farm. The staff our father had acquired to do the farm work became very supportive to her, which is a most unusual response toward a woman," continued Jonathan.

"But she impresses me as a very humble person," I said.

"You are right and she has always managed others with gentle firmness, including me." We both joined in laughing. "I do not worry about her when I am gone but recently I acquired additional land and staff; so, the load is a little heavier. However, the acquisition of Julian was a miracle. He knows how to manage people and from Jesus's teachings he has learned humility and love."

"Maybe, if you took a wife, she would become more interested in a marriage for herself with another woman in the house," I suggested.

"I doubt it because she has always wanted a sister, and she now has that with Bernice." "What about you? Is marriage in your plans for the future?" Jonathan asked.

"Now, you have turned the tables. Well, no. I do not have such thoughts. If I married, she would have a lot of problems, Martha would become her supervisor and Mary her little girl. Now, tell me, what woman would want to deal with that?" I said.

"Don't be so hard on your sisters. They are two wonderful people," said Jonathan.

"You are exactly right, but I am trying to be honest with them for their benefit and for my sanity," I responded. "Now let's get some sleep and put those sisters out of our minds for a little while.

We had two days of rather hard traveling. The temperature had turned hot and the donkeys needed not only a lot more water but more rest time. Once, we stopped and bathed them in cool water, which pleased them a great deal.

There was a very small community at the southern end of Lake of Galilee. We were passing slowly through that little community when Jonathan called my attention to some very unusual baskets and other works that were for sale.

We stopped and mingled among the houses. I began to make some significant purchases and then a large number of merchants suddenly appeared with their wares. Jonathan really became amused at my frustration, and I asked him to begin making an evaluation of some of the items and either buy or reject them. We began to work our way out of the community and were soon on our way up the west bank. Some of the people followed us for a long way trying to make a sale.

When we arrived at John's house, he was not there but his wife, Priscilla, told us that he was in the area with Jesus and should be back soon.

"Where is Jesus staying?" I asked.

"Now, that is always a good question. Last night he was here, but I have not been told if he will stay here tonight. Let me suggest that I take you next door where I think you can find a room for the night."

That would be wonderful. Do they have any shed where we can keep our donkeys," I asked.

"Yes, and those donkeys will find two new friends in that shed," Priscilla said.

"That is just what they need to make them feel better," I said.

So, we went next door where we met Anna who graciously agreed to have us and showed us a very nice room. We soon settled in, fed the donkeys, and brought them water. Those donkeys seemed very happy with their new friends.

There was a considerable rise in the noise level outside the house, and Anna said, "There comes Jesus and his disciples. They can be very noisy at times."

Jonathan and I walked to the door and there they were. There was no sign of Jesus. We went back in Anna's house, then Jesus appeared in the doorway at Anna's looking in our direction. Upon seeing us, he immediately came to us and greeted us with joy and excitement. All of my weariness suddenly disappeared.

"What has taken you so long to return?" Jesus asked.

"We celebrated the Passover in Jerusalem and Jonathan joined us," I said. I watched Jesus as he smiled, obviously very glad to see both of us.

"Jonathan, when do you plan to go home?" asked Jesus.

"Probably tomorrow, I really need to get back and see what is happening on the farm and with Abigail. Have you heard that Julian, Bernice, and Zechariah are living there with her?" he asked.

Jesus looked at him and said, "Everything there is fine; and Abigail is happy, but she will be very delighted to see you."

"And likewise, I will be very glad to see her." Jonathan stopped in his tracks, looked at Jesus as though he had a question on his mind, and wondering how did he know about Abigail.

Jesus looked at him, smiled and winked, then said, "Jonathan, I would like to come to your house in three days and have a little time for relaxation and meditation. Do you think Samson, our "littlest shepherd" would be able to join us for a couple of days?"

"I will immediately send one of my servants to ask him," responded Jonathan.

"Thank you," said Jesus. "Lazarus I hope you can stay for a while."

"Yes, I will be at Jonathan's."

"Wonderful," said Jesus, "Now, tell me, how are Martha and Mary?"

"They are fine and I will tell you more when we are at Jonathan's," I said.

"I will look forward to that and to hear about your mother, Sarah."

With that Jesus swept out of the room. All of the disciples followed him along with a few other people to go to Peter's house.

The disciple, John, remained with us, and we walked over to his house. We began to talk about all that had happened since we had last seen Jesus. Priscilla served us some hot herb tea, and we all began to feel much better.

"You will never believe some of the happenings in recent weeks," said John. "It has been a little wild and frustrating but always filled with astonishment and excitement even Judas showed some emotion and joy."

"Can you share some of it with us?" I asked.

"Of course, you want to hear some of the details? Sometimes, it is hard to tell about the works of Jesus in a way that satisfies me. I always feel that I leave some of the important things out."

"But what you share will feed both our souls and our curiosity," said Jonathan.

"We have just returned from the coast of Tyre and Sidon," said John

"Wow, you went a long way. Why?" inquired Jonathan.

"Jesus became very tired, and one day he just started walking toward the west he walked and walked," John said.

"In the evening, we would stop and some of us would go with Judas and purchase something to eat and drink. Jesus did very little talking and he didn't relate to any strangers. In fact, we were soon out of the territory where people would easily recognize him and still he kept going. He stayed quiet and prayed a great deal. Sometime after the noontime break he would sit and answer questions."

One afternoon, Nathaniel said, "Good Master, would you..."

Immediately, Jesus interrupted him, "Don't call me good. There is only one who is truly good and perfect, and that is our Father God, the Creator of the universe and all that has been and will be made. He is good. Now, Nathaniel, continue on."

"You made a number of comparisons of 'Happy are the pure in heart', 'Happy are the sorrowful for they shall find comfort,' he said.

"Nathaniel, stop right there, I did not say 'Happy.' And I would not have said 'Happy.' I am sure I said 'Blessed,' that is not 'happy.' Are all of you listening? The word 'Blessed' is a word filled with meaning and promise. It tells of a blessing on earth which springs from the promises and the soul of God the Father in heaven. Such blessings are the greatest gifts we ever receive. So, it is and always will be 'Blessed are the pure in heart, for they shall see God. To see God may not bring happiness because you may only experience him as a judge. Nathaniel, and the rest of you, why, have you made an adjustment to the word I have used so many times during my teaching?"

"Thank you," said Nathaniel.

"Thank you for asking," said Jesus. "Those who have ears. Let them hear. Don't ever expect that you will be happy because you are my disciple. If you carry the burdens and weight of the world in your heart, the heartbreak of all those who are burdened with pain, hunger, and sorrow, it may be hard to be happy. You can be blessed and that may bring you greater joy than any other experience or feeling in all this world."

That really caused a lot of discussion among us that evening. In fact, we have continued to discuss it at great length. Jesus sensed our conversations and one evening asked 'Why are you having so much trouble understanding the significance of blessedness?' We all got very quiet.

Jesus picked up on our conversation by saying, "You think of time and eternity as being two totally different and separate identities. They really are one. Make a fist with one of your hands; go on Philip make a fist with one hand or the other. Hold that fist up before you, so that you can see it. Now take your other hand and spread your fingers straight and wide...wide...fingers spread apart. All right, bring those fingers and securely wrap them around your fist and squeeze tight. The fist is this world but the fingers and palm of the other hand shows how we are surrounded, encircled, embraced by eternity. We live in both simultaneously. You cannot separate one from the other. Each of you are creatures of this earth, but you are also a child of eternity."

When I tell you, "Lo, I am with you always. It is because I will always be here, as near as your breathe from eternity into time."

Judas said, "We need you here all the time and never somewhere else. What would we do without you?" He was almost yelling. "Jesus, you cannot leave us, your kingdom is here. You have told us to pray 'Thy kingdom come on earth as it is in heaven,' and I do that several times each day with great joy and excitement; so, you cannot consider going somewhere else."

"Jesus sat very quiet," said John.

Judas started again, "Tell him Peter. John, he may listen to you. Suddenly all of us wanted to disappear. Jesus got up and walked over to Judas with that quiet smile on his face and took Judas by the arm and the two of them walked away. I must admit that we were very relieved."

John stood still for a few moments caught up somewhere in a memory that he seemed not interested in sharing. He quietly walked away and looked for his wife, Priscilla.

Jonathan and I went outside to share in the beautiful day. There was a quiet relief from the pressure and tension of the last hour. We just stood still and soaked up those warm rays of sunshine.

"Jonathan, I really have a lot to do before I come to your house, and it is going to be hard to get it done. Do you think you can help me tomorrow morning by contacting some of the people who have crafts for sale? Then you would be free to leave for home in the early afternoon, and perhaps take one of the donkeys that is loaded with merchandise?"

Jonathan was a little slow to respond, "I am eager to get home as Jesus wishes to see Samson; and I must arrange for him to come, but let's wait and see how tomorrow works," he said.

"Wonderful, let's make a list of those you can see, and others that I can visit and meet for something to eat in the early afternoon."

"We better start those lists now before John returns," Jonathan said.

"You are right," So, we rather hurriedly reviewed those merchants who were in a close proximity to each other and soon had our morning contacts planned when John returned.

"Oh, there you are," he said, "I was so wrapped up in the push and shove with Judas that I did not tell you about one of the most interesting experiences that we had in the area of Tyre and Sidon. Come let's sit down, we have some time before Priscilla serves us dinner."

We sat as John spent a long time arranging some pillows.

He began, "One morning I kept noticing a woman following us, listening, and observing. I had never seen her before. She kept working closer and closer to where Jesus would be teaching or praying. Jesus went into a house and she followed him,

> *Immediately that woman,*
> whose little daughter was
> possessed by an unclean spirit,
> heard of him, and came
> and fell down at his feet.
> Now the woman was a Greek
> a Syrophoenician by birth.
> She begged him to cast
> the demon out of her daughter.
> And he said to her,
> "Let the children first be fed,
> for it is not right to take the
> children's bread
> and throw it to the dogs.
> But she answered him,
> Yes, Lord; yet the dogs
> under the table
> eat the children's crumbs,
> And Jesus said to her,
> For this saying you may go your way;
> the demon has left
> your daughter.

That evening Jesus drew apart with Peter and me and talked about the Syrophoenician woman and the conversation between the two of them.

Jesus said, "I was so tired, my mind was not thinking, my spirit was numb, and I was insensitive to the cry of a mother. I have been thinking about the love of my mother for me and the family. That mother was in pain with a broken heart but I was only tired."

"Father, forgive me; dear woman and mother, forgive me. Now, I know what was meant in the Torah when it says several times that 'God Repented'. God suffered a deep sorrow that afflicted his whole being, he repented. So, I, too, repent and feel a sorrow that reaches beyond the depths of my mind and soul.

"I should have been able to measure the deep need of that mother and child. Then I should have been able to lay aside my intense longing for the people of God to come into a new relationship with the One who calls to them. God wants so much for his chosen people to fully claim their position and God's love for them.

Jesus sat for a long time with tears in his eyes.

Neither Peter nor I knew what to say in that moment. It had really been said by Jesus, so we sat there with him and quietly shed tears with him.

"Lazarus, I kept thinking about what Jesus said, 'and God repented.'"

"John, I have not thought anything about that, and I will take my questions back to the Rabbi at the Temple in Jerusalem, who trained me for my Bar Mitzvah. I am sure Rabbi Levi will have his opinion, and it will be worth considering. But did you ever ask Jesus about it?" I asked.

"No," said John very shyly, "he was so upset that we did not want to harass or bother him as he was working through his sorrow. That is what he called it—a deep sorrow that consumed the divine being, so I am sure he felt consumed."

John continued with the story.

"Peter and I got up and walked quietly away which I guess was our avoidance of the issue. When we returned, Jesus was gone and we had no idea where he went. So we returned to the disciples and Jesus was not there either. That caused a lot of questions, which we could not answer. Then several of the disciples left to try and find him. Before any of them returned, there was Jesus in our midst. He took off his outer robe, rolled it up and lay down with that robe under his head and went sound asleep.

"The next morning Jesus was up meditating before any of us. Suddenly, there was the mother of yesterday, her husband, and their daughter in our midst with cheese, bread, and a wonderful jug of sweet goat's milk. The daughter came to Jesus and just looked at him with a smile that was more radiant than a sunrise. Jesus kissed her on the cheek and embraced her. She raced away to pass out the bread to all of us. Her bright smile and cheerful voice was a special blessing to all of us. Everyone became more cheerful.

"The young mother and her husband walked over to Jesus with their heads down. Jesus put his hand under their chins and raised their faces, kissed both of them on the cheek, and embraced them with a warm compassion that radiated respect and love.

"As we left, that young girl walked with Jesus holding his hand for a long ways before she stopped, bowed, and turned to run back to her family. Jesus watched her and then waved to her family as he turned and set his face toward the east.

"Jesus never made any announcement about stopping to see his mother and family in Nazareth, but all of us expected it.

"It was the usual happy reunion and very soon Jesus and his mother disappeared. I am sure they had gone to James's house just to be alone for a little while. When Jesus's reappeared he was ready to leave for Capernaum. He left so quickly that five disciples were left behind and had to catch up. Jesus did not say a word from the time we left the region of Tyre and Sidon until we walked into Peter's house. Of course he had greeted his family in Nazareth, but that was it.

"A simple late night meal was shared and very quickly everyone scattered to find a place to sleep. Before any of us got up Jesus was watching the sunrise and people were beginning to join him on the little beach. I am not sure that I had ever known anyone who enjoyed God's creation more than Jesus. He could sit for hours and just watch the unfolding of all of God's glory."

Thus, John ended his story of Jesus's travel to Tyre and Sidon.

The next day, Jonathan started early to visit merchants in the area, and then he would go home. He was very eager to get there, see Abigail, check on the farm, and send someone to bring Samson to see Jesus. I would not see him until tomorrow or the next day depending on how quickly I could make my visits to other merchants in and outside of Capernaum.

When I joined Jesus on the shore of Lake Galilee, he was playing with four children. They were holding hands and skipping around in a circle one way and then they would reverse the direction and skip the other way. When Jesus sat down, the children were right in front of him watching and waiting.

He asked, "Do any of you know a song we could sing?"

They all sat in silence waiting to see if Jesus knew a song. Other children were running to join them and soon there was a large semi-circle of children surrounding Jesus. All were sitting on the ground.

Suddenly, Jesus did start singing just like the canter in Jerusalem:

> Praise the Lord!
> Praise the Lord from the heavens,
> praise him in the heights!
> Praise him all the angels,
> praise him, all his hosts.
> Praise him, sun and moon,
> praise him, all you shining stars!
> Praise him! you highest heavens,
> and you waters above the heavens!
> Let them praise the name of the Lord!
> For he commanded and they were created.
> Praise the Lord!

When Jesus stopped, one little boy spoke up and said, "You left some of it out!" Many laughed and the youngster became embarrassed, stood up, and ran to his father.

Jesus motioned for him to come back and come to him. His father encouraged him and very slowly he walked to where

Jesus was sitting. Jesus reached out and took his hand and drew him closer.

"You are exactly right. There was much more to that Psalm and all of it is very beautiful. But sometimes it is all right to use only a part of a Psalm or some other scriptures to praise God. And sometimes that is the way a Rabbi will help us grow in our faith. So, thank you for reminding us all that there was more to that very beautiful Psalm."

I could not linger long before leaving, so I approached Jesus and told him I must go. "I will look forward to seeing you in three days," I told him.

"I will be there," he responded.

Then I was gone. I always dreaded leaving, but it was necessary for many reasons and Jesus knew it.

I worked hard all the rest of that day and into the evening. Then it was too late to go to Jonathan's. So, I went back to the disciple John's house and was kindly given a place to sleep. I left early the next morning.

I had bought too much and the donkeys were rebelling and refusing to walk under the weight of all that merchandise. There was no place I could buy another donkey, so I would take extra time to rest and let them graze. I was making progress, but it was very slow. During one of my stops, I was surprised to see Julian appear with another donkey. We made some changes and the donkeys were much happier; and so was I.

"How did you know to come," I asked Julian.

"Jonathan said that he left more merchandise than he should have and sent me to see if I could find you."

"Thanks to both of you because I was facing outright rebellion on the part of those donkeys. They were getting angry enough to either bite or kick me when I got close to them. I am too tired to fight."

Julian laughed his big hearty laugh that made the air ring with joy.

"Julian, the Roman soldiers must have loved to hear you laugh."

"O, I never laughed in those days. I was always serious, always angry, always fighting with everyone around me. Would you like to see how I can fight?" he asked.

"I will take your word for it. I am sure I would lose any fight with you," I said. "Now let's get on with this trip. I am hungry and I hope Abigail has something to eat."

"She always does, and she has made Bernice a wonderful cook" Julian said.

So, off we went and soon we were starting down the hill to Jonathan's.

"Peace be with you," Jonathan called when we drew up to the house.

"Peace will be fine," I said. "But to be very honest I would much rather have some bread and cheese made by your wonderful sister, who is such a good cook."

"She is ready for you; so leave the care of the donkeys with Julian and the servants, and you go in the house to rest and talk with Abigail," Jonathan said.

"Did you get lost Lazarus?" she asked as she set before me some bread, cheese and goat's milk.

"No, but I was facing rebellion by my donkeys because of their overload of merchandise, so I was in a major crisis when Julian arrived. I was glad to see him."

"Lazarus, you look exhausted, are you all right?" she asked.

"I am not really sure, but let me say yes. I am all right but very tired."

"When you finish those few things, "said Abigail, "Let me suggest that you go straight to bed, and I will bring you something hot to drink.'

That is the first time in my life I did not rebel about going to bed very early. So, when I finished my cheese and bread I immediately went to my little sleeping area and virtually collapsed. Abigail came in with a hot drink, which did not really taste good, so it took me forever to drink it.

Jonathan came in saying, "Abigail says you are sick and we must take care of you. Lazarus, have you eaten some food that was spoiled?"

"I don't think so, but who knows? When you are away from home it is hard to know what you should eat and what you shouldn't eat. And sometimes, I am so hungry after traveling that I will eat anything put in front of me, no questions asked. But Jonathan, I admit that I do not feel well."

"Then you try to sleep late tomorrow. We will take care of the animals and repack and store your merchandise," said Jonathan.

"Thank you, Jonathan," and with that I am told that I fell sound asleep without having finished my sentence.

It was late the next day that Abigail told me how Bernice kept applying cool clothes to my hot forehead until finally my fever left.

The next day I didn't awaken until mid-afternoon when I was startled that a cold cloth was washing my face. Bernice was still caring for me. She gave me a drink of water and I sat up for a few minutes before I was able to stand up with Julian's assistance.

Abigail prepared some kind of hot broth which she told me to eat very slowly and I obeyed her orders.

That evening Samson appeared. He had been summoned by Jesus through one of Jonathan's servants. We visited for a long time and then took a short walk and I felt much better. When we returned Abigail had a very wonderful meal prepared for us and just as we started to eat Jesus was there in our midst. He had Nathaniel and Philip with him.

Jesus looked at me and said, "Lazarus, I feel weakness and restlessness from you. Are you all right?" I walked over and Jesus took my hand.

"I was sick during the night. And Jesus, if you ever experience that, I would advise you to come here for the kind care of Abigail and Bernice. To answer your question, I am a little weak and tired but will improve with your presence and friendship."

"Let's all gather around Lazarus," Jesus said, "Put your hands on him, and let's pray."There was utter silence but a warmth flowed from those hands that made its' way to my very inner being.

I heard Jesus' voice, "Thank you, Father, for filling my beloved friend with your strength from our faith and love." Again, there was absolute silence. When Jesus spoke, he said, "Come Lazarus, the two of us need to take a walk." He stepped out of the house and I followed and off we went toward the high hill to the east. Neither of us said a word and Jesus set a brisk pace. When we arrived at the crest of the hill Jesus stopped and sat on a rock and motioned for me to sit also.

"Lazarus, I am concerned about you," he said.

"Why Jesus?"

"You are so faithful to me; and you are trying to run your business and care for your family. Martha is becoming more and more distressed about your welfare while Mary thinks you are indestructible. How are you going to make it home with the load of merchandise you have at Jonathan's?"

" Perhaps, I should leave some of it with Jonathan."

"But, you still have more animals than one man can manage and there is danger on those roads."

"Yes, Jesus, I am well aware of the danger, and, sometimes, I push sensibility aside."

"Can you get one of the men here to go with you?"Jesus asked.

"But then they would have to make the trip back, and I feel that is most inconvenient for them," I said.

"Do you mind if I ask them for ideas for someone who might help?"Jesus asked.

"Jesus, that is not necessary, but if you wish, I will agree."

We spent the next hour talking about family, and it was a wonderful rest from the last few weeks. Jesus has a laugh that springs from the very depth of his soul and his eyes can be alive with joy.

We made our way back to the house, and we heard some rollicking laugher before we ever got there. It sounded like a party, and we were both laughing when we arrived.

I moved immediately to Jonathan and told him that I must start home tomorrow. He informed me that Julian and another servant would be going with me. The remainder of the night I kept withdrawn to the side of the activities and after a good night's rest Julian, Saul, and myself started toward home. I was amazed how much merchandise I had to transport.

I did not have to lift my hands to help. Each day I felt my strength grow.

The whole way back I kept repeating, "And God repented." I will be very glad to see Rabbi Levi and bring his wise words back with me to share in our group discussions.

Martha was so glad to see me that I was a little overwhelmed by her warm greeting. Mary dove into the merchandise to see what she could find that interested her.

Julian and Saul didn't even spend the night. They left immediately and young Judas arrived from his house just as they said "Good-bye and Peace."

Accusations and Threats

There were times when I wished I did not know Jesus. There were even times when I wished he was not my best friend. It was a heavy load to carry in my heart and mind. I worried about him and his family; yet, I loved all of them. I looked upon them as and extension of my family. What a wonderful privilege and blessing.

Jerusalem was my business arena, and I greatly enjoyed my visits to the Temple. Then, sometimes, I would visit the Beautiful Gate into the city and listen to all of the tumult and fuss of the elders debating. After listening to those discussions and intense arguments, I would sometimes go home crying. At other times, I would be trapped deep in puzzlement; a few times I would actually skip along laughing at all the grand and silly ideas expressed at those Gates by supposedly learned men.

There was one thing that would always make me catch my breath and withdraw into the deepest sanctuary of my soul. More of the leaders of Israel were expressing anger and frustration over the teachings of Jesus, and some would voice violent threats against him and his followers. That made me very uneasy.

One day, I was worshipping at the Temple and the crowd was phenomenal. I had to push and shove, slide this way and that, before I ever got into the sanctuary. Once there, I decided it would be just as well to stay toward the back.

My mind and spirit became enchanted with the beauty of worship and this day there was a cantor whose voice made the Psalms come alive. His voice was clear and soared to the heavens and came back with all of the joy and wonder that makes those words so inspiring. I closed my eyes and just listened.

I soon became aware that a small group of men behind me were whispering rather loudly. I wanted to turn around, tell them to hush, and remind them where they were. But then I heard the name Jesus, I tuned in to their conversation as best I could, rather than the canter. It was not immediately evident how many were involved in the conversation, but two of them had spent several days recently observing and listening to Jesus in Galilee.

One of them soon made the accusation, "he's a disturbing heretic." The other said, "I think something needs to be done immediately to close him down." Now, they had my full attention. I listened to their accusations, threats and desperate attempts to find avenues to destroy Jesus. They saw his healings as frauds and his teachings were dangerous. His disciples were mindless idiots, who didn't have enough sense to make a judgment about what they were calling "the Jesus cult" that seemed to be growing. One almost shouted, "It must come to an end now."

The crowd in the sanctuary had thinned a little and about that time Rabbi Levi came pushing through to where I was standing, "Lazarus, what is the latest word you have on Jesus? There are so many different opinions it is hard to know what to believe or not to believe. Since you are his close friend, I know you can help me filter through all this trash talk going around."

"Greetings Rabbi! I have just been standing here for the last hour listening to a conversation about the heretical mission of Jesus from four or five men who obviously are deeply concerned.

But I can tell you, they do not know the truth. I was sure they did not want to hear anything different from me, so I remained very quiet and listened."

Rabbi Levi looked very startled; and I thought he might run, but I put my hand on his arm and said, "That's all right, Rabbi. I am sure they are well away from the Temple." The Rabbi and I moved out of the sanctuary where we could talk more openly.

When we were away from the sanctuary I said, "Rabbi, I really do not have any recent news about Jesus; but the last time I was in Galilee, the crowds were bigger and the disciples seemed very adjusted to their role in relation to Jesus.

"Why are these people, whoever they are, against him? There are other spiritual leaders with their disciples who teach and presumably perform healings?" said the Rabbi.

"I really don't know, but there are many who are seemingly threatened by Jesus. But I can tell you, he teaches love, peace, and about God's righteousness. He is one of the most mild mannered people I know," I said.

"Then there should be no objection to him."

"Rabbi, he does talk a lot about the Kingdom of God, but it is an inner kingdom over which God presides. He does not raise any threats toward Rome or any civic or religious leaders. It puzzles me that there are those who think Jesus is talking about overthrowing the established government. I can assure you completely that such an idea is not on his mind," Lazarus said.

"Thank you, Lazarus, what you have told me is a great help; and I will try to share it wisely with the right people," said the Rabbi. "I must be off to do my duties, and I will look forward to seeing you again soon."

"Can you let me ask you an important question?

"Why, yes," said the Rabbi.

"One of Jesus's disciples, named John, was telling me about an experience when they were in the region of Tyre and Sidon. A Syro-Phoenician woman came to Jesus because her daughter was afflicted with demons and she asked for help. Jesus was very tired and he spoke with a sharp tongue saying, 'I did not come to give bread to dogs,' and the woman responded, "but the dogs are willing to gather up the crumbs under the master's table.'"

"That surprises me," said the Rabbi. "I would not have expected such a sharp rebuke to have come from Jesus."

"But wait, listen to me for just a moment. The disciple known as John said that Jesus struggled with what he had said. When several of them were alone that evening Jesus was still reflecting on this incident and he suddenly said out loud, "Now I know what it means in the Torah that God 'repented.' He explained to me that it meant God felt a deep sorrow. Then in their presence Jesus asked God's forgiveness. He also in his prayer time asked for his mother's forgiveness and the child's mother's forgiveness. But I am still puzzled about the meaning of God repenting?"

"Jesus is exactly right when he says, "God repented" and, yes, that means a deep soul searing sorrow. God repented after he had created human life. He again repented after the flood because he had destroyed humankind. He repented for making Saul king over Israel. God can feel a deep remorse, a cutting, painful soul sorrow. God created us after the divine angels who have all the character traits of God. So, as God grieves; deeply and repents so do we. I hope that gives you something to share with Jesus's disciple John," Rabbi Levi said.

"You have been a great help, thank you so much Rabbi. I always enjoy seeing you." He was gone but I enjoyed my usual brief encounter which was extended long enough for me to gain his insight into the meaning of God repenting. I moved away from the crowd surrounding the Temple and started home.

I was getting close to where I would leave the city when I became suspicious that I was being followed. I have never had any feelings like that before, so I stopped and looked behind me and saw four men stop and walk to the side of the street. They, however, kept glancing my way. I stopped several more times acting like I was looking at some vendor's products, and it was always the same. Were those the men who had been standing behind me at the Temple? Did they overhear my conversation with Rabbi Levi about Jesus? I moved off into a side street and after counting to ten, I walked briskly back out on the main street, and turned in their direction. We almost ran into one another and I stepped across the street, into a little café with which I was familiar. I went all the way through the building and out the back door. I then walked quickly, and once outside the city, I moved down the road to where I entered the Garden of Gethsemane. I then halted to see if they would appear. I did not want them to follow me home.

I was very grateful that I was alone and soon came to Bethany and our home. Mama greeted me and let me know that the evening meal would soon be ready.

That night, it was a long time before I went to sleep. Why were those men following me? If they were following me, what might they want? Is it possible that I would see them again? Is it possible that they would find Rabbi Levi and ask him about me? Perhaps, I should talk with him, but then again, I do not want to alarm him or frighten him. So, I drifted off to sleep with a lot of questions on my mind.

The next morning I awoke with the same questions rattling in my mind. At breakfast Mama asked me, "Lazarus, didn't you sleep well? Your mind does not seem to be with us today?"

"Well, I have been thinking about going on another buying trip," I said. "Will you go toward Galilee?" Mama asked.

"No, I haven't been south and to the Great Sea for a long time, so that is the direction I am planning to take," I said.

"The first thing I must do is see if Judas is available to go with me. I have gotten so that I depend on him and he also seems to expect me to continue using him. Plus, he relies on my leadership in setting up those major trips," I told Mama.

"Lazarus, don't you think it may be time to encourage him to make buying trips on his own. He appears to be a very responsible young man. You have trained him well and he has been attentive to do things as you want them done."

I was encouraged by Mama's comments, "You are right he has worked hard to do things in a way that will please me."

"Now, who are we talking about," said Martha as she swept into the room. "Do you think Jesus is going to work to please you?"

Mama said quietly, "Martha he is talking about Judas being such a good helper and doing things in a way that pleases and helps Lazarus."

"You better watch him; he's a young man; and one day he may take off with everything, donkeys, merchandise, and even the money."

"I trust him completely," I said, "and, what's more, I have been thinking about making him a full partner. That would mean he could make decisions on his own and that would make things easier.

Mama jumped in quickly, "I think that is a good idea, Lazarus. Perhaps, the two of you can talk about that while you are on this trip."

"That is a great suggestion, Mama. I will be back in a little while," I said as I walked out of the room to go see Judas. I heard Martha start to disagree with me but Mama quieted her down.

Judas was home and he seemed very glad to see me. He was even happier that I wanted to go on a buying trip. We talked about all that needed to be done before we left and Judas as always said, "I'll take care of that."

Let me give him the credit that he is due, "He did it all and in two days we were ready to leave on the next morning."

The donkeys seemed excited that we were leaving; and I wasn't sure if what my sister, Mary, might be found perched on the back of a donkey when it was time to go.

All was ready and we turned south toward Hebron. Judas was wanting to stop all along the way especially in Bethlehem, but I kept our little caravan moving until we were in Hebron. I was disappointed that we did not find anything new. It was merchandise that we had seen before and I suggested that we move on toward Beersheba.

I began to inquire about Moses who scared us so much on one of our earlier trips. No one seemed to know him and they would always change the subject when I brought up his name.

"Judas, do you think that Moses got into trouble and the people are afraid to say they have known him?" I asked.

"Well we saw him as trouble," responded Judas.

"It seems that I remember he lived close to a small town north of Beersheba," I said.

"That's it, we were on our way to Beersheba and when we had trouble with him, it was then that we turned west."

"Then let's ask in that community when we get there tomorrow."

We found a good place to camp that was protected and had both water and grass. Our donkeys were glad to stop and we started a small fire to make something to eat. We had plenty of dried meat and bread.

While sitting there and I was dozing off to sleep when Judas asked, "What is it about Jesus that keeps you so interested in him?"

I caught my breath and thought, I have missed a great chance to share the "Good News" with someone who is very close to me, and I had not thought about it. "Judas what have you heard about Jesus that has aroused your curiosity, I asked?"

"Well, I hear little bits of things around your house. You personally seem to be very close to him, but in Jerusalem he is called a heretic; and some say he is a crazy man who plays tricks on people."

"Let me..." I started to say.

"But let me be clear," said Judas, "I do not think you would be interested in any crazy man. However, recently I have been hearing more that is negative about him than I hear good. So, I need someone to help me."

"Judas, I am not sure that I have time to tell you everything, but I can talk along the way on this trip. Let me just say two quick things. I have known Jesus since we were boys. We even trained for the Bar Mitzvah together under Rabbi Levi and were confirmed in the Temple. Jesus is my best friend and I strongly believe he is the Son of the Living God."

"That is a lot and I am impressed," said Judas with a sense of awe and excitement. "Tell me one thing that he teaches."

So, as we moved south toward Beersheba I began to share some of the teachings of Jesus. "He teaches a lot about the Kingdom of God and his righteousness."

I realized that Judas was very focused on what I was saying. "God's righteousness always relates to us through his Justice and Mercy, and we are to do the same in our relationships to others. When you think of God's Righteousness, always remember, it means Justice and Mercy. Justice means God knows the whole truth about us. He knows every thought and action. Mercy means that God loves and forgives us for what we do and is working to redeem us and draw us into his Kingdom. God never gives up on us and we are not to give up on others because we are God's child and must work to be like him in the way we live."

"Stop, right there, Lazarus, and let me think about what you have shared and possibly ask a few questions," Judas said.

"It takes a while to sort through what he teaches us, so take your time. But I cannot promise you that I will always be able to answer your questions."

"Fine," said Judas, "so, we can grow together and when you see Jesus you can ask him a question for me and bring it back."

He curled up on the ground with a robe balled up and tucked under his head like a pillow and he got very quiet. Every now and then I would hear him say, "Justice… Mercy," then he would get quiet until he would say it again.

"Lazarus, you said that God's knows everything about us?"

"That's right Judas, everything. He knows both our thoughts and our deeds and he still loves us."

"That is a lot like my Mama," said Judas.

"I think you are probably right."

He got quiet again and I heard him say again, Justice…Mercy.

It was a very little while when both of us dropped off to sleep pondering about the

Justice and Mercy of God. I think Jesus would have been very pleased and certainly young Judas had grown in his faith and knowledge. I was pleased that I was given the opportunity to be a witness and isn't that being a disciple?

We were up early and on our way and quickly moved our little caravan south toward Beersheba. I kept wondering about Moses and the mystery that surrounded him.

We came to a little community just north of Beersheba which looked very familiar and Judas turned and said, "Here is where we met Moses."

We moved off the road to begin making our rounds of the merchants in that area. At the first stop I asked, "Can you tell me about Moses who lived in this area?"

The man stopped, waved us to get away, and disappeared into his house as he pulled the curtains at the doorway. I looked around and there was no one on the small street with us. Everyone had vanished and as we walked through that little village it was as though the people had dissolved and any merchandise had disappeared with them.

"Come on Judas, let's get out of here. Don't mention the name of Moses again."

In Beersheba, we went about our business and for the first time on this trip had reasonable success. When we ventured a little closer to Egypt we were thrilled at the discoveries me made of new crafts. Also, things were a little cheaper and that encouraged us to buy more than we anticipated.

We spent four days in the area and on the second evening I asked, "Judas, we have talked about God's righteousness, would you like to deal with another area of Jesus' teaching?"

"Yes, please," he replied.

"All right, let's clean up this campsite then we can sit and talk about the Kingdom of God." So we busied ourselves, had something to eat, and sorted some of our purchases, and discussed buying another donkey. We were going to need another beast of burden after another day's purchases.

"Lazarus," Judas asked, "have you ever thought about buying a camel? They can carry so much more, and I could care for the animal at my house in that big shed when we are not traveling."

"Well, that's an interesting idea. Let me pose another idea, what would you think about us becoming business partners? That would include the idea of you making buying trips on your own when I am away in Galilee. And, after each trip we would split the profit half and half."

Judas sat there looking at me, "Well, Jesus' teachings stir the mind and spirit but you have just shocked my whole being. Are you serious?"

"Yes, Judas, I am very serious!"

"Lazarus, you said a full partner?"

"Yes, Judas, because I think that is the only way for it to work and be fair to both of us. Plus, I trust your business sense, both of us enjoy working hard and we have strong support from our family. The way I see it, I have nothing to lose and everything to gain."

"That is a lot of responsibility for me," Judas said.

"You're right," I said, "but there is a selfish side for me. Someday, before very long, you will want your own business, and I would rather work with you and not in competition with you."

Judas laughed the biggest laugh I had ever heard out of him. "You are certainly full of surprises. I thought you were going to talk about the Kingdom of God. Are you still up to that?"

"Oh yes," I said, "Jesus keeps mentioning it over and over. In a prayer he gave us he prayed 'thy Kingdom come on earth as it is in heaven' and again he said 'Seek you first the Kingdom of God and his righteousness and all things will be added unto you.' You cannot get away from the Kingdom issues in his teaching. But it is not a physical Kingdom like Rome, it is a spiritual kingdom that is within. We are God's kingdom children. God reigns within us and his Kingdom is real and vibrant within us."

"You are telling me, Lazarus, that I can be a member of that Kingdom, but still give my loyalty to Rome and our home area of Judea. That there is no conflict by being a part of both?"

"You can abide by the spiritual laws of God's Kingdom and that does not make you less Judean or Roman. But, yes, there are certain moral and spiritual laws that you must incorporate into your life. God comes first not Caesar or some Roman governor. Plus, as Kingdom children, we live differently than most people. Jesus calls on us to be humble, merciful, to hunger after God's righteousness, to be a peacemaker, to keep our heart pure and morally straight, to bear the sorrows of other people in this world, and always be willing to listen to others.

"He says for us to expect to be misunderstood by others around us. Plus, there is a possibility that we may be persecuted for our beliefs and actions. Also, he calls upon us to be a light in the world to help others find their way. There is much more but maybe I should stop there," I said.

"Lazarus, how am I to do all of this? I am only one person trying to do what is right every day," Judas said.

"And Jesus says to you, 'Lo, I am with you always.' He will be the friend who will always be close to guide, strengthen, and comfort you. Judas, let's stop because we have shared a lot this evening. Sleep on it and tomorrow will be a new day."

"Sleep on it. I will be awake all night struggling with the meaning of a possible partnership and the teachings of Jesus as they apply to my life. Good night, Lazarus." With that Judas walked off to be with himself.

After two days we came back by Beersheba and cut west toward Ziklag and the Great Sea with a caravan that was going to Gaza.

When we came to a big well, west of Ziklag, I recognized it immediately. "Judas this is where we left the road and stayed with Malachi and his sons. Over there is their house and we even bought some things from them."

"You are right. Let's stop and see if they know anything about Moses," he suggested.

"I agree." So we moved in the direction of that house. Malachi saw us coming and came out of his house to meet us. We had a happy reunion and talked business with him as he showed us some crafts and we made some purchases.

Finally, I ventured, "Malachi, we have gotten some strange responses from people when we have mentioned Moses. Would you have any answers about the reasons?"

I noticed a quick hesitancy and his sons stopped and looked at him.

His voice got much quieter and his sons looked around as if to see if anyone was listening. "Lazarus, all I wish to say is that he had a major clash with Roman authorities, and he and his friends were crucified not far from here. There, that's as much as I am willing to say," said Malachi.

We visited for the rest of the day, saw a few more craftsmen that his sons brought to his house, and he invited us to spend the night. Nothing else was said about Moses even though I had many questions. Judas and I left early the next morning for Gaza.

The rest of the trip was routine except that we bought a camel. I had forgotten how much a camel was capable of carrying. Judas was thrilled with the purchase and he and that camel became very good friends. At night, Judas would sleep leaning up against that camel and talk to him about Jesus.

One evening I said, "Judas, Jesus often talked about prayer and its importance to our life. In fact, I heard him say, 'we ought always to pray,' but he urged us to pray privately and not put on some show of our piety. I really liked that and Jesus lives that way. His prayers are private and quiet. It is our time with God the Father and we should cherish that opportunity. Also, he told Martha one day when she asked about prayer. He said, 'When you pray you are not standing outside the gates of heaven appealing to God on the inside but, you go in those gates to the very throne of God and bring your petitions and requests right before God himself...' That impressed me a great deal and ever since then I have imagined myself standing in the presence of God the Creator and Redeemer and talking with him. I do not share with him the trivial of life but those bigger issues where I or someone else needs a lot of help."

"That is wonderful," said Judas, "I can hardly wait to get home and share that with Mama because I know she will like it. Jesus said, 'we ought always to pray.'"

"But," I interrupted, "that does not mean we shut our eyes, we can pray while we work or walk. It doesn't mean long sentences, it can be short thoughts. But God is always listening."

"That is wonderful and helpful," said Judas. "I will think a long time about that before I go to sleep tonight, and I will tell Melchizedek about it."

"You will tell who?" I asked.

"Oh, I didn't tell you, that is the camel's name."

I roared with laugher, "Melchizedek?"

"You don't like his name?" ask Judas.

"It's fine," I said. "It suddenly reminded me of Jesus and his donkey. When he was twelve he had a donkey name Methuselah and everyone though that was so strange and funny. So now we have Melchizedek, the camel. I can hardly wait to tell Jesus. I really think that will please him."

"Maybe I will get the opportunity to tell him myself," said a wistful Judas.

"Maybe you will."

So he wandered off with Melchizedek and they settled down for the night.

While we were still on the road, at night before he would go to sleep I would hear him saying quietly "justice...mercy" and then after a little while he would come out with several other words: humble…merciful…peacemaker…sharing someone else's sorrow… always pray without ceasing." He really struggled with these spiritual issues in life and from time to time he would ask a question.

The trip continued to go well, and we would talk more and more about a partnership. At first, Judas was skeptical, but he began to share positive thoughts about it until he was saying he could hardly wait "to tell Mama about this potential and exciting arrangement."

We ended up buying so much that we bought a second camel. It was a little skinny and I worried about it but Judas kept saying, "Mama will fatten him up."

"Tell me, Judas, are you going to name this new camel?"

"I already have," he said, "his name is Mordecai, after my grandfather."

"I hope when you get married that you have daughters. Maybe you would do better with girls' names," I said.

We both laughed.

Two weeks later we arrived back in Bethany with two camels and six donkeys loaded with a great variety of merchandise.

My sisters became very involved in looking through what we had bought. Judas and I began the job of sorting the merchandise, then packaging that merchandise for particular merchants that we would visit, and make a presentation to them. You soon learn about your clients and their interests.Martha and Mary took several things in the house, but before the day was over Mama brought all of those things back except one. There was a little vase that we had purchased south of Beersheba and it really caught her eye and interest. It was a very simple gift for a very wonderful woman and I noticed that Judas took one of the same to his Mama.

It was great to be home, but all of the questions rose in my mind about being followed by those men from the Temple when I was last there to worship.

The next day was the Sabbath and I returned to the Temple. There was Rabbi Levi, but I did not want to talk with him today, so I avoided him. I am not sure that he saw me and that was helpful.

It was good to hear the Cantor singing the Psalms. As I was listening, I suddenly thought, why didn't I invite Judas to come with me. Then I promised myself that I would be sure to invite him next week, and I must ask about his Bar Mitzvah. That made me remember that I had said something to Jonathan about his Bar Mitzvah and activities surrounding Jesus had so consumed our time that I had not been attentive to Jonathan.

The next day Judas and I went our separate ways to make our sales and it was a very good day. When we returned to the house I said, "Judas, it looks like we should have bought a lot more."

Judas laughed as he said, "We must begin gathering our own caravan and take four or five more people with us."

"Let's think about it, but right now let's finish our present sales work. Plus, Judas, would you be interested in going with me to the Temple next week for Sabbath worship? I would really like to take you with me.

"Well," said Judas, "no one has ever asked me and I have never been there. I guess it is because my father died when I was very young and no one has taken his place for religious training."

"Then you have not had your Bar Mitzvah?"

"No, but not because I haven't wanted to celebrate it."

"Then, let's talk about that also, and I can work with you."

After another day of sales I returned to Jerusalem in hopes that I could talk with Rabbi Levi. I have never been to the Temple when there have been so few people there or in the city as well.

I was there for about an hour in worship when Rabbi Levi came from a side entrance and I watched him. He spoke with one of the cantors and then left by the same way. I quickly slipped out an entrance and turned to the right in hopes of catching him. He was nowhere to be seen. I walked around slowly and then returned to the sanctuary. There he was again. This time I worked my way forward until he saw me and by sign language I let him know that I wanted to see him.

He pointed toward the opposite side of the sanctuary, and I made my way out and around to the left.

In just a moment, he was there greeting me.

"I am so glad to see you. I need to talk with you about several things. Do you have the time for me now and is there a place where we can be private?"

Rabbi Levi hesitated and then he simply said, "Follow me."

He surprised me. We went out of the Temple, down the main street, and turned into a little alley. He opened a small door into a small intimate café. Immediately, he went into a small booth, pulled the curtain and soon two cups of hot tea where placed before us.

"My, I did not know that you have a hiding place," I said.

"There's a lot you don't know about me, Lazarus. Now, you seem to be rather urgent in your request."

"Yes on two counts," I said.

"So full of problems today?" he asked and chuckled.

"Rabbi, when I was here a few weeks ago and told you about the conversation I heard whispered in the sanctuary. Those men followed me after I left the Temple. I lost them and have been on a buying trip. But did they ever come and question you about me?" I asked.

"As a matter of fact they did," he answered.

"Well, I hope your friendship with me has not gotten you in trouble with those people who are intent on harming Jesus," I said.

"I simply told them you are Temple trained and remain in constant contact with us. That your professional work takes you into Galilee and your reports about Jesus are of a great help in allowing the Temple staff to know what is going on. But I did not say anything like you are a spy," he said.

I started laughing and couldn't stop. "So, I am now the informant."

"Call it what you will, but they have not returned."

"Thank you, Rabbi. You pulled me out of one hole, but it seems to me that you have pushed me in another."

"Not at all," said Rabbi Levi, "you are in the clear and I am glad to be seen with you at anytime. Now, what is the second issue?"

"I have a young boy working with me, Judas by name. He is talented and works hard for both of us. His father died when he was very young and his mother is still single with no immediate family living in the area. He would very much like to celebrate his Bar Mitzvah. I am willing to sponsor him, but I need a Rabbi to train him and enable this to happen."

"And you are asking me to take that job. Bring him before me and let's see if he can pass my examination, and we will go from there. But I assure you that I am making no promises," the Rabbi said.

"When will you have time to see him?" I asked.

"Right after high noon tomorrow; bring him here to this cafe. I will see you then."

With that Rabbi Levi was off to his next appointment, and we would be one of those appointments tomorrow. I felt good about his answer to both questions. Now, I knew that I must get home and talk with Judas.

I left the Temple area and moved on toward Bethany. For some reason I kept looking behind me to see if I was being followed, but there was never anyone there. I felt good about both issues I had discussed with the Rabbi. I am already looking forward to our meeting tomorrow. It will be like reliving the study program with Jesus. Of course, Rabbi Levi is considerably older, but he has the same enthusiasm and his voice has even gotten more mellow. It will be good to hear him quoting scripture again.

I went straight to Judas's house, and both he and his mother were there. I asked if we could talk for a few minutes. I explained to his mother, Judith, about our conversation concerning the Bar Mitzvah and she acknowledged that they had talked about this.

"Today I talked with Rabbi Levi at the Temple. I studied under his tutelage years ago and found him exciting and helpful in every way. He would like to meet with us tomorrow at high noon at the Temple."

Judas's eyes got big and he said, "So, soon, Mama I…"

"Judas, there is no use dragging something out that should have happened in your life years ago. He will be ready to go with you, Lazarus. Let me thank you for your interest and help. Judas expressed real excitement about this, and I can assure you I am just as thrilled for him. Plus, he talked about a possible partnership between the two of you. At some time I would like to talk at length with you because Judas gets so excited that he finds it difficult to talk," Judas's mother said.

I could tell he was very excited. I rose and excused myself.

"Yes, we must talk about several things. Come to the house by mid-morning Judas and we will go," I said.

Walking home I realized that I was as excited as Judas. When I told Mama, she looked at me and beamed. I am so proud of you doing those things for Judas. "Now, for the Bar Mitzvah, we must be the ones to plan his party."

"Good Mama, but don't jump so far ahead."

"Lazarus that takes considerable planning, and I will talk with Judith after things are moving along."

I returned to the shed to do some sorting and I was surprised to find Judas already there. He looked at me with the brightest smile.

"Thank you, Lazarus! I will try hard not to disappoint you. I will study and work very hard."

"I know you will," I said. "Now, let's get on with the work here."

The next day Judas was at our house almost a little after dawn. Goodness, he had on a beautiful robe which caught the eye of both my sisters. We were eating and Mama invited him to sit down and join us. Judas eats enough for two people and probably would have eaten much more if Mama would have put it before him. I have never heard him laugh so much and Mary kept encouraging him to laugh by telling funny stories. It was one joyful morning.

We left early for the Temple. Judas began walking so fast I thought I was going to have to run to keep up. I kept trying to remember if I was that excited when we first went to meet with Rabbi Levi. I decided I was when I remembered that Papa had told me to slow down. Judas kept laughing a nervous giggle that was a little distracting.

When we arrived at the Temple, we went directly to the sanctuary. There was no laughter now but Judas found it difficult to stand still. We stood in the back, listened, and watched as the great beauty and mystery of holy worship unfolded. As the time came for our interview, I pulled on Judas's sleeve, and we moved out of the sanctuary, toward the great front door to go to the café. Rabbi Levi was just outside the door, when I spoke from behind him, he jumped, then moved quickly to the side, and told us to follow him. Rather than going to the café we went to a little office area and then he greeted us and suggested that we sit down.

He looked at Judas for a few moments and then spoke in Hebrew to him. Judas tried to respond to him, but he became very confused, so he switched to our native Aramaic and said, "Rabbi, I'm sorry, but I have not had any formal training in Hebrew since I have no father at home."

So, Judas," responded Rabbi Levi, "you cannot quote any of the Torah or the Psalms in Hebrew?

"No, sir," he said with his head down."

"Well, that is going to make things a little more difficult but not impossible. Lazarus, I do not know how busy you are, but you must spend some intensive time with Judas studying Hebrew. Begin teaching him the Torah and the Psalms. It is my understanding that the two of you go on buying and sales trips together. Only speak Hebrew to each other. Begin memorizing Psalms one and two, the creation stories in Genesis and the laws given by Moses in Exodus. When you have completed that come back and see me."

"Thank you, Rabbi," said Judas, "I will do my best."

"I am sure you will and Lazarus will be a good teacher. Judas you are blest to have him as your mentor and teacher."

With that Rabbi Levi was out the door and gone with both of us staring after him. There are times he seems like some vision appearing and disappearing.

"Come on Judas. It is time for us to go home, but first let me take you by the Great Gate into the city and we will listen to the elders argue and debate for a little while. I always enjoy this, and you will hear only Hebrew."

We made our way through the crowds in the city streets and soon arrived at the Beautiful Gate. Judas became so fascinated by the crowd pushing and shoving, always trying to get closer so as to hear better that he was not listening himself.

I patted his shoulder and said, "Listen to the words, the Hebrew. See how much you can understand?"

Judas got very quiet, and I could tell that he was straining. Suddenly, I thought he was going to cry, "Come Judas, it doesn't really matter at this time. Together, we will get it."

I took his arm and pulled him away from that scene. It was mistake on my part and we made our way home. But Judas was not going to let go of his failure.

"Lazarus, I really did not understand a thing they were talking about."

"That's fine, Judas. It was a deep theological debate they were having and many of the words I did not understand myself. The two of us will begin tomorrow to work on your learning Hebrew."

I am not sure I convinced him, but I would not take him back to that Gate.

We arrived back in Bethany and Judas went on home after we set a time to meet in the morning.

When I went in the house Mama asked how the day went.

"Our interview with Rabbi Levi went well, but I made a terrible mistake. I took Judas to the main gate of Jerusalem to let him listen to the rabbis debating. He could not understand a thing and he became so discouraged. I felt he might back out of the study

program with Rabbi Levi. Mama, the look in his eyes was frightening."

"He will be all right," Mama said, "I will go over and talk with his mama tomorrow and together we will plan a way to encourage and support Judas."

I went out to the shed, worked with the donkeys, and cleaned the whole shed. Mama brought me something to eat. Sister Mary came out and started helping me put things back in the shed that I had taken out. She never said a word and when we finished I went back in the house and went to bed. There was some bread and cheese when I awoke and I know Mama had put it there.

I wrestled with myself all night and kept waking up and having terrible dreams that had no connection with my problems with Judas.

I left the house before anyone was up and walked to Jerusalem. I went to the Temple and sat down on the steps. I prayed to God, talked to Jesus, and fussed at myself, but the hollow feeling in my heart would not go away. I finally walked back to the Garden of Gethsemene and found the rock where we had stumbled on Jesus with that bird I had knocked out of the tree.

I had hardly settled on that rock when one of those birds appeared and perched on a low tree limb right in front of me. That bird started singing with its head held high. I was so intrigued and pleased. I was startled when someone sat beside me, and when I looked it was Mary, my sister. What a gift, a beautiful song and a loving sister. My life was suddenly full again and I started laughing. Mary joined me laughing and took my arm and laid her head upon my shoulder.

"How did you know where to find me," I asked.

"I just asked myself, if I was feeling frustrated and confused where would I go and here I am."

"Thank you for coming. Look at that bird. It is still sitting there looking at us. Come, it is time to go to our house," I said.

So we started walking with that bird leading the way. When I got home, Mama prepared some food for me and I found new strength in the food I ate and in the warm love of my family.

There was a startling noise outside, and Mary and I ran to see what it was with Mama and Martha following. There was Judas in the shed looking very confused. "That donkey tried to kick me several times, and he kicked the wall, instead. I think I will leave this shed for a little while."

I said, "Good idea. Come in and have some breakfast with us."

He didn't need another invitation and we were all sitting around eating, talking and laughing. What a wonderful scene, I thought.

We then began to plan a buying trip and decided to go toward Jericho.

"Give me two days and I will have everything ready to go," said Judas as he went out the door. I soon followed him and in two days we were off to Jericho. I was teaching him to learn to speak short phrases in Hebrew, and Judas was beginning to answer. In the evenings, we would practice writing Hebrew using the old piece of slate that I had used with Rabbi Levi. I found my tutoring job very interesting and exciting. Goodness, I found myself feeling like a father and I am sure I was acting a little like one. It suddenly came to me that I needed to be careful. Judas and I were developing a partnership in our business and I could not mix paternal attitudes with business needs. So, I pulled back and we continued to get along fine.

By the time we returned to Bethany Judas was beginning to blossom in his Hebrew studies. I was amazed with his natural ability with the Hebrew language. Again we went to the Beautiful Gate and listened to the debate. He was amazed at how much he understood, and we stayed for about three hours without any complaint from him.

The next day we were scheduled to work on sorting and dividing our merchandise in preparation for our sales routes around the city of Jerusalem. Judas did not appear and

had not come by high noon that day. I walked over to his house and discovered from his mother that he had left for the Beautiful Gate early in the day.

That evening Judas came to the house apologizing for abandoning me but telling me about what an exciting day he had had listening to the rabbis. He stayed until dark working with me in organizing his part of the crafts.

The next morning we left and went our separate ways to sell and listen to the needs of the merchants to find out what we should buy on the next trip. When Judas returned he was excited because when he had finished his sales he took the donkeys right up to the Beautiful Gate and listened for a long time.

We returned to the Temple the next day and had some time with Rabbi Levi. He was so pleased with Judas's progress that he scheduled his first class and gave him his student supplies, which included a new slate board. Judas was thrilled. All the way home he was quoting the Creation Story, Exodus 20 and a number of Psalms. Judas was on his way toward his holy hour, the Bar Mitzvah.

Every now and then, I would correct the way he pronounced a word or suggest a slightly different emphasis on a phrase to give it added meaning. I could see that these next weeks would be busy and exciting. So when I got home I suggested to Mama that she and the girls had better begin planning for a big celebration. Judas was on his way.

She put her arm around me and said, "I'm so proud of you."

I hadn't felt that good for a long time.

Love and Forgiveness

No one could miss the urgent pleas Jesus made for us to join the kingdom of God. Jesus's teaching was a Kingdom message but none of us were clear about what that Kingdom was and where it might be.

To Jesus that kingdom seemed as near as his breath; but to us, who listened to his teaching, we were ready to march to some other place to find and join it. We seemed incapable of hearing him when he would tell us over and over "the kingdom is within you;" plus, he kept referring to children in that kingdom. That would be fine as long as they stayed out of our way. Children would be a nuisance if you were called upon to fight for the kingdom wherever it was. Again, Jesus confused us more than once by saying, "You cannot follow me unless you accept my kingdom as a little child.

Whenever some of us would be gathered in debate or discussion, we would always find ourselves talking about 'the kingdom." It was much later that we learned and accepted the kingdom of God as a spiritual kingdom within each of us and not some earthly establishment with princes and lords, an earthly government, castles and especially some army equipped to fight wars and to control and manipulate the people.

Jesus was constantly challenging our mental self-images. We thought we knew who we wanted to be and how we were going to get there. But then we would be off together for a time of teaching and meditation, and it seemed that every time "the Kingdom" would be our central focus. We kept struggling with our own "kingdom images" and they were far removed from what Jesus taught.

I remember so clearly when Jesus said:

> *Truly, I say to you,*
> unless you turn
> and become like children,
> you will never enter the kingdom of heaven.
> Whoever humbles themselves
> and becomes like a child,
> he is the greatest in the kingdom of heaven.
> And, whoever receives one such child
> in my name receives me;
> but whoever causes one of these little ones
> who believe in me to sin;
> it would be better for them
> to have a great millstone
> fastened around their neck
> and to be drowned
> in the depth of the sea.

Jesus never hesitated to speak of judgment. Sin is an abomination to him. There is a price to be paid for wrong choices on our part, and we are responsible for our daily choices. Life is serious business for all of us and especially for our corporate living in every community where people live. Discipline, commitment, responsibility, and service are all tied together and he did not hesitate to remind us that punishment was harsh and swift. But it is never God's Will that any of us be lost from his forgiveness and love.

One evening while he was teaching, he said:

> *What do you think?*
> If a man has a hundred sheep,
> and one of them has gone astray,
> does he not leave the ninety-nine
> on the hillside and go in search
> of the one that went astray?
> And if he finds it,
> truly, I say to you, he rejoices
> over it more than
> over the ninety-nine that
> never went astray.
> So it is not the will of my Father
> who is in heaven
> that even one should perish.

Peter had been listening very intensely and he asked:

> *Lord how often shall my brother* or friend,
> sin against me, and I forgive him?
> As many as seven times?

Jesus was quiet a few minutes and with a warm smile he looked at Peter and said, "Peter, are you listening to me?"

"Yes, my Lord."

"Are all of you listening?" We knew it would be something very important. He paused for a long time and seemed to be in prayer before he answered Peter and spoke to all of us. Then with real force and command he said,"

> *I do not say to you seven times,*
> but seventy times seven.

There seemed to be a quiet grumble that rumbled across the group listening to Jesus and he very forcefully repeated:

> *Seventy times seven.*

"Peter, let me ask you to reflect on this question, how many times has God forgiven you and how many more kindnesses will you receive from him in your lifetime? Jesus paused for a long time as he watched Peter and then said very quietly;

Seventy times seven.

Those who were standing around were looking back and forth at each other. Several were talking and others were struggling in prayer. Jesus had a way of pushing you into a sudden prayer experience. It was natural when you couldn't understand or when your mind rebelled, you were inclined to leap into a prayer mood. That could really be very helpful. Then when you felt a moment of enlightenment you would turn and look for the very person with whom you wished to have a very intense conversation about the issue that had just been raised.

On this occasion I turned and looked for Nathaniel. He was very obviously in an attitude of prayer, and I started walking slowly toward him. At the very moment that I reached where he was standing, Philip also arrived and our warm greeting to each other startled Nathaniel. He turned toward us and motioned for us to follow him.

"Let's find a place to be alone," he said.

We continued walking until we came to a small olive grove and then Philip said, "Stop here. We are separated from the group, but we can see Jesus in the distance; and if he decides to move on, we will see and can follow him."

Nathaniel spoke very quickly, "Seventy times seven…seventy times seven…it seems to me that Jesus is saying, never stop forgiving…Seventy times seven."

"That is a heavy cross to carry," I said. "But it is the only way that we can prove we are willing to make a difference in our personal life and in the lives of others around us and eventually in the whole of our society.

"What if we are kind? Is that forgiveness?" asked Philip.

The three of us became quiet in very serious thought.

"No," said Nathaniel, "Kindness is not the same thing. Forgiveness springs from the very soul of God and it heals and renews. Kindness is an attempt to do something nice, and, perhaps, even important, but it leaves an open door for you to back out of your commitment. Kindness just does not go far enough."

We got very quiet again. Suddenly, Jesus spoke and he was right there behind us. We had not seen him come our way.

"The three of you seem so very serious in your discussion while most of the others have gone on their way. So, I came to join you. Nathaniel, you have captured the meaning and significance of forgiveness. It is one of the most important attributes of God's righteousness, his mercy. Kindness can be a simple human excuse to do something nice for a show that others may see you, and then you withdraw from the situation. Forgiveness is an act of love that seeks to redeem the worst situations in life. It is absolutely the best of the spiritual gifts of heaven that heals and enriches relationships on earth. And remember, it never gives up."

"Jesus," I said, "will you let me try and work through all that you have just said in my own words?"

"All right, Lazarus, put what I said in your own words, and let's have Nathaniel and Philip judge if your insight is the same as mine."

"Now you have frightened me, I have no intention to speak for you," Lazarus said.

"You are not speaking for me, you are sharing with us your understanding of a very important spiritual insight," said Jesus.

There was a long silence while I lifted my hands in prayer seeking for God's guidance. Jesus, Nathaniel, and Philip honored my silence and joined me in prayer as they best felt it might help me.

"I eventually turned and faced all three of them, "Forgiveness is a spiritual gift that pours forth from the very throne of God. It is that part of the divine righteousness of God that flows through us and becomes a powerful instrument of our service to others and help for ourselves. It brings new life and kindles hope and positive purpose in the midst of fractured and despairing relationships.

"Kindness, on the other hand, is our earthly attempt to perform personal service where pain or personal need are evident. But since it is a human attempt to do good without God being involved, we find it easy to cancel or withdraw our commitment without any feeling or remorse. Kindness too often is only a momentary gesture that can be withdrawn or forgotten in a flash. That makes it an imperfect effort on our part to do God's will when the deep needs of life are crying out for God's forgiveness to bring new life, healing, peace and joy." I remained silent and removed from the group.

Nathaniel spoke quietly and said, "Lazarus, I like your explanation."

Jesus came up to me and put his arm across my shoulders and said, "Thank you Lazarus; you seem to clearly understand the differences. You have done well. Now, let's all go to Peter's house and discover what the others are saying."

With that, all four of us turned and made our way back into Capernaum where we would be blest by rich fellowship in a gracious home with which we are all very familiar and comfortable.

When we arrived I realized that Jesus seemed very excited about seeing someone whom we did not expect. I stood for a moment and watched and then realized Jonathan had arrived at the house in our absence.

I immediately greeted Jonathan and he startled me by saying, "Lazarus, you look frustrated and even confused. Is something wrong?"

"We will talk later," I said, and turned to greet some others that I had not seen earlier in the day.

Later that afternoon, Jesus was seated at a table and the room was filled and overflowed out into the street with many people other than the disciples. He began to talk and everyone beyond the room was straining to hear what he was saying. After some additional greetings and light talk, Jesus got very quiet. He raised his hands in prayer and we all became quiet and there was a great sense of expectancy as those outside were still trying to push in.

> *The Kingdom of heaven*
> may be compared to a King
> who wished to settle accounts
> with his servants.
> When he began the reckoning,
> one was brought to him
> who owed him ten thousand talents;
> and since he had no money to pay,
> his lord commanded that he be sold,
> with his wife and children
> and all that he had,
> and payment be made.
> The servant fell on his knees,
> imploring him,
> 'Lord have patience with me,
> and I will pay you everything.'
> Then the lord of that servant
> was moved with compassion,
> released him and
> forgave him the debt.
> But that same servant
> as he went out,
> came upon one of his fellow servants
> who owed him a hundred denarii;
> and he seized him, took him by the throat,
> saying, 'Pay me what you owe.'
> So this fellow servant fell down
> at his feet and begged him,
> 'Have patience with me
> and I will pay you all of it.'
> He refused and went

and had him put in prison
till he should pay the debt.
So, when his fellow servants
saw what had taken place,
they were greatly distressed,
and they went and reported
to their lord all that
had taken place.
Then the lord summoned
that servant and said to him,
'You wicked servant!
I forgave you all that debt
because you asked me;
and should not you have mercy on
your fellow servant,
as I had mercy on you?'
And in anger his lord
delivered him to the jailers,
till he should pay all his debt.
So, also my heavenly Father
will do to every one of you,
if you do not forgive
your brother from your heart.

Jesus stopped and was very quiet. He looked around the room with a very concerned look on his face. No one spoke and it seemed that our breathing had almost stopped. Then Jesus said very slowly, *Seventy times seven.*

Judas got up and walked toward the door. John was standing there and he made an attempt to engage Judas in some conversation, but Judas shook him off and left. John started to follow him, but he returned to his place by the door and closed his eyes as though he was in prayer.

Jesus got up and worked his way to the door and spoke to John. He then looked at both Jonathan and me and motioned us to come. By the time the two of us had struggled through the crowded room and managed our way outside, John and Jesus were almost out of sight on their way to John's house. We didn't catch up with them until they were at the house and going inside.

John's wife was so glad to see us and Jesus immediately asked her for a cup of water and then withdrew to a bedroom and pulled the curtain.

We started talking in muted tones feeling that Jesus was either resting or praying.

"John," asked Jonathan, "Where do you think Judas may have gone?"

"He seemed very upset," responded John, "and I have no idea where he goes when he leaves the group with such anger filling his heart. I have talked with him but I don't think he was ever interested in talking with anyone."

"Do you think I could find him down by the lake and would he talk with me?" inquired Jonathan.

"You could try but often in such times when anyone seeks to engage him in conversation he will insult them and walk off again," said John.

"Come Lazarus, let's see if we can find him." said Jonathan as he walked out of the house with me trailing along behind him.

We arrived at the lake shore in a very brief time and stood looking both ways for any signs of Judas. There was no one in sight that we could see.

"Let's walk down to where Jesus has taught several times," said Jonathan.

We walked, talking very quietly, and watching for any signs of Judas. Jonathan put out his arm to stop me and then pointed away from the lake. There was Judas walking by himself, kicking clots of dirt, little branches, anything that got in front of him.

I asked Jonathan, "Are you sure you want to try and engage him in any conversation."

"That's why we came down here. All he can do is ignore us or try to send us away," responded Jonathan.

So we walked toward him. I know he saw us but he did not acknowledge our presence. Jonathan was the first to speak, "Judas, may we join you?"

Judas growled like an animal, "What do you want?"

He stopped and looked at us and hissed, "Why are you here? Just leave me alone." With that he started walking again.

Jonathan spoke quietly, "We will leave you alone if that is what you want, but sometimes when I am frustrated I find it helpful to have a friend around."

"What makes you think I am frustrated? And you are certainly no friend of mine. What does Jesus see in the two of you anyway? You were not called to be disciples and I don't happen to be calling anyone to follow me," he replied heatedly.

Jonathan ventured to continue the conversation, but he switched the subject, "That was a heavy load Jesus put on us, seventy times seven."

"Dumb, impossible, out of reason, where does he come up with that stuff?" Judas asked grumbling. He was silent for a few moments. "That has nothing to do with establishing a kingdom in God's Name and to his Glory. Why doesn't he just lead on and let's get the job done, the kingdom established." Judas turned and faced us, his face was flushed with excitement, and his eyes were on fire.

I ventured to respond to him, "It will be exciting when that kingdom becomes real for all of us."

"Right, Lazarus. That is what we should be doing right now, and not sitting around talking," he said. Lazarus also felt like Judas was mumbling to himself, "Seventy times seven, a waste of time and energy, a total distraction."

"Jesus talks a lot about a kingdom, what do you think he means?" asked Jonathan.

"Haven't you been listening Jonathan. He is going to lead us into a new kingdom that is eternal. None of this Roman stuff with false gods and Caesars and stiff-necked centurions giving us orders and killing our people. What a great day, a new day, a glorious day of victory," said Judas in a most commanding voice as he marched around in circles with high steps and head held high.

"But," I interjected, "what about that kingdom within that he so clearly talks about?"

"Lazarus, think," Judas startled me, he was yelling so loud almost in my face, "that is his way to keep the Roman government off his back. That Centurion, whatever his name is, who sometimes follows us around is a spy searching for the right moment to call in the Roman soldiers and strike, and we must be ready."

"Are you talking about Julian," asked Jonathan, "and what are we to be ready to fight for and with whom?"

"We will fight when they come to arrest Jesus," said Judas in a delighted tone of voice that revealed his excitement at the thought of some sort of brawl.

"How, now, would you ever suggest that we engage in any fight with Rome?" I asked in utter amazement.

"But we can," said Judas with assurance, "we can! I have been getting ready for months by enlisting mensome of whom are always present at our larger gatherings. I have more than a hundred horses for immediate use; plus the necessary armor to equip those who volunteer. We are ready and I will lead that fighting unit to glory, all in Jesus' Name."

"Have you talked with Jesus about this? asked Jonathan.

"Of course not, he wouldn't understand and he doesn't need to be bothered with such things," retorted Judas. "You two must be ready to help. I have a horse and enough armor for each of you, and you will be given a special leadership position in his kingdom," said Judas with a very brave look and tone.

There was none of the sulking in his demeanor that was usually seen. Judas was walking like he was on a battlefield and his sentences were rapid and commanding.

"I wish you would talk with Jesus about this Judas. It is important for him to know what is planned and available as a support to his kingdom," I said.

"No, I told you he would not understand, I am absolutely convinced of that," Judas said.

Jonathan suddenly changed the direction of the conversation. "Judas, thank you for sharing these exciting plans with us. You have worked hard to be ready. I am so glad we came to talk with you, and we will not say a word to anyone. You are the one to decide on the time and the place."

"Thank you, Jonathan," said Judas, "I am glad you are seeing things my way and we will talk further very soon. Plus, let me thank you for your generous gift to the cause of the kingdom. It is safe with me and will be used wisely for the kingdom. Glory to God and praise to the Name of Jesus."

"Judas, I am sorry to break up our meeting but Abigail will be looking for me at home, and Lazarus is going with me. We will be in further conversation with you as Jesus continues gathering more people to teach and heal and lead them into his glorious kingdom." said Jonathan. He turned to me, "Come, Lazarus, it is time for us to go home."

As we walked away Jonathan whispered, "What an amazing discovery that was. Judas has made such elaborate plans to bring the kingdom in for Jesus but on his terms."

I remained quiet not knowing what to think at that moment. Actually, Judas frightens me the more I get to know him. I was glad to get away from him even though I knew I was fleeing some distorted idea about what Jesus meant in his teaching on the Kingdom of God. Judas needed to be confronted and dealt with immediately. But how many other people were distorting and even destroying the vision of Jesus just as Judas was prepared to do? It was frightening!

Jonathan and I walked back up the beach of Lake Galilee and did not speak a word. I felt stunned, and I hoped that he felt much the same way.

We became aware that John and Nathaniel were walking toward us on the beach. I panicked because I absolutely could not talk about what Judas had just revealed to us.

John immediately asked, "Did you find Judas?"

"As a matter of fact, we did," responded Jonathan, "and he is fine and will probably return to Peter's house sometime this evening."

"Did he talk with you?" asked Nathaniel.

"He did and he is struggling with the very heart of Jesus's teachings," said Jonathan. "We didn't talk long because I know that Abigail is expecting me home this evening; and Lazarus and I must be going over the hill toward home, right now."

"Thank you, Jonathan," said John, "I was beginning to be worried about Judas and the two of you as well. But, since all seems to be well, Nathaniel and I can return to my house for the night. Are you sure you two don't want to join us?"

"Thank you, John, but just as your wife is expecting you; so is my sister, Abigail expecting us. She is waiting and will want a full report on all that has gone on today."

We continued to walk together and engaged in rather meaningless dialogue until we came to the road that ran west and that is where Jonathan and I said "Shalom" to John and Nathaniel and went our separate ways.

"Jonathan, you amazed me by not giving away what Judas shared with us. I would have probably told them about some of his wild intentions and that would not have been fair to him. There is no way that I could explain Judas correctly," I said.

"Let's be sure not to say anything about our conversation with Judas when Abigail can hear. It would upset her terribly," said Jonathan.

"I agree with you but at some time I would like for us to take stock of what we heard Judas saying and give thoughtful consideration about what we should do, or possibly not do, even if we do nothing," I said. "He has frightened me, and I fully believe that Jesus needs to be informed."

"You are right and it is not going to be easy," Jonathan said.

Both of us became uncomfortably silent and I was glad that we soon crested the hill and saw Jonathan's house in the distance. The moon gave it a quiet glow and that is always the way I thought about his house and friendship.

Abigail received us warmly, "Goodness, I had about given you up. I am so glad to see both of you. Please, share with me anything that is important while I fix you something to eat."

Jonathan spoke quickly, "Abigail, it is late and we don't need anything to eat but a hot cup of tea would be gratefully received with a piece of bread. Lazarus, do you want anymore?"

"Tea will be perfect; I am tired and need to soon find a place where I can lie down and rest," I responded.

"Well, we certainly have plenty of places for you to sleep," said Abigail. "We can talk tomorrow; plus, your friends Julian and Bernice are very eager to see you and hear news about Jesus."

"Goodness, I had almost forgotten them in all of the push and shove of our activities," said Jonathan. "Are they all right and have they been helping you?"

"Jonathan, they are the greatest gifts I have ever been given. Julian is in the fields everyday from early until late and all of the servants like him. Bernice is a sweet blessing in helping with the house needs and assisting with feeding the servants and bringing water from the well. I never have to go to the well!"

"All of that pleases me since I have been gone so much. And Zechariah, what about him?"

"He is the sweetest child and so very funny. He has a pet lamb and they spend hours butting each other," said Abigail with a chuckle. "But we can talk about all of that tomorrow. Your tea is ready. Lazarus, if you would like to take it to your room that would be fine. Would you like a basin of water to refresh yourself?"

"Please Abigail, that would be most helpful," I responded.

I took my cup of tea and went to the room that I always use. Abigail soon appeared with a basin of water and a towel. "Thank you, Abigail. I look forward to the morning when we can visit."

"Good night, Lazarus."

It had been a long trying day and after bathing and stretching out, I went sound asleep and didn't waken until the sun was getting rather high in the sky. I was so surprised and when I went to the basin there was warm water in it and a fresh towel. I soon went into the main part of the house and there was Abigail and Bernice working together in the kitchen area. When I spoke they both jumped in surprise.

"I did not know you were up," said Abigail. "I hope we did not waken you.

"No, you were both very quiet. Bernice, I am so glad to see you." She looked down at the floor avoiding any eye contact.

"Give her a little time and she will conquer her shyness," said Abigail. "Now what would you like to eat?"

There was a sudden explosion at the door as little Zechariah came running in. He stopped momentarily and then ran to his mother and grabbed her legs burying his face in her robe.

"It's all right, Zechariah. Lazarus is our guest and you may remember him. He was with Jesus when your mother was healed," said Abigail.

Zechariah turned to look at me as he held on to his Mama's robe and used a portion of it to cover the lower half of his face. Slowly there was a sign of recognition.

"I am so glad to see you again Zechariah," I said very cautiously.

His grip on his mother began to relax and then he ran to Abigail. His mother still had not said a word. She stood with head down, slightly turned, and not a muscle moved.

Abigail took Zechariah's hand and moved over to the fire-pit stove. She gave him a piece of bread which he put in his pocket. Then she gave him a second piece and pointed to me and very slowly he came toward me with his arm extended to give me the bread. I knelt down and took the bread, "Thank you, Zechariah. You are a very helpful boy, and I hear you have a pet lamb?"

With the mention of the lamb a smile broke across his face, but he didn't move. Finally, he looked at his mother and back to me. "Jesus touch Mama. She stops crying." He then ran to his mother. She knelt down and whispered something in his ear and

Zechariah turned and looked at me and started walking my way. When he was almost to me he held up his arms and embraced me and kissed my cheek.

"Thank you, Zechariah," I said, "that's the nicest welcome I have ever received." With that he embraced me again and kissed my cheek and then ran back to his Mama while we all quietly laughed.

"What a fine young man you have Bernice," I said.

"Thank you," she responded without ever looking up.

"Abigail," I asked, "Where is Jonathan?"

"He and Julian have already gone to the fields. There was a small problem that Julian wanted to show Jonathan and together they would work to solve it. Come, sit down here at this table, your morning food is ready. Perhaps, Jonathan will come back and join you."

I had almost finished my meal when Jonathan and Julian came in the door. While we greeted each other, Abigail and Bernice quickly prepared additional food for the two men. I kept looking at Julian, he was a totally different person. He had lost his stern look and there was happiness spread across his face.

He asked about Jesus. "He is fine," I said, "and his teaching takes on a new intensity almost every day. His most recent emphasis has been on forgiveness and he has created a big stir among his disciples."

"How could Jesus cause a big stir?" Julian asked.

"Peter asked him," said Jonathan, "How many times he should forgive a person who had committed a wrong against him and then Peter suggested seven times? Now, listen to this; Jesus, after a few minutes of prayer and contemplation quietly said, seventy times seven."

"Oh, that is quite a requirement," said Julian.

"I can assure you that it caused a lot of discussion and some rather sharp disagreement," I said.

"Go on and admit it Lazarus, there were heavy, almost angry discussions," said Jonathan.

"Plus, there were attempts to qualify who that applies too in life, but Jesus would not let them qualify it. He kept saying after all of our variations about who we should forgive *seventy times seven,* he said it over and over and over."

Suddenly, Bernice ran over to Julian and knelt down beside him and pleaded, "does that mean I must forgive those men who stoned me?"

We all froze as we looked at Bernice and then at each other.

"Must I forgive those men?" she cried. There was almost desperation in her voice.

Jonathan very quietly spoke to her as he might speak to a child, "Yes, Bernice, Jesus would say that you must forgive them all."

She buried her face in Julian's side and began to cry, "How, how…Oh, how…How can I ever forgive them? Oh Julian, the pain has come back. I can see the evil intent in their eyes and feel the hot anger of their shouts. The stones pounding my body had death written on them, and they hurt. How, Jesus…How, Oh how?"

We all sat there feeling some of her pain and wanting Jesus to be present and help explain just how she could forgive those men.

Jonathan turned to me and very quietly said with pleading in his voice, "Lazarus, we need you to pray for understanding."

They all looked at me and I was very startled. I sat there thinking and quietly, without words, praying about what I should do. Help me Jesus, I thought. It was like my hands and face were being drawn upward. Everyone was very quiet as they listened to the sobbing of Bernice. Jonathan told me later that the same light that shines around Jesus began to flow and glow over me.

"Father, God and Savior, Creator of life and our ever present Guide in this life. Be our shield and defender, our help in time of trouble. Forgive us when our minds and spirits are shallow and narrow. Open our eyes that we may see what Jesus has seen. Open our love that it may be as big as Jesus's love for us and others. Seventy times seven seems so out of reach. Stretch our faith, empower our ability to forgive, enable us to love the unlovable, to embrace those who have brought us pain and sorrow. God of Love and Kindness, each of us has brought you pain but your righteousness continues to forgive, right now heal and love us. Give us the power to do the same for all others. It is to your glory and for the benefit of the world that we offer this prayer. Amen"

As I lowered my hands, I felt exhaustion sweep over me and then there was new life that surged around me from within. It was the most amazing and uplifting experience I had ever known. I opened my eyes and everyone was watching me.

Bernice was crying quietly, still kneeling beside Julian. She looked at me with a new expression of beauty and peace, she started speaking very quietly and her voice grew in intensity, "I forgive them. Yes, I forgive them! Please, tell Jesus that I forgive them." A smile broke over her face and she stood up and pulled Julian to his feet and startled us all by saying, "Yes, Julian, I will marry you!"

The two of them stood there laughing and embracing while we were looking at each other.

Bernice turned to us while clinging to Julian's hand. "He had asked me to marry him and I told him 'No.' Thank you for that prayer Lazarus because during that time I realized how much I hated those men who stoned me. I hated them so much that I also hated Julian because he is a man. I forgave those men during your prayer and a gift of love for Julian swept over me that made me want to be his wife and companion in love through forgiveness...seventy times seven."

That big muscular man swept her into his arms with tears flowing as he kept saying, "Thank you, Jesus for setting us free."

Bernice suddenly pulled away from Julian, she faced him and firmly said, "Now Julian, you must forgive Rome for all the things they required of you and that would make our love complete."

Julian looked stunned and then angry. He shouted, "how can I forgive an evil empire with a sinister, evil, pagan ruler? How?"

His fists were tight and thrust at the heavens. "How?" Somebody tell me "How? Seventy times seven, I can't do it even once! How?"

His last outcry was like a lion's roar. It frightened Bernice so much that she ran to Abigail and clung to her, with Zechariah holding on to his mother. It was a scene of anger, fear, and panic as we all stood there listening to the outcry thundering out of the very soul of Julian.

He suddenly dropped to his knees and I walked over and put my hands on his shoulders, "Julian, the peace and power of Jesus is with you and his forgiveness is working in you. Receive him! Receive him Julian and be free."

I did not move but kept my hands on his shoulders. I stood and watched him as perspiration poured off of his face like a river and he shook like a great earthquake. He raised his arms with his fists still clinched tightly. He was agonizing in his search for peace and forgiveness.

We watched as Zechariah slipped away from his mother and came up to Julian and put his arms around him. Julian was so startled that he appeared about to fight. Then he opened those big hands of war and death and slipped his arms around that little boy and simply spoke, "I'm free…Zechariah, I'm free…" He gently put his hands on either side of Zechariah's face and in almost a whisper said, "I'm free…Praise be to God…Rome no longer owns me…I'm free."

He stood with a start and looked around the room. His eyes fell on Bernice, and he started walking toward her. When they came together in yet another embrace, again he cried out, "Bernice, I'm free!"

Julian turned to me and said, "Lazarus, you must pray again. Please, now…Pray, Lazarus…I'm free Lazarus…Pray!

Everything got quiet. I raised my arms and realized that everyone in the room was raising their arms.

"God of forgiveness and love, touch this moment, embrace each of us in our need. Enable us to grow in our understanding of who we are, your earthly child. Help us to hear your son Jesus challenging us, 'unless you become as little children.' Teach us to trust in your power. Help us to grow in your love. Enable us to grow in our understanding of your forgiveness, seventy times seven. Lord bless these your special children of this hour, Julian, Bernice, and Zechariah. Wrap them in the strength of your eternal arms and may they grow in love together and out of their love for you, may they serve others. Set them free to be what it is you want them to be and may their freedom be the light that brightens the way of those around them day by day. This we pray to your glory and for our strength. Amen.

Slowly our arms were lowered and all was very quiet.

The first thing we heard was a child's voice, "Julian, I love you."

Julian and Bernice dropped to their knees and Julian embraced both mother and son, lifted his face toward the heavens and cried out, "Thank you, God. Thank you. Thank you!"

What a celebration we had. The freedom of love and forgiveness filled the air.

Julian stopped and his booming voice still filled with the quality of command said, "Do you think Jesus would bless our union of love?"

A voice said, "You should ask him!" There was Jesus and Nathaniel standing in the doorway. He had the biggest smile on his face and his eyes seemed to be dancing. I had never seen Jesus look like that in all these years. He walked toward Julian and Bernice and took their hands and joined them. He wrapped his fingers around their hands and raised his face toward heaven:

"Father, you made man and woman for each other. Fill Julian and Bernice with a special gift of love that binds them together. May their love bear the fruit of children. May their commitment to you bring a special ministry of service to all those around them. May they live free and forgiven lives as they reach out forgiving and blessing others with your mercy and love." As he continued to pray, he knelt down and embraced Zechariah in his arms.

"Bless Zechariah who enriches all of our lives and your kingdom. Make him an instrument of joy. All this and more we pray in your gracious and holy name. Amen"

Zechariah's childish voice spoke loud and clear, "And bless Jesus. We love him. Amen!"

Everyone was more or less stunned by that little boy, but he and Jesus were wrapped in a big hug and were laughing joyously with each other. When Jesus stood up, he picked Zechariah up with him, and the two were dancing across the floor as all of us were clapping in time with Jesus's steps. Then Julian and Bernice joined them and eventually everyone was singing and clapping as we danced around the room.

For three days we remained at Jonathan's. I have never seen Jesus so relaxed and happy. Many times I wished that Aunt Mary and my sisters Martha and Mary were there to enjoy this happy time with us. There was a lot of individual prayer time when people would slip off to be alone, but we would all come back for meal time.

Jesus and I walked together out in the vineyards and grazing fields with the sheep.

Several baby lambs took an immediate liking to Jesus and he to them, and it was fun to watch them interrelate with each other.

I told him about Judas, my young partner, and my sponsoring him with Rabbi Levi. He asked a number of questions about both persons and seemed to find satisfaction in my being a father figure for young Judas. We talked about Jonathan working toward his Bar Mitzvah. Jesus was at first surprised that this had not been cared for by his family, but then we talked about his earlier handicap and it all fell into place.

"Perhaps I should say something to him, and encourage him," Jesus said. "Do you think he would want to join you in Bethany and work with Rabbi Levi?"

"That is a wonderful idea but I am not sure he would want to be away from this farm that long," I said.

"Well," said Jesus, "he now has Julian to help here and that might allow him to consider it. Jonathan would like Rabbi Levi, and I can see the two of them getting along very well. And just think Abigail could come for his Bar Mitzvah, and she has not been away from this farm. What an experience for her."

"What a wonderful idea for both of them. Let's be careful in presenting it. They just might find that reasonable and exciting," I responded.

We stopped then for another time of quietness and prayer.

"Jesus, I thank you for this time together, but let me raise what for me is a very serious concern and it troubles me."

"And what is that my friend?"

"I find myself listening to accusations and serious threats against you, even plots toward you at the Temple. Are you using the care you need too for your safety?"

"It is interesting that you raise that concern because several other of my disciples have brought that up with me and so has Jonathan. But my heavenly Father assures me that his plan is supreme and I am not to alter directions."

"Then I will not raise it again," I said.

Julian and Bernice were two of the happiest people I had ever known. Jesus spent a lot of time with them, and during those times Zechariah would always be sitting on Jesus's lap, sometimes playing with his beard. Jesus referred so many times to Julian as Zechariah's father that eventually the child started calling him father. Both Julian and Bernice would beam when he called him father, and then they would try to do something special for the child.

It was time for me to go home, and I didn't want to leave. Then I rose for the day and found that Jesus and Nathaniel had left early to go back to Capernaum, and that turned my thoughts to Nazareth and Bethany. I had much to tell Martha and Mary. It was my plan to stop for a brief visit with Aunt Mary and Jesus's family. That meant I would have even more to share when I finally got home.

It was always hard to say good-bye to Jonathan and Abigail. We had become such good friends. One day he totally surprised me by suggesting that I move my whole family and business to a place on his property where we could build a nice home and other needed buildings for my work. It would put me closer to Jesus, but it never felt like God's plan for me. So I just kept making my circuits to buy merchandise, and then I would go home. Judas and I would then go out and sell all we had purchased to merchants around Jerusalem. My sales routines gave me plenty of time to spend at the Temple, and I enjoyed that greatly.

When I spent time in Galilee, I greatly missed the high and beautiful worship at the Temple. Those times furnished me with great inspiration and personal satisfaction. I would always tell Jesus about my visits when we would get together.

Thank you God, Jesus and friends, my life is very good, and I will do all I can to protect and nurture it!

The Pressure Grows

Jesus's teaching was taking on a new intensity. I would meet people in Jerusalem who had just returned from Galilee, and they would talk about the urgency in Jesus's voice. Many asked me why I thought that was happening; and I would very honestly reply, "I don't know."

That never satisfied anyone, but what else could I tell them without making up something that would not properly represent Jesus. He had enough to manage without me making up things about him and his future intentions, but the pressure seemed to be growing in his ministry and mission.

I had been with Jesus so much recently that it was time for me to earn a living for my family. They are most patient and as interested in Jesus as I am, but there is work to be done, and it must be done now.

In the evening I arrived back in Bethany, it was a happy reunion. I also realized that Judas was standing off to the side with a sly grin. I grabbed and hugged him, and he was surprised but pleased.

After things settled down a little, I looked at Mama and asked, "Are you and my sisters all right? I have really abandoned you, and I must not do that again."

Mama looked at me with a bright smile and said, "We have been fine with the help of your partner."

"Judas, you have been working?"

"Of course, what else did you think I would do? Since you have been gone I have made three buying trips, immediately sold all the merchandise that I purchased, and have given your share of the money to your Mama, but I have a report for you."

I stopped in my tracks and looked from Judas to Mama and both of them had a bright smile on their faces.

"Lazarus," said Martha, "we have found a new brother who isn't running around all the time."

"He has maintained the property, earned us money, repaired the house, and helped with a lot of errands. We aren't sure we need you anymore," Martha added.

I just stood there looking from one to the other as they all laughed at me.

"Lazarus," said Judas, "tomorrow will be your day of discovery, and I hope you will be pleased. Now, you probably need some rest. I will be back in the morning. See you then Mama 2 and sisters dear."

"Mama 2 and sisters dear, what is he talking about?" I asked.

Mama laughed and said, "Those are the names he has given us, and we rather like them. Come, Lazarus, let us prepare you something to eat and tell you a few things that have happened while you have been gone."

"Also," said Mary, "we want all the news you have about Jesus, and what is happening with those disciples of his?"

I sat down at the table in our eating area and Mama brought me a cup of goat's milk. After drinking that, I looked at her and said, "I am very tired. Would the three of you mind if I went to bed?"

"Of course not," said Mama, "we can talk all we want to in the morning. And we can have a good laugh over your surprise about Judas and his successful management of your business."

They all laughed; and I left just shaking my head in disbelief, but at the same time I was very pleased.

I was amazed that I did not awaken until almost noontime and to be very honest I was more tired than when I went to bed. Mama kept insisting that I go to bed again after I ate but that seemed useless. The best suggestion came from sister Mary, who said we should take a long walk in the Garden of Gethsemane, and I looked at her and said, "I'm ready. Let's go!"

The two of us walked all around and when we came to a nice grassy area, I lay down and was surprised that I fell into a sound sleep. Mary claimed that I was very restless, but she was not going to disturb me.

She looked at me and asked, "Do you want to talk about Jesus?"

"Jesus and his disciples are fine. People keep coming to hear him teach, and they press him for healings and special blessings. Mary, I am not sure where he gets all of his energy. He is up early, goes hard all day, and ministers to the needs of people into the night. I have seen him get extremely tired, but he recovers quickly," I said.

"Prayer feeds him spiritually and physically. He is an amazing, wonderful person, who is at home both here on earth and in the spiritual Kingdom of his heavenly Father. His teachings are most exciting, but there are those who would disagree with my assessment. Now let's return to the house and I will begin to find out what has been happening here."

We walked in silence but I was thrilled with Mary walking beside me, holding my hand and singing quietly some of the Psalms. For the first time, I realized how beautiful her voice is. How blessed I am with such a wonderful family.

When we got back to the house, I made a rather quick inspection of the property and house. I was surprised that I found everything was well cared for, and no noticeable repairs needed my immediate attention.

When I went in the house, I looked at Mama and said, "It is time for me to get back to work."

"First, let Judas tell you what he has been doing," Mama said with a sly smile on her face.

I started eating what Mama had prepared for me, and there came Judas, "Good morning, Mama 2. I am here to give a report to Lazarus."

He came to where I was seated, grabbed a couple of pillows, and sat down in the corner of the room. He then started telling me what he had done while I was gone.

"Almost immediately after you left for Galilee, my Mama and I worked to repair all the merchandise you and I had stored that needed some help. Every piece of that merchandise was carefully repaired and sold. A few pieces were beyond repair and we have disposed of them. Let me assure you, I did not sell anything that would embarrass you because it was of poor quality.

"Also, I have made three buying trips of my own. I first went to Jericho and then across the Jordan River to several communities, Esbus and Medba. Daniel told me there were excellent craftsmen in those communities and he was right. I was surprised how much I bought from those local markets.

"Plus, I was surprised now much Daniel had stored and was waiting to show you in the hopes that you would buy it. All of it was of very high quality; I bought all of it; and that has been sold. I have also made two other trips, one to the south to Hebron and two communities where we had not been, Adora and Engedi. I found many excellent products, which I felt were worth buying.

"The third trip was to the west toward the Great Sea area. Each time I stored all of the purchased merchandise here and worked out of your sheds. I always had 'Mama 2' inspect what I had bought and ask any questions that would enable her to understand what I was doing."

I was too stunned to interrupt, so I just sat and listened.

"Now, if you have any questions Lazarus, please stop me. I will do my best to give you adequate answers," he said.

"You are doing well Judas, continue on," I said.

"On the third trip, I felt I needed some help. I knew a friend, Jonah, who spoke Hebrew, and I invited him to assist. I paid him the same amount you paid me on my first trip. He worked out fine, and I think we could use him again if you think it necessary. It was great that he spoke Hebrew. He was harder on me than you ever were.

"After each trip, when I finished selling all the merchandise, I took out my expenses and then split the remainder in half and gave your part to 'Mama 2'.

"Lazarus, I was amazed at how much he gave me," Mama said as she turned, picked up a box, and put it on a table beside me. I could tell that there was considerable weight to it.

"What is this?" I asked.

"Open it and you will see," Mama said.

When I opened it, I sat there amazed. It was almost full of money, Jewish, Roman and even Egyptian.

"I am sorry that I did not go by an exchange table to have it converted to one kind of money," said Judas.

I just sat there because I did not know what to say. I picked up some of the coins and let them drop through my fingers back into the box.

"Judas, this is a huge and happy surprise. We are perfect partners and I will never regret making you my business associate. Plus, you have been a true son to 'Mama 2'." Everyone started laughing and Mama was shedding a few tears.

"Judas, I never want you to stop calling her 'Mama 2'. That is a proud name you have given her, and it shows your respect and affection for her."

That really set Mama off and both she and Mary were bawling.

"All right, let's talk about your Bar Mitzvah. Have you been able to work with Rabbi Levi?"

Judas brightened, "he is the most wonderful man I have ever met. We work together twice a week unless I am out of town. Then when I return he makes it three times a week until I make up what I missed. He says I will be ready for my Bar Mitzvah in about a month. Can you believe that, a month to go."

"Judas," Mama said, "you haven't told us that; we must get busy to plan your celebration after the Temple service."

"My Mama has been working on the celebration, so why don't you go and talk with her, and I am sure everything will fall in place," said Judas.

"Judas," I almost yelled, "you can't go on a buying trip if you are that close to your Bar Mitzvah."

"Well, I thought about asking you if you could take Jonah with you this time, and I will complete my work with the rabbi," said Judas.

"Lazarus," interrupted Mama, "I think you better make it a short trip. We really need you here."

"I was planning another trip," said Judas, "perhaps, Lazarus, you can go north as far as Sebaste and shop along the way, but my ultimate goal is to see Daniel. He always seems to have a lot of craftsmen set up for us to see. The merchants here are asking for those little candles that we purchase in that area, and I wanted to buy as many varieties as I could find."

"Fine, I will go that way and turn around and come back. We can probably accomplish all we need to do in one week. So if you can check with Jonah, I would like to leave day after tomorrow," I told Judas.

"I will go check with Jonah right now. I will bring him back here to help me get things ready for the trip and you can meet him. I am supposed to meet Rabbi Levi tomorrow, so I will not be available then until middle of the afternoon," said Judas.

"Judas, the most important thing for you to do is to complete your studies and memory work for your Bar Mitzvah. I can take care of the buying trip, but if Jonah is available to go, he will make a big difference."

"I want to ask you something, Judas. That old storage shed seems to look very different, but I cannot put my finger on what exactly is different," I said.

Judas, Mama, and my sisters laughed.

"Well," said Judas, "that old shed started leaking and I was trying to make repairs and suddenly it collapsed. It came very close to catching me inside."

"That would have been terrible," I said. "So what did you do?"

"Well, I took it all apart, piece by piece and rebuilt it exactly like it had been. So, you have what can be called an old/new shed; but, it doesn't leak. Oh, let me get out of here and see if I can find Jonah. I will hope to be back in a little while." Off Judas ran, and we all just stood there and watched him go.

I turned to Mama, "I am amazed at his report and success. There is no way that I would ever be able to let him go. If this Jonah is a good worker and can help us, it will free me, and I can even spend more time with Jesus. Are you comfortable with that Mama?"

"Of course, but I hope you don't leave us completely."

"Mama, I would never do that. This is home and you are our "Queen" in the castle."

Everyone started laughing. Mary said, "Now, Mama, you have another name. You are our Queen."

"Now, let's not be silly," said Mama. "All I want you to do is love me as your mother." We all laughed and gathered around hugging her.

"I need to go check on the animals for my upcoming trip. Are the camels still with Judas?

"Yes, and they are well cared for," said Mary. "I'll go with you, and perhaps there is something I can do to help you get ready."

"Come on," I said as we went out the door.

It is always a joy to have Mary around anytime she will go. I really wanted to take her on the buying trips because her happy spirit would always make things easier, but it would not be safe.

When we arrived at the animal shed, one of the donkeys immediately came up to me and wanted to be rubbed behind his ears, but the other one remained aloof and watched me from a distance. I was checking the harnesses when here came Judas with Jonah in tow. Jonah was a big strapping boy with a pleasant look and not any shyness about him.

"Jonah, this is Lazarus; and I will say in front of him, you can believe anything he tells you. It is fun working with him, and this is his sister Mary."

"Well, thank you, Judas, and I am very glad to meet you, Jonah," I said.

"The same here," he said.

"Are you able to go on a buying trip day after tomorrow for a week?"

"Yes, I will be delighted to go."

"It will be a short, fast trip for only a week."

He nodded his agreement and for the remainder of the day we worked to line everything up to be ready to go. Since Judas could not help tomorrow until late in the afternoon, it was best to try and complete all the preparations today.

"Judas, do you think we should take the camels or just the two donkeys?"

"I would take all four animals because I think you are going to be surprised how much you will buy. There is no use having to buy another animal."

I paused and thought and then said, "I agree."

Jonah, I am assuming that since you have gone on one trip with Judas that you are familiar with these animals and have made friends with them."

"Yes, except for Mordecai. He does not seem to want me to do anything around him, so you may have to manage him," Jonah said.

"That is no problem. All right, daybreak day after tomorrow!"

"I'll be here," Jonah said.

"Come on, Mary, I want to spend the rest of the afternoon and evening with you, Mama, and Martha," I said.

"Now, that will be a change, and we may not find that much to talk about."

"Oh hush, come on, let's go," I said.

We all needed a relaxing and delightful afternoon and evening. We took a long walk and chatted. Then Mary and I went to the well for water. The next day I went into Jerusalem to visit the Temple and I was thrilled to hear the cantor.

> *I will lift up my eyes unto the hills.*
>   from whence does my help come?
> My help comes from the Lord,
>   who made heaven and earth.
> He will not let your foot be moved,
>   he who keeps you will not slumber.
> Behold, he who keeps Israel
> will neither slumber or sleep.
> The Lord is your keeper;
>   the Lord is your shade on your right hand.
> The sun will not smite you by day,
>   nor the moon by night.
> The Lord will keep you from all evil;
>   he will keep your life.
> The Lord will keep your going out and your coming in
>   from this time forth and even for ever more.

All my days of weariness were swept away. I wanted so much to raise my hands and arms like we did in the presence of Jesus, but I knew that would create some kind of negative scene. I did not want the excitement in my heart to be turned into some form of ridicule that would be frowned upon by those standing around me. So I stood there with my eyes closed, my heart jumping with the joy of my faith welling up to the very top of my being. I slipped through the crowd and out of the Temple making my way to the Beautiful Gate.

The elders were there arguing issues of theology. In fact, there were five or six different discussions going on. Today, there seemed to be a lot of excitement. Every now and then one of the elders would jump to his feet and make a fervent speech and there always seemed to be a challenger. I went home feeling that all was in good order at the Gate Beautiful.

When I got home, I called, "Mama 2, where are you?"

"I believe you know my name," she said with a firm, clear voice.

I laughed and said, "Mama, I am so impressed with the way Judas has become a part of this family, and all of you are so comfortable with his presence."

All of a sudden we heard, "Mama 2, are you here?"

"Of course, I'm here, where else would you expect me to be?"

"I am back from the Temple. Oh, Lazarus, Rabbi Levi told me I am ready and he will schedule my Bar Mitzvah three weeks from today."

"Wow, that will pressure us on this trip, but we will be back. Mama, are you and Judith going to be ready for the big celebration?"

"We are ready right now, but I am willing to wait for three weeks." said Mama.Judas shared his news with Martha and Mary, and they congratulated him and gave him a big hug which startled him.

The whole time I was thinking of canceling my trip, but I figured I needed to get out of the way. So early the next day, Jonah and I left for Sebaste. Since we started at daybreak, we made excellent time. There were few people on the road at that time of day so we moved around Jerusalem and away from the city. Once on the main road going north, I became very satisfied with our progress.

We had been pushing our animals hard all day and the day was fading quickly. We saw a small grove of trees and moved off the road. The camels immediately lay down and the donkeys began to graze on the small amount of grass that was there.

Jonah and I had a few bites of cheese and some water. Soon it was time to move on even though it was beginning to get late in the day. We had not traveled long when to my surprise, there beside us—I recognized that path that we followed years ago when I was eleven years old. Our intention was to set up camp for the night and that would be a most suitable place.

I suggested to Jonah that he wait a few minutes and allow me time to see what was now down that path. It was obvious that it was still an area where others camped, so I searched around and found a very nice place to stop and spend the night. I confessed that I looked for that escape route of years ago, but there was no alternate path out of that place.

I even walked out to the main road and looked along it for where another path might come out. I was standing there pondering this mysterious occurrence when much to my surprise a voice said "Lazarus, what are you doing here?"

I turned around and found myself facing Julian.

"Julian why are you here?" I asked him.

It was a most happy reunion. I took him to our camp and introduced him to Jonah. We chatted while Jonah made a fire after he had collected some wood.

"Lazarus, let me answer your question. I am here because Jesus sent me. He would like for you to return to Galilee as soon as possible."

"Is something wrong?" I asked.

"Not that I know of, but he just seems to like having you close by," Julian said.

"Julian, I cannot return for four weeks. My business partner, Judas, is having his Bar Mitzvah, and I am his sponsor. That means I am taking the place of his father who died many years ago. So Jonah and I are on a quick week's buying trip. We will then have several days to make our sales before we share in the ceremony at the Temple. After that I will be free to return to Galilee, which I was planning to do. But I am obligated to two families to see this through. In fact, they will not accept Judas for his Bar Mitzvah at the Temple unless I am there.

"So if you would please return and tell Jesus that I will be there in about five weeks," I told Julian.

"That is…" Julian didn't have a chance to finish what he had to say.

Jonah yelled, "Look behind you."

Julian and I turned to face four Roman soldiers spread out as if for an attack.

"What do you want?" asked Julian. His eyes were like steel.

"Your money and the animals. Plus, we will take that boy. If you resist or fail to obey our command, you will immediately regret it," one of the soldiers said.

Julian started walking very slowly toward them. "Stay where you are," shouted one of them. One of the soldiers started walking in a circle to get behind Julian, and he was approaching him with a drawn broad sword. Things happened so fast. At that point, I really did not see what happened.

All I really remembered about those first few minutes was that Julian suddenly spun around, grabbed the soldier behind him, took his broad sword, pushed him off about a foot, and ran him through. The soldier dropped. Julian wheeled around and was on the attack. The soldier closest to Julian charged him. That soldier raised his sword to strike Julian and with one horrible slash Julian cut his arm off and then ran his sword through him. He was out of it. At that moment, Julian yelled to us, "Run."

We turned and did just that as I heard another groan from one of the other soldiers, and I knew Julian had taken him out. I quickly looked around from the bushes and Julian had the path blocked to keep the other soldier from escaping. He turned to run into the wooded area and without flinching Julian raised the sword he had taken, threw it as straight as an arrow, and buried it in the back of the running soldier.

Everything was quiet, and there stood Julian with his head down, shaking violently, "What have I done. Dear God, I am still a killer. Forgive me, Lord. Save me, Jesus." He was weeping.

"Julian, you were protecting us, and there was no choice. Thank you for your protection and God understands. You are forgiven, Julian," Lazarus said.

His eyes were still like steel. He was breathing very hard; it was like deep gasps. He dropped to his knees, "Bernice, come... come, Bernice, and heal me with your love."

I almost yelled, "Julian, we need your help. Please, Julian, come back to us and help us. We are desperate, Julian."

He shook his head and kept batting his eyes as he looked at me as if I was some stranger. "What is the matter?" he whispered.

"Julian, look around you. There are four dead soldiers and their horses are here somewhere. We are going to be caught and crucified immediately if you don't help us do something very quickly," I said.

Julian jumped to his feet and looked around. "What's your name boy?"

"Jonah," he responded.

"Lazarus, help him take this soldier's clothes off and put them on. Jonah, be quick!"

We started taking his clothes off while Julian started moving the other soldiers out of sight. Jonah looked a little strange in those clothes and Julian collected a helmet and put it on his head. "Come with me," said Julian.

I could hear Julian talking very fast to Jonah telling him to bring the soldiers' horses one at a time back here from the main road. Walk slowly as though nothing is wrong. Jonah started down that path, and he walked strangely wearing that soldier's armor.

Julian immediately picked up the soldier we had stripped and carried him behind the trees. Julian then told me to bring the first horse to where he was going behind the trees that he pointed out to me. He then sent Jonah for the second horse. We soon had everything away from the main road. We were all out of breath from the excitement and the rushing around.

"Jonah take those clothes off," Julian commanded.

Julian then circled the area several times. "Come quickly," he said, "Here, take these shovels." He removed them from the horses' harnesses. We went a little ways and he said, "Here, start digging, fast! We will bury the soldiers here."

We started digging while Julian was stripping the horses of everything but the bridle. Julian then went a little ways from us and started digging.

"Hurry," he said. He walked over to where we were digging and said, "Make those holes deeper. Jonah, go back and put out the fire, and see if you can move your animals away from that area! Run!"

Julian started digging, and I was amazed how much dirt he could move in a short time. He pulled one body and dropped it in the deepest hole. Then he ran and went to the area where he had fought the soldiers. He broke a branch off a tree and started swirling it around and around on the ground covering all tracks.

I came back to the camp after leading the four horses off to the area next to the low cliffs. It was a grassy area and the horses immediately began to graze.

"Come, Lazarus," Julian said, "let's finish that burial job with Jonah."

We dug fast and finished burying the bodies. The clothes we buried with the armor in the first hole that Julian had started. He told us to find any dry branches and bring them and he dropped them over the raw dirt of the graves. He did everything possible to make things look natural. "Come and bring the shovels." He looked at me and said. "Now, take us to where you left your animals."

"What are we going to do with their horses?" I asked.

Julian froze, "I had forgotten them. Come, let's go get them."

We led those horses back to where I had left our camels and donkeys. When we got there, Julian was very impressed with how beautiful the area was. "Now," he said, "we have to get out of here very quietly without calling any attention to ourselves. Take the bridles off the horses, and I hope they are going to stay here for the grass and water."

It was almost dark. The moon was extremely bright, and it was amazing how much light we had. Suddenly, there was that mysterious path again. I knew it was the same one we had used years ago. Why hadn't I been able to find it in years past?

"Take this path, and it will bring us out farther up the road," I said.

We had gone a short distance and there was a small open area. Julian suggested that we stop for the night, and perhaps we will be hidden and safe. I am not sure Julian nor I slept very much, but Jonah snored all night long. Every now and then I heard Julian say, "God, forgive me. Jesus, please forgive me. Bernice, help me." I will never forget that night. Julian is still an efficient Centurion, and I now know how he earned that position.

At daybreak, we did find ourselves at least a little refreshed both our body's and most of all our attitudes. Julian was up earlier than either of us, and he had found a small spring which he had cleaned out so that the animals had a small pool from which they could drink.

We slipped out of that hidden area into the flow of what little traffic was that early in the morning.

Julian said, "Don't get in a hurry. We are not running from anything that anyone else knows about. So from time to time he had us stop. Once there was a small roadside stand selling food, and we stopped to purchase some things to eat. He suggested we talk and laugh. "We must have been the picture of three happy merchants with nothing to fear."

Once a patrol of four Roman soldiers galloped by, Julian wandered off to the side of the road. He later told me that he never knows if there may be some soldier who perhaps would recognize him. It is a simple precaution I take when I am on a main road.

We arrived at Daniel's house just south of Sebaste a little before noon. He was surprised but pleased to see us. I introduced Julian as one of the followers of Jesus who was returning to Galilee to be with Jesus and his disciples.

In just a few minutes, we were brought before a table that was spread with a lot of very wonderful food. Jonah's eyes became very big when he saw all of that food. We had a most delightful time sharing a meal and engaging in delightful conversation mixed with a lot of questions about Jesus.

That afternoon and evening we visited five craftsmen in the immediate area of Daniel's home. We saw and bought some very beautiful merchandise, but I did not see a single candle.

"Daniel, where are the candles like the ones we have bought before," I asked. "Judas, who is now my partner and is finishing his work on his Bar Mitzvah, says that the merchants around Jerusalem are asking for them."

"You should have asked when we were at the house," said Daniel, "I have some for you there, and we can get more. But we must go a little farther east for those, and we will be there tomorrow. This evening I will show you what I have for you to take with you," Daniel said.

We had brought the two donkeys and two camels and we had already bought enough to completely load them. I was amazed how quickly we were collecting quality crafts.

That evening I checked what Daniel had and he was right. He had collected a beautiful assortment of candles. I think Judas will be very happy.

Daniel started asking questions about Jesus, and I was surprised to find Julian answering his questions and sharing his thoughts.

"Jesus talks a lot about forgiveness. One evening he talked a lot about the prophets and he quoted the prophet Jeremiah:

> *This is the covenant which I will make*
> with the house of Israel
> after those days, says the Lord:

> I will put my law within them,
> and I will write it upon their hearts;
> and I will be their God,
> and they shall be my people.
> And no longer shall each man
> teach his neighbor
> and teach his brother,
> saying, 'Know the Lord,"
> for they shall all know me,
> from the least of them
> to the greatest, says the Lord;
> for I will forgive their iniquity,
> and I will remember their sin no more.

Everyone sat very quiet. I was amazed that he, a Roman, was beginning to memorize the words of the prophet Jeremiah.

He continued, "And Jesus shared with me the wonderful words of Isaiah when he said to his people:

> "I have swept away your transgressions
> like a cloud, and your sins like mist;
> return to me for, I have redeemed you."

Julian looked at me and for the first time since our confrontation with those Roman soldiers, a bright, happy smile swept across his face. He had found his forgiveness and healing.

"And," I said, "Jesus really caused a stir among his disciples when Peter asked him how many times he should forgive his brother, and Jesus said *seventy times seven.*' Peter had suggested that we forgive seven times, but Jesus had a much broader vision of love and forgiveness."

Daniel's amazement showed as he said, "Did you say 'seventy times seven"?

Julian responded, "That's right and that is what he meant. I understand he has talked about it a number of times since, and some of the disciples have tried to get him to change it. One evening the disciple, Judas, started to bring it up, and Jesus looked at him and quietly said, *Seventy times seven.* My impression is that you do not change Jesus's mind; yet, there are those who are always willing to try."

"Lazarus, I understand he constantly talks about a kingdom. What is that all about?" asked Daniel.

"It is not an earthly kingdom. It is God's kingdom, and that kingdom is within us where God longs to reign supreme. Jesus has said several times in his teaching and in conversation:

Seek first the kingdom of God
and his righteousness, and
all things will be added unto you.

"We are to seek that kingdom through prayer and meditation and we exhibit its presence within us to the world. We reveal it to people around us by the way we live and how we act toward others."

Julian jumped in again, "Jonathan shared with me how we must be a light in the world by bringing to people an understanding of God's truth, forgiveness, and love into the midst of the darkness in this world."

Daniel said, "Jesus is amazing. I wish I were able to go listen to him, but I am going to have to let you be my ears and then share his teachings."

"But Daniel that is exactly what he is training us to do.

Jonah suddenly spoke, "I don't know about you, but if I am to work tomorrow I need some sleep."

He was shown where to sleep and the rest of us began to close out our conversations.

Julian said, "I wish I could stay longer and share more about Jesus with you Daniel, but I must leave early in the morning. So thank you, and don't worry about me I will be gone before you are up."

I spoke up, "Julian, please, give Jonathan my regards and tell him that I will be there as soon as I can. Then either you or he can tell Jesus that I will be there in about five weeks as soon as

I complete my obligation with Judas's Bar Mitzvah. Thank you for coming, Julian, and blessings and peace on your return home. Please, give Bernice my shalom and tell Zechariah I have a toy for him when I get there."

"If I tell him that, he will come and get you," said Julian.

The next morning Julian had gone; and Daniel, Jonah, and I left for another buying trip, and I felt that if we were successful we might be able to go home tomorrow. We again returned with two donkeys fully loaded, and we began to separate all the merchandise with a load for each animal and some for our backs.

I invited Daniel to go for a walk and shared with him the near tragedy on our way to his house, and how Julian saved our necks and our lives. He was amazed and frightened for us.

"So, is there another way to Jerusalem that is not far out of the way that we can go home and avoid that area of the main road?" I asked.

"Come, said Daniel, "let me draw a map in the sand for you. This road will bring you to Bethany on the right side of Jerusalem."

It was really a very easy way, and early the next day, we were on our way. Twice we ran into Roman patrols but they did not bother us at all. We kept going until we arrived in Bethany long after dark. When we got there, I sat down on the ground from nervous exhaustion.

Martha appeared in the doorway of the house with a spear in her hand. And looking over her shoulder were Mama and Mary.

Mama asked, "What are you doing arriving home at this time of night?"

I interrupted her, "Mama, I am not interested in giving you a reason for the late night trip at this time. So, we will unload these animals and be in the house for just a little food and something to drink and then go to bed. Fix a place for Jonah, there is no reason for him to go home until tomorrow."

I must have sounded firm because when we got back to the house all was ready and very soon we were in bed. I am not sure I have ever been so tired and Jonah was snoring before I laid down.

The next morning we were a little late getting up. I was surprised to find Judas already working through our purchases and beginning to divide them for our sales contacts. He was really excited to find the candles and was especially interested in some of the small unique baskets.

I went back in the house and invited Judas to come for our morning meal. Jonah was already at the table and the young men were most happy to see each other.

It wasn't long before Jonah said, "Judas you should have been with us for some of the greatest excitement I have ever experienced."

Jonah looked at me, and I nodded for him to continue. He began to tell the story of Julian. Before he finished Mama, Martha, and Mary were gathered around us.

"You mean to tell me that Julian killed all four of those soldiers by himself?" asked Judas.

"That's right," I said, "and it must be understood that we tell this to no one else or Julian might be hunted down by the Roman authorities, and Jonah and I could be crucified with him. Julian did not want to do what he did but he had no choice. He was defending our safety."

Judas couldn't stand it, "Where did Julian get his sword?"

"No more, now or ever," I said with a very firm voice. "Do you understand me and why I am saying this?"

Everyone nodded.

"It is now time for us to get to work on that merchandise," I said, "Judas is everything in place for your Bar Mitzvah?"

"Yes, and my Mama is so very excited. She says the celebration is all in place. Guests have been invited and food planned," he said.

"Wonderful! Then, let's get busy and move this merchandise," I said.

Judas jumped up, "Lazarus, Jonah and I will take care of that job. We will manage the sales. You just stay here with Mama 2 and your sisters. If we need you, we will ask for your help. Rest a little," said Judas.

"Is that the younger partner's order,' I said as I laughed.

"Just a suggestion; plus, I would like to be familiar with what you bought," he said as they walked out the door.

They were gone and we all stood there and pondered the new relationship I was developing with Judas. And I will admit that it felt very good.

Mama came over to me and broke the silence, "Lazarus were you hurt in that fight with those soldiers?"

"No Mama, and neither was anyone else, and amazingly neither was Julian," I said.

Martha asked, "Why was Julian with you? Where did he come from?"

"That is interesting," I said, "I met him on the road on his way to Bethany to tell me that Jesus would like for me to return to Galilee as soon as it was convenient. I could not have been more surprised."

"We were preparing to camp for the night, and he stayed with us. It was a good thing that he did. I don't think I have been so scared in all my life and I remind you that everything happened so quickly. It was over before I had realized what was happening. But that must be the end of it for the protection of Julian."

I went outside to see what the boys were doing and they were fine. They had everything divided out and ready to sell.

"We will leave tomorrow," said Judas. "Why don't you go to the Temple Lazarus and see Rabbi Levi. He seems eager to see you."

The next morning the boys were gone before I got up, and I made my way to the Temple. I stood looking at that beautiful sight as always. It always impressed and thrilled me. The worship service was in progress and I listened to the cantor.

I went to the outer court; and after a little while, I spotted Rabbi Levi and made my way toward him. He saw me and the two of us met and greeted each other with joy. "Come," he said. And we walked off to a little conference room.

"I am so glad you are back and that you will be here for the Bar Mitzvah. Judas is a very unusual boy who learns quickly. He is so thrilled with you and your leadership in getting him to work for this special event in his life."

"I am thrilled with him and he is making a great partner in my business," I said.

"That is wonderful" said the rabbi, "Judas has told me that a celebration has been planned at his home. In fact, I have been invited. Lazarus I hope you have remembered that you should present him with a tzedakah box at that time?"

"Oh, rabbi, I had not thought of that, but I have time to find one. At least, I hope I have time," I said.

"Your have time and there are some nice ones for sale outside the Temple. That may save you some time."

"Again, thank you, rabbi. You are still my guide," I said.

"Lazarus, remember that you perform all the roles of the father in the service," the Rabbi reminded me.

"I will come to several of the services this week and learn exactly what I am to do," I said.

"Lazarus, I'm sorry, but I must go. Come back in two or three days. Shalom!"

"Shalom," I said.

I went outside to the outer court and there were many people with the tzedakah boxes for sale. They varied greatly in size, cost, and beauty. I was amazed and puzzled. I decided that I would go home and look at mine very carefully before making a decision.

I shared with Mama about my day and the conversation with Rabbi Levi.

"Oh, Lazarus, your papa spent many hours making your tzedakah boxes. He actually made three and chose one to present to you. Wait here."

Mama went to her room and in a few minutes she came back with two boxes. "Here, these are the others. I have kept them over all these years. Now, they are yours and perhaps you would like to present one of them to Judas.

I took them and set one down and slowly examined the one I held. It was beautiful. Then I picked up the second and turned it over and over and looked inside the box, "This one I will give to him. I like the Star of David etched inside the top of the lid."

"Goodness, let me see. I did not notice that," said Mama as she peered inside. Now, let's put this away until the day and I will polish it to enhance the color of the wood. You have made a good choice, Lazarus. It is going to be a wonderful day."

Often in the evenings Judas and Jonah would sit with me and ask questions about the teachings of Jesus. We talked a lot about God's Righteousness and then we moved on to forgiveness. "Seventy times seven" had Judas both amazed and puzzled.

"How can I forgive anyone that many times? Why would I even want to forgive someone that many times?" he stammered.

"Because it is God's way and it is the way he deals with you."

"Do you mean to tell me that God will forgive me 'seventy times seven'? But why would he even want to? What a waste of his time and spiritual energy?" asked a bewildered Judas.

"He forgives you because you are his child, and he loves you so much that he is willing to forgive you that often," I said. "Plus, your forgiveness of others is your way of sharing God's healing grace with others around you. It may be hard to imagine, but you are an extension of God's love, forgiveness, and grace."

That's frightening," said Jonah.

"No," I responded, "it's challenging!"

"You sound like Rabbi Levi," said Judas.

"Now, there is a true impossibility. I could never bring all those Hebrew lessons to life with the excitement that Rabbi Levi does."

Judas thought for a moment, "No, Jesus goes beyond those lessons of the Torah, and you are a gifted teacher of what he is saying."

"Thank you, Judas. That is a real compliment you have given me, and I do not take it lightly. You have just challenged me to do even better."

The days leading up to the Bar Mitzvah for Judas went quickly. That day brought the two families together, and we marched to Jerusalem for the big celebration. When we arrived at the Temple, Rabbi Levi was waiting on us and immediately took us inside. In just a few moments, he took the women to a place where they could stand and watch the service. When he returned, he asked us to follow him and we began making our way toward the front of the sanctuary. The cantor was singing and there was a lot of coming and going in the worship area.

I looked at Judas and he was so handsome in the new robe his Mama had made for him. He was standing straight and I had not realized how tall he was. There was a brief break in the worship service and Rabbi Levi looked at the two of us and quietly said, "Follow me."

I was a little overwhelmed when my mind took into account how long I had been following him in a variety of ways. It is going to be fun and helpful to continue sharing our experiences with that wonderful rabbi.

My attention shifted as the Bar Mitzvah began and my full attention was on the rabbis and Judas. He read and expounded on the scripture with clarity and excitement. Before I knew it the service was over and Rabbi Levi was leading us out of the sanctuary to join his family that were waiting on us. The walk to Bethany was filled with excitement and joy.

The celebration at Judas's home was wonderful. I could not believe all that had been prepared for this day. My thoughts went back to the day when I stood in the Temple, and I hoped that Judas would enjoy visiting that place as much as I do.

I was yanked out of my "wash" of memories when Mary grabbed my hand and pulled me into the circle of dancers. It was a glorious time and I was so glad to see all of my family so filled with pride and excitement.

A break came and I found Mama standing at my side with the tzedakah box. I presented it to Judas, and suddenly realized that I was to put the first gift in it and I had no money. I looked at Mama and Martha, and it was Mary that slid in beside and put some gold coins in my hand. I fulfilled my obligation and then and kissed Mary on the cheek. Others began to surge around to fill his box which he would use for the rest of his life to help many people in need.

"Mary," I said, "Where did you get that money?"

"You had showed it to me several days ago and explained what it was for. I saw it in your room just before we left, and I picked it up in case you needed it," she responded.

"Thank you. I would have been greatly embarrassed if you had not been thinking for me," I said. "Now, all my obligations are over with, so, let's dance."

Mary took my hand and we got in the circle of friends and began clapping and singing with everyone else. I noticed that people were still congratulating Judas and putting money in his tzedakah box. What a great Day!

When it was appropriate, I walked off from the celebration and was thinking about Jesus having Julian come to ask me to come to Galilee. Mary appeared and took my arm and walked with me toward home.

"You are thinking about Jesus, aren't you?" she asked.

"Yes, I have performed my duty here, and I am ready to go to Galilee," I said.

"Can I go with you?" Mary asked. "I promise to stay out of your way."

"Let's plan on that the next time, and we will spend time at Nazareth."

We walked on to our house and sometime later Mama and Martha came. I was scolded severely by Martha for leaving the party. She was right, but I felt Judas would understand.

Two days later, I was on my way to Galilee. Judas was there to see me off and told me about his plans for Jonah and him in the weeks ahead. I promised him I would be back to help before long. I took one donkey and was on my way. I could not walk fast enough and was soon at Daniel's and then moved on to Nazareth.

My Walk Through the Valley

My trip back to Galilee almost wore me out. I was in too big a hurry, stopped very late in the day, and was on the road early the next morning. By the time I arrived in Nazareth, my donkey was rebelling. He would sit down in the middle of the road and start braying. People traveling would start laughing and caravan leaders would become angry because he would absolutely block the road.

Upon arriving in Nazareth, it was James who spotted me coming toward their house. The greetings from Jesus's family were warm and joyful. Aunt Mary was beautiful. The twins who happened to be there were so much like their mother that I could not take my eyes off of them.

"Jesus will be glad to see you," said Aunt Mary. "But you had better get a good start early in the morning because we understand that Jesus is soon taking his disciples and going to Judea beyond the Jordan," said James.

Aunt Mary added, "But you must stay here for the night. You can leave early in the morning after a good night's rest and a full morning meal." The donkey seemed to understand what was being said and brayed loudly. Everyone looked surprised and laughed. Aunt Mary told James to take care of the donkey and invited me inside.

That evening was a delightful visit filled with a lot of stories and laughter. I really did not want to go to bed because we were having a rollicking good time and all my weariness was forgotten. I told them all about Mama, Martha, and Mary. Juda became excited when he heard I had a business partner and he asked me a lot of questions about our working relationship.

Aunt Mary listened with great interest and then she decided it was time for me to go to bed that I might face tomorrow. She closed the visiting and said, "I will lead us in an evening prayer." She was quiet for a long time but I knew she was praying because a word would slip out every now and then. After a considerable time of meditation, she spoke. "God of us all, Father of my son, Creator of the world in which we live. May mercy and love be your gifts this night. Pour out your spirit upon each of us in accordance to our needs. Give us rest to face the new day you will give us. Discipline our thoughts and use our love to bless others. Push us in your righteous ways that tomorrow we will better meet the opportunities before us to serve those needing our faith, service, and prayers. To your glory, we pray. Amen."

She remained very quiet for a long time. No one moved until she raised her head and with that beautiful, serene smile on her face she said, "Shalom."

James motioned for me to come with him, and we went to his house. It was adjacent to the back of Aunt Mary's house. It was small, but adequate for his wife, child, and him. His son was asleep, so I moved in very quietly and was shown where I would sleep in an area that had been prepared for me.

The next morning I rose just before daylight. James greeted me, and I loaded my donkey just as Aunt Mary called me to come eat. It was a perfect meal with a wonderful assortment of food and quiet laughter to brighten the new day. I started out for

Capernaum planning to make a brief stop to see Jonathan. He was not at home, so I visited with Abigail and Bernice before continuing my trip. Julian was also in the fields working, and I asked that he and Jonathan be given my greetings.

Upon arriving in Capernaum, I went straight to John's house. Priscilla received me but encouraged me to immediately leave, so I could catch Jesus and his disciples before they got too far ahead of me. "Leave your donkey here," she said, "I will see that it is put in the shed, fed, and watered."

Priscilla pointed the direction I should go. I quickly removed my pack off the donkey's back and swung it around my shoulders. I started a slow trot down the hill toward Lake Galilee. When I came to the shoreline I could see a large group of people walking and quite scattered along the north shore. I slowed to a fast walk. I became aware that someone at the back of the group seemed to be waving to me. Soon, I realized that it was Jesus. He waved and waited until I got there. We had a very happy reunion as the disciples began to drop back and gathered around us.

"Thank you for coming," Jesus said, "I sensed that you must be close by. Lazarus, things will be a little easier now."

His last comment intrigued me, but I simply said, "I bring you warm greetings from your family."

I was panting a little from being out of breath just as someone handed me a flask of water.

"You stopped and saw Mother?" Jesus asked with surprise.

"Yes," I responded, "after all you must remember they are my family also. I spent one night and everyone sends you their warmest greetings. Your mother prayed a beautiful bedtime prayer. I love to hear her prayers. It is like her words slipped off the tongue of an angel as she spoke ministered to our hearts' spirits."

"You are right, Lazarus. Now, let's use our breath for walking. We have a considerable ways to go," Jesus said.

After a while, John swung in beside me. "John, your wife was a great help to me. She directed me where to go to find all of you. Without Priscilla's guidance, I would have missed all of you. Plus, she took charge of my donkey and that allowed me to leave immediately," I told John.

"I am so glad she could help you, and it is good to see you. I know Jesus is pleased. He has talked about missing you," John said.

We came to a town name Bethsaida that was just east of the Jordan River. Jesus called some of the disciples and suggested that we camp for the night just south of the town close to Lake Galilee. Then he directed that they go with Judas, who had our funds and buy some food from the local vendors for everyone. A few of the disciples and several friends scurried off to take care of their assignment while everyone else sat down and rested.

When they returned with the food, we moved just out of town and settled in a small olive grove close to the shore of the lake and set up a small camp. In the quiet of the evening, there were those who wanted to question Jesus. There were always some Pharisees that had Biblical questions, and Jesus always drew them into the circle of his friends.

"Jesus," called a voice out on the fringe of the group.

"What do you say:

> Is it right for a man to divorce his wife
> for any reason that pleases
> *and seems reasonable to him?*

Jesus pondered the question for some time, and then he got up and slowly walked back in the direction from which the question came. "Your question comes from our modern culture that tends to accept divorce, even when there may be a very simple solution to a simple disagreement between a man and his wife. But,

> Haven't you read that the one
> who created men and women,
> from the beginning he made them
> male and female and he said,
> marriage shall cause a man

to leave his father and mother,
and he shall cleave to his wife:
and the two shall become one flesh!
They are no longer
two separate people but one.
No person shall separate
what God has joined together.

"Then *why*", that same voice countered, "*Why did Moses command that a man could present his wife with a written divorce notice and dismiss the woman? It was because you know so little about the true meaning, requirements and disciplines of love that Moses allowed you to divorce your wives!*
But, are you listening:

That was not the original principle.
God was very clear,
anyone who divorces his wife
on any grounds except her
unfaithfulness, and marries
some other woman,
commits adultery.
His disciples after some discussion
among themselves said to Jesus,
If that is a man's position with his wife,
it is not worth getting married.
Jesus responded, It is not everybody
that can live up to this,
only those who have a special gift.
Some are incapable of
marriage from birth,
some are made incapable
by the action of people,
and some have made themselves
so for the sake
of the kingdom of heaven.
Let those who can accept

what I have said,
let them accept it as God's Will
and his position
on the issue of marriage.

There began a very noisy discussion between individuals and groups of people about what Jesus had just said. Obviously, some rather meekly agreed and others strongly disagreed. Some left the group they had been talking with and just wandered off by themselves. There really was considerable confusion and disturbance. A few turned and looked at Jesus and mumbled their frustrations, then turned, and disappeared.

The children in the crowd were not interested in those discussions, and they took advantage of the moment and began to encircle Jesus, and he was obviously very pleased with their presence. A few parents brought their children to Jesus and asked him to bless them.

The disciples were not pleased and tried to move them away from Jesus but he stopped them,

> *Let these children come to me,*
> and do not hinder them,
> for to such belong
> the kingdom of heaven.
> Then he began laying
> his hands on all of them.

Jesus got up and walked among the people as they were eating. Every now and then someone would hand him a morsel of bread or a piece of cheese, he usually smiled and accepted it.

Most of the crowd remained quiet and people would keep looking at Jesus as if expecting more from him.

A man slipped out of the crowd, moved past the disciples, and stood in front of Jesus:

> *"Master, what good thing must I do*
> to secure eternal life?

Jesus looked at him, lifted his face in prayer:

> Why do you ask me about what is good?
> One there is who is good.
> If you would enter eternal life,
> keep the commandments.
> And the man said to Jesus, which?
> Jesus said,
> You shall not kill,
> You shall not commit adultery,
> You shall not steal,
> You shall not bear false witness,
> Honor your father and mother,
> and, you shall love your neighbor as
> you love yourself.

The young man said to Jesus with considerable excitement, "All these I have observed since my youth; what do I still lack?"

Jesus smiled at him quietly and put his hands on both of his shoulders, looked him squarely in the face and said quietly, "if you would be perfect, go, sell what you possess and give that money to the poor and you will have treasure in heaven; and come follow me."

Judas was immediately at Jesus's side whispering. I feel he must have been suggesting that the young man give his money to their funds. Jesus just looked at him and shook his head "no."

The young man stood very still and looked at Jesus for a long time and went away with his head down. We learned later he had many possessions. Judas followed him but we never saw that young man again. I often wondered about him. I did ask Jesus about him, and he told me that the young man had been following along with them for several weeks, had engaged some of the disciples in conversations, had raised some very direct questions, and was getting more and more interested about what he might do.

"Lazarus, it is not easy for anyone when he or she must make the hard decision. It will always be that way. Even you are torn between your friendship with me and your responsibilities at home. I constantly find a tear in my heart because of the push and pull between my love for my mother and family and the mission to which God calls me."

"Jesus you have seen into my heart and sometimes I hope we can talk about this some more. It appears the people here are waiting for you to continue."

Jesus looked at the scattered groups and walked toward the middle of those in the area and called, "Gather round; you have had a nice break; and I trust that you are now refreshed and ready to struggle with additional issues facing your life and faith."

He had them all in a good mood, so he stopped, prayed, and then began: "You may find it hard to understand and agree with what I am about to say to you again. Listen very carefully:

> It is very hard for a rich person
> to enter the kingdom of heaven.

Think with me:

> It will be easier for a camel
> to go through the gate called
> "the eye of the needle"
> than for a rich person to enter
> the kingdom of God.

There was a lot of frowning and noisy murmuring among the crowd. Everyone was astonished at such a suggestion and someone spoke up:

Who then can be saved?

And Jesus firmly responded, "Moses kept reminding the children of Israel to remember…So remember…A person's wealth may doom them, condemn them, push them away from the kingdom, but remember, God is always working to draw you close to and into that kingdom. Again, I say to you remember:

With God all things are possible.

Peter spoke up right beside Jesus:

We have left everything and followed you.
What then shall we have?

Jesus turned and looked around at his disciples:

Truly I say to you, in the new world, when the Son of Man shall sit on the glorious throne, provided by God and *render judgment over all peop*le.

Are you listening!

Everyone who has left houses or brothers or sisters
or father or mother or children or property,
for my name's-sake, you will receive a hundredfold,
plus you will inherit eternal life.

A kind of hushed buzz moved through the crowd, especially the disciples.

Jesus interrupted the confusion, "However, remember: Many who consider themselves first in life will be last in *eternity.*

Are you listening? There are those who will be considered last in life, who have nothing, but they will be first in God's kingdom. Where will you be?"

It was beginning to get dark and Jesus urged everyone to leave for home. "Shalom, children. I will see you again soon on one of God's glorious day's."

Jesus motioned for John, Nathaniel, and me to come with him. We walked a ways along the shoreline.

"Lazarus, let me thank you for coming when Julian called you. He shared with me a little of the fright you had at that camp where he happened to meet you. It reminded me of an earlier trip we took together a time long ago."

"Yes, Jesus," I said, "It was just as frightening. Julian protected us and even risked his life. I am sorry that it reminded him of earlier days when he fought in the Roman Army, and that it brought such grief to his heart and mind."

Jesus quietly said, "He wept through his description of that hard, brutal action he took. It was in the tender embrace of Bernice that he found his healing. He talked a long time about his past. Life had not been easy for him and he was struggling with both who he was and what he had done. Bernice brought him comfort in both heart and mind and Lazarus, he sees you as a great friend." I was surprised and said, "If he sees me as a 'great friend,' I will try and let our relationship grow in a way that may be helpful to both of us."

"Just allow yourself to be a little more relaxed around him," said Jesus.

"I guess you are right. I have been somewhat afraid of him knowing who he was and what capabilities he has. Seeing him perform at that camp didn't diminish that feeling. One man against four and the four lost."

I realized I was almost out of breath talking about him.

"Lazarus, slow down," Jesus said. "Always remember that Julian is a child of the living God, and he needs your ministry. He looks to your leadership in his life."

There was a sudden and intense silence.

"Thank you for sharing that with me," Jesus said.

"Jesus let me share one more thing," I said, "That same path suddenly appeared for our escape. I had actually looked for evidence of that path, and there was no sign of any place where we could cut through those woods. But when we were ready to leave, there it was."

"Make it one of your blessings in life," said Jesus.

"Nathaniel, let's get back to the camp and find a bed for tonight," suggested Jesus. "Tomorrow may be a long day of new excitement and discoveries."

So off we went—back to the camp where the other disciples were assembled. Most had retired for the night, and it didn't take us long. Jesus disappeared, and I was sure he needed his time of prayer and meditation.

The next morning Jesus told the disciples to pack up what they had, and they would go north toward Mt. Herman. I sat down and in prayer and deep thought I struggled for a long time about what I should do. There seemed to be a strange and different call in my heart. So when it was time for them to leave, I spoke briefly with Jesus and decided I would go to Jonathan's and meet up with Jesus and the disciples when they returned.

Abigail and Bernice were glad to see me, and I immediately asked for water and a place to rest. They told me that Jonathan and Julian were again working in the fields, but would be in at the close of the day. I stretched out and was surprised that I fell into a sound sleep and was awakened by Jonathan's happy greeting.

We visited and had dinner and again I asked if I could rest.

Abigail looked rather sternly at me and asked, "Lazarus, are you all right?"

Bernice came in where I was sleeping several times during the night to ask if I needed anything. I slept later than I expected, and when I came into the kitchen area it seemed they were having a quiet conference about me and my needs.

After talking with them for a few minutes, I announced that I was going home and Julian immediately responded, "You're not going alone, I will accompany you to just north of Jerusalem."

The farther we went the worse I felt. Julian cared for my every need. By the time we got near to Jerusalem it was evident that I was getting weaker and weaker. When we came to Jerusalem,

Julian told me he would not leave me until I was home. By that time, I was riding on the donkey with Julian holding me up.

Bethany looked very good, but before I got home, I rested, drank some water, and walked to the house. Everyone was surprised to see me and especially to see Julian.

"Lazarus," said Mama, "I did not expect you so soon."

"And Mama, I did not expect to be here so soon. Jesus and the disciples were going north toward Mt. Herman, and I just did not want to make that trip. Julian was kind enough to accompany me home and has helped me when I needed a strong arm to lean on."

Martha had a very puzzled look on her face as she walked to me, "Lazarus, you seem very tired, and perhaps you need a good meal after your long walk. Come here and sit down."

"Where is Judas?" I asked.

"He and Jonah are on a buying trip to Gaza and the coast. They have been gone a week, so they should soon be back," Mary informed me.

Mama and Martha were scurrying around fixing something for Julian and me to eat. I really did not feel hungry, but I sat there and stirred what was on my plate, and ate very little. I told Mama it was wonderful. Julian savored every bite and let Mama know how much he enjoyed it.

"Julian," Mama said, "Thank you for taking care of my boy and bringing him home. You must stay here tonight before you leave.

"Thank you," said Julian.

Mary butted in, "Julian, can I bring you anything else to eat."

"You have already fed me well and I appreciate it," Julian said.

I think Julian really wanted to stay for a few days, but it was a busy time at Jonathan's farm, and Julian felt he should be there working in the fields.

I decided to go to bed early. Mama kept moving in and out of my room very quietly, and I knew she was, for some reason, checking on me. In the middle of the night, I jumped up, ran out of the house, and became very sick. I heaved so hard that I dropped to my knees.

Mama was right there, "Lazarus, I knew you were ill when you came home. Have you been sick like this before you arrived here?"

"No Mama, I think I am just very tired. I will be fine in the morning."

The next morning Julian was soon on his way home. I had asked Mama not to tell him about my sick spell during the night.

Several days had gone by when Judas and Jonah returned home from their buying trip, and I tried to help them prepare for the sales rounds without any success. They had three days of successful rounds in visiting merchants surrounding Jerusalem and in the city as well. They sold three quarters of their merchandise and Mama prepared a celebration meal, but I had to leave before it was over. In the middle of the night, I again ran from the house because I was sick. Mama followed me and became very upset when blood was very evident in what I had thrown up.

She helped me back to bed and the next day I did not even attempt to get up. Everyone was upset and the old doctor who prescribed herbs gave me something which made matters much worse. He looked at me and shook his head and said, "And he's so young."

Mama nearly threw him out of the house. I heard them talking about Jesus and Mary went to Judas's house and asked him to come. Mama, I was told, asked him to go and find Jesus, and tell him, "Lazarus is ill and we need you to come immediately."

Judas was gone for eight days and when he returned they expected to see Jesus with him, but they were told he would soon come.

Mary screamed at poor Judas, "Why didn't you bring him?"

Mama took Mary into the next room and talked with her for a long time to calm her, but she was nearly hysterical before the day was over and still no Jesus.

I kept getting weaker. Judas offered to go and find Jesus again, but Mama said no.

"I am sure he will come," she said.

Much to our surprise Julian appeared at the door and asked if he could see me. From that moment he never left my side. He took care of my every need day and night and prayed continuously. When I died, Mama said that Julian wept profusely for two days, and he refused any kind of food.

> *Now, when Jesus arrived I had already been in the tomb*
> four days. Bethany is very close to Jerusalem, less than
> two miles away. There were many people who had come
> out to comfort Mama, Martha, and Mary and to weep
> over my death.
> Jesus came in from the Jericho road having come down
> the Jordan River. Martha went out to meet him.
> " If only you had been here, Lord," said Martha,
> "My brother would never have died. And I know
> that, even now, God will give you whatever you
> ask from him."
> Jesus embraced Martha, looked at her and quietly spoke.
> "Your brother will rise again."
> Out of frustration she almost shouted,
> " I know, I know, he will rise again in the resurrection at
> the last day, I understand that."
> Jesus took Martha's hand
> and they walked to the house as Jesus spoke.
> "I myself am the resurrection and life.
> Martha anyone who believes in me will live
> even though he dies, and anyone
> who is alive and believes in me will never die.
> Martha, is it possible that you can believe that?"
> "Oh, Yes Lord, I truly believe. You are the Christ, the Son
> of God, and he is coming into this world," Martha said.
> Martha where is Mary?
> "She is sitting at the house angry with you for not coming
> before our Lazarus died."

Jesus picked up his pace and said, Come let us go to her. But, Mary had left the house to find Jesus because someone had said to her, the Master is here and is asking about you. Jesus was some ways from the house in Bethany but Mary jumped and ran to meet him with the mourners following after her.

Then Mary when she saw Jesus, she spoke through her sobbing voice. "If you had only been here, Lord, my brother never would have died."

Martha began to sob as well and Jesus was deeply moved by the depth of their sorrow.

"Where have you put him?" asked Jesus.

Lord come with us and see. And as Martha and Mary took his hands to lead him he too was weeping.

The mourners were very touched by Jesus's emotion and they began to weep even more.

And some asked, "if he could open the eyes of the blind, surely he could have saved Lazarus."

And when Jesus came to the tomb,
it was only a cave, and a stone
had been placed in front of it.
He stood there and turned to Martha
and said, "have them move the stone."

Martha responded, "but Lord he has been in there for four days and the odor will be terrible. I cannot endure that smell knowing it is my brother."

"Move the stone," said Jesus.

So some men moved the stone.

Jesus raised his face toward
the heavens and said,
"Father, I thank you that you heard me.
I know that you hear me always,
but I am saying this for the benefit of those
who are standing nearby, that they
may believe that you have sent me."

When Jesus had said these things, he said in a very loud voice, "Lazarus, come out!"

And I came out, my hands and feet still bound with bandages
and my face draped with a cloth. Jesus said, "Take off his restrictions and free him so that he can go home."

All of this was shared with me over and over again by my family, Julian, and my partner, Judas. The highlights were related to me many times by Julian, and we rejoiced again and again with Psalms and songs of praise.

Jesus walked up to me. There were tears in his eyes. "Lazarus, my best friend, come and let's go to your home. There we can praise God together."

He then gave me a warm embrace.

I took Martha's hand and Jesus took Mary's hand as he put his arm across my shoulders. Together we walked to Bethany, with me still wearing my grave clothes, and Julian leading the way. It was like a resurrection parade. Some people when they saw me ran because they were afraid, but others fell to their knees and gave God the glory.

Mama was at home. She came to the door when we were a short distance from the house. She squealed like a young girl and started running. I met her partway and we embraced. Martha, Mary, and Jesus joined the embrace when they came to us.

Mama started praying, "Eternal God, Creator of life, Sustainer of life, and the Giver of new life…Thank you, Father God… Thank you, Eternal Spirit…Thank you, gracious Redeemer. A short while ago my son was dead but you have brought him to us alive. Empower us all with new life. Bless each of us with the power to live as new children of the Kingdom. Help each of us to appreciate the gift of life more each day. Help us to use our life as your humble servants. This we pray to your glory and in praise of your holy name. Hallelujah! Amen."

People began to come from every direction, so we quickly moved ourselves into the house. Mama would not let me far from her. From time to time she would stop, turn me toward her, look very intently at me, and kiss me on my cheek. That day I was showered and blessed with a mother's love. I will never forget it and will always cherish it.

Julian and Judas maintained tight security at the door to give us our privacy. The buzz from the growing number of people outside kept mounting. There was a mixture of prayers, singing and calling to one another.

Julian allowed John to enter the house, but he continued to stand there blocking all entrance by anyone.

"Jesus," said John with a voice of concern, "I heard some Pharisees very openly-plotting against you. They were saying that some specific action must and will be taken against you during the Passover. It sounded like a direct threat. Perhaps we should return to Galilee where they have little power and influence.

"John, I am now in the hands of my Father; and if he wants me to move back to Galilee, he will tell me. Where are the other disciples? I have not seem any of them during the last several days," Jesus said. "Jesus, when we came off of the mountain," said John, "you announced that you were going to Jerusalem. It was then that Thomas announced: *Let's go with him and die with him there.*"

"Yes, I remembered that," said Jesus, "and they all seemed inclined to want to go home and be in Jerusalem for the Passover."

"They were going to take care of some family and business needs and join us here. They should all probably be here by tomorrow," responded John.

At that moment Peter, Andrew, and James entered the room and greeted everyone.

"What is all the excitement about," said Peter. "There is a constant rumbling of voices and we heard them repeating over and over, Lazarus."

John walked over to the three and started talking in a quiet voice about Lazarus being raised from the dead. The smiles on their faces was very special and then they came and greeted me with a prayer by Peter. "Lord of life and Lord of death. Our voices are raised in praise to you that Lazarus lives. Keep him bound to earth for his service to your kingdom among those who need his commitment and ministry to the merchants of life. Let us lift our voices and sing your praises. Amen."

Mama spoke to Martha and Mary and they moved to the kitchen area and began preparing some food.

Jesus looked at me and motioned for us to go to the room we shared when he would come to Bethany. He closed the curtain and sat in his corner of the room. Mary slipped in and handed each of us a small cup of goat's milk which was greatly appreciated.

"Lazarus, let me tell you that events are going to start moving very quickly. But before it goes too far, I would like to plan a Passover meal with my disciples. I want all of them there. Do you think Julian would be able to find at least some of them and bring them here?"

"Let me go and talk with Julian and John."

I slipped out of the room and pulled the curtain closed behind me.

John was talking with Mama, and I went over and waited until they finished their conversation. "John, I need to talk with you and Julian."

We moved to where Julian was still standing by the door. I was amazed when I glanced out the door. For as far as I could see, there were people and the noise was almost overbearing. "Julian?" I asked, "What are we to do with all these people? Do you think we can get them to go home this evening?"

I asked Julian to come with me. Then I directed my partner Judas and Jonah to protect the door. John, Julian, and I went into Mama's room, and I suggested that they try and locate the disciples and bring them to our house.

"Where do you think they are?" asked Julian.

"I have no idea, but I hope they are coming this way from their homes," I said.

Julian asked, "Is there anyone besides John who will know them all?"

"Peter is here, take him with you," suggested John.

"We will find them if they are in this area," said Julian as he left the room.

John and I went back to my room and when I looked in Jesus was sound asleep. We backed out and left him. "Lazarus, I will go and help Julian and Peter and return as soon as possible."

"That is probably a very good idea, and I will see if I can disperse some of the people outside our house. If the disciples come we will need some time for Jesus to be with them."

John left the house, and I went with him to the yard. Suddenly, there was Nathaniel and Philip.

I said to them, "Jesus wants to gather the disciples here at our house, have you seen any of them?"

They looked at me with a blank stare and shook their heads "no."

"Then, let me suggest that you move from here to the Gate Beautiful at Jerusalem where the elders are debating and discussing issues of faith. And after you have checked there, go to the Temple and see if any have gone to be there for worship. When you return, come by the well and see if you can locate any of them, and tell any you find to come here. But be sure to return here by the time it is dark."

They left very quickly, and I moved slowly toward the Garden of Gethsemane.

They were very successful and by evening all of the disciples except for Judas had gathered at our house. They were quietly seated outside talking to one another when Judas suddenly came running into the area looking very disheveled and almost disoriented.

Mama saw Judas and walked over to him and asked if he would like something to eat and drink.

"Oh please," he responded.

She motioned for him to follow her into the house, and it wasn't long before he joined the group.

Jesus was watching all of this and waited until Judas returned. Jesus then sat down and the disciples gathered about him and he entered a time of quiet prayer. We all joined him except for Judas who got up and went back in the house.

I started to go see what he needed, but I knew Mama would care for any need he had. So I watched the door just in case Mama looked out and called for me.

Jesus was still praying when everyone was startled by seeing Aunt Mary with Jesus's brother James and Juda appear on the path from Gethsemane. We all waited for Jesus to finish his prayer. John got up and went to Mary and embraced her and greeted the brothers. They walked very slowly toward Jesus.

Jesus opened his eyes and there stood his mother. They locked eyes and were very still. It was the most amazing thing to watch—their expressions. They were talking without saying a single word. The love that flowed between them was exciting and amazing.

Jesus rose and embraced his family with great excitement and then everyone joined in. As this was going on, Judas the disciple, suddenly ran out of the house and raced off in the direction of Jerusalem without saying a word to Jesus or anyone else. Mama followed him out of the house, but there was no stopping him. He disappeared down the path toward Jerusalem.

Jesus saw Judas come out of the house and paused to watch. It was obvious to me that Jesus was offering a prayer for Judas.

Jesus then turned and looked at all of the people that had been gathering. "Tomorrow is the Sabbath and I urge everyone to be present for worship at the Temple. It promises to be a glorious day with God revealing his greatness and glory."

With that brief announcement he took his Mother's hand and walked into the house with Aunt Mary, James, Juda, and me. Mama was waiting at the door and drew Aunt Mary into her embrace, and we disappeared for the evening to be a family.

A Grand Parade

When the Sabbath dawned, it promised to be a beautiful day which the Lord had truly made. The breezes from the south were sweet and warm. There were delicate clouds floating lazily in the dark blue sky. The birds announced their joy with the day as they flew from tree to tree while sharply banking in their flight and doing dips in the air. Our house came alive very early. Jesus had already left, and I felt sure he was in the Garden of Gethsemane praying. We did not know until Martha came out of her room that Mary had gone with Jesus.

Our morning meal was being prepared by Mama and some of her friends and we were about to pray when Jesus and Mary returned.

Mama asked Jesus if he would have a prayer and much to our surprise Jesus turned and said, "Mary will lead us this morning." All became quiet as Mary had a silent time before her prayer.

Jesus put his hand on Mary's arm to quietly stop her as he made her aware that others were joining us and it would be best to wait just a moment. Aunt Mary and more of Jesus' family were coming down the path where they had been camping with the

Galileans who came for the Passover. They stopped at the edge of the assembled group and Mary closed her eyes and lifted her hands toward the heavens. Many of us joined her as we regained our composure.

"God of the ages...Father of all people...Lord of the Sabbath...You called the prophets and David...Bless us in this day, a day that belongs to you...Challenge us with your righteous spirit...Bring quietness to our restless hearts...Challenge our faith in you and through Jesus may we come to know what you would have us be and do...Inspire our dreams and our service to your kingdom. Let the worship we experience this day be the dawning of a new understanding of your kingdom. Come Spirit of God...Come!...Bless the food we now share, bless our families, May it all be to your glory. Amen"

Aunt Mary walked through the gathered people and went straight to Mary. She hugged her with a long embrace and sealed it with a kiss.

Mama invited all to come to the tables with assorted food and drinks and then she joined Aunt Mary and my sister Martha in sharing warm and happy greetings.

Jesus was standing close to Mary and those around him were startled by the flapping of bird wings. Jesus looked up and raised his hand and a beautiful dove rested on his hand and very intentionally looked him straight in the face. Everyone froze in their place and watched. Jesus stroked the head of the bird and it made a quiet chirp or two and flew away.

In all the excitement of our greetings and congratulations of Mary for her beautiful prayer, then stopping to watch the bird that landed on Jesus's hand, absolutely none of us realized that standing in our midst were the twin sisters of Jesus, Esther and Naomi, and their children.

It was Esther who announced their presence, "Cousins Mary and Martha we have come with our families to celebrate the Passover with you. I am Esther and here is Naomi."

Mary and Martha dissolved in tears and engulfed them in hugs and joyful greetings. Martha suddenly turned, "Where are your children?"

Esther responded, "This is Joseph and there are two you have not met, Mary and our baby, Moses."

Oh, how beautiful," Mary said.

Naomi quickly jumped in and said, "Here are our twins Rebecca and Naomi and we also have a son, Amos."

Both Martha and Mary froze. Then Martha said, "Amos? Our Papa's name?"

"Yes," said Naomi, "He is named for your papa who was very special to us."

Very quietly Mama started crying and stood still staring at him. My sisters knelt down and embraced a confused little boy.

Naomi said to Amos, "We will explain this to you a little later, be patient."

"Come and eat," said Aunt Mary, "It may be a long day."

Mama and Martha took the younger children by the hand and helped them find what they wanted to eat while Mary took care of the twins and the older children. Everyone was so very happy and there was much laughter and hugging.

The disciples gathered closely around Jesus as he ate with a high sense of expectancy. He began talking to them as we all listened:

> *The kingdom of heaven is like*
> a farmer going out early in the morning
> to hire laborers for his vineyard.
> He agreed with them on a wage
> of a silver coin a day and sent them to work.
> About nine o'clock, he went out and saw some
> others standing about in the
> marketplace with nothing to do. You go to the vineyard too,
> he said to them and I will pay

 you a fair wage. And off they went.At about midday and again
about three o'clock in the afternoon
he went out and did the same thing.
Then about five o'clock he went
and found some others standing about.
Why are you standingabout here
doing nothing, he asked them?
Because no one has employed
us, they replied.
You go off in the vineyard
as well, he said.
When evening came the owner
of the vineyard said to his foreman,
Call the laborers
and pay them their wages, he said,
beginning with the last
and ending with the first.
So, those who were engaged
at five o'clock came up and
each man received a silver coin.
But when the first to be
employed came they reckoned
they would get more,
but they also received a silver coin
for each man.
As they took their money
they grumbled at the farmer and said,
these last fellows have only put in
one hour's work and you've treated them
exactly the same as us who have gone
through all the hard work and heat of the day.
But he replied to one of them:
My friend, I'm not being
unjust to you.
Wasn't our agreement
for a silver coin a day?

Take your money and go home.
It is my wish to give the late comer
as much as I give you.
May I not do what I like
with what belongs to me?
,Must you be jealous
because I am generous?
So many who are the last
now will be the first then and
the first will be last.

Then Jesus sat for a long time and watched the disciples and others who mingled in with them. Martha brought him a flask of water which he shared with others sitting around him.

Jesus rose and went in the house and I followed him. He picked up his outer robe that was in the room where he had slept and put it on.

"Lazarus, go and have the disciples come inside a few minutes before we leave."

I went outside and passed word that Jesus would like the disciples to come inside.

Matthew informed me that Judas had left only a few moments before, and he did not know where he had gone, or how long it would be before his return.

Upon assembling inside I shared the news about Judas and Jesus made no sign of concern about his whereabouts. He began speaking:

We are now going to Jerusalem,
and soon the Son of Man
will be handed over to the chief priests
and the scribes
—and they will condemn him to death.

Peter started to object but Jesus stopped him before he even got a word out.

They will hand him over
to the heathen to ridicule and
flog and crucify.
And on the third day he will rise again.

There was considerable confusion among the disciples. Peter was showing anger while others exhibited resignation.

The mother of the sons of Zebedee had been standing with Mama in the corner of the room. She moved quickly to where her sons were standing, grabbed their sleeves, and pulled them before Jesus. She had been listening to Jesus and decided that she wanted a personal favor from him. He listened to her with a rather puzzled look on his face. You could tell he was not comfortable with what she was whispering and her sons seemed extremely restless. Jesus gently stopped her and trying to understand clearly what was being asked he very kindly asked:

What is it you want, he said.

Their mother immediately responded:

Jesus, please say that these two sons of mine may sit one on each side of you when you are king!

The other disciples were about to make an objection when Jesus raised his hands and called for quietness. Everyone became very attentive at that point.

Jesus looked at the three of them and said:
You don't know what it is you are asking.
Can you two drink what I have to drink.
Yes, we can, they answered.
Ah, you will indeed drink my drink, said Jesus.
but as for sitting on either side of me,
that is not for me to grant
– that belongs to those for whom
my Father has planned it.
When the other disciples realized

fully what was happening
they were highly indignant with the two
brothers and their mother.
It was then that Jesus called them close
to him and said,
you know that the rulers of the heathen
lord it over them
and that their great ones
have absolute power?
But it must not be so among you.
and if anyone of you wants
to be first among you,
he must be your slave
—just as the Son of Man
has not come to be served but to serve,
and to give his life to set many others free.

With that said, Jesus stood and started walking toward the door. Several of the disciples would like to have asked questions, but Jesus had other priorities. When he passed through the door, he was surprised how many people had gathered so early in the morning. He turned and spoke to the disciples, "Come, it is now time to go to Jerusalem to celebrate the Sabbath in the Temple. The children ran to him and he greeted each one.

As he started walking toward Jerusalem he came across two blind men sitting by the roadside:

> *Hearing that it was Jesus who was passing by,*
> they cried out,
> Have mercy on us, Lord, you Son of David!
> The crowd tried to hush them up,
> but this only made them
> cry out more loudly still.
> Have pity on us, Lord. you son of David!
> Jesus stood quite still and called out to them,
> What do you want me to do for you?
> Lord, let us see again.

And, Jesus deeply moved with pity,
touched their eyes.
At once their sight was restored,
and they followed him.

A great shout of joy rose from the crowd that observed the healing. The number of people in the procession and along the road were growing and there were many others waiting for him along the way before he even got there. Peter and Julian were leading the way making a path for Jesus, his disciples, friends, and family.

As they approached Jerusalem
and came to Bethphage and the Mount of Olives,
Jesus sent Philip and Thaddeus ahead
telling them: Go into the village in front of you
and you will find there a donkey tethered
and her foal as well.
Untie them and bring them to me.
Should anyone say anything
to you, you are to say,
The Lord needs them
and he will return them to you.
So Philip and Thaddeus went off
and followed Jesus's instructions.
This took place to fulfill
what was spoken by the prophet,
saying, Tell the daughter of Zion,
Behold, your king is coming to you,
humble and mounted on a donkey,
and on a colt, the foal of a donkey.
Philip and Thaddeus went
and did as Jesus had told them;
they brought the donkey and the foal,
and put their garments on them,
and Jesus took his seat.
Then most of the crowd spread

their own cloaks on the road,
while others cut down
branches from the trees
and spread them in his path.
The crowds who went in front of
him and the crowds who followed
behind him all shouted:
GOD SAVE THE SON OF DAVID! BLESSED IS
THE MAN WHO COMES IN THE NAME OF THE
Lord!
GOD SAVE HIM FROM ON HIGH!

There is no way I can describe all that was going on. The crowd was enormous. Children were running in an out of the procession, old men were waving their canes and walking sticks and women were dancing in the road. The women took off their head scarves and spread them in the path of the donkey. There was singing and praising God, the most High.

A child tripped and fell when running across the road and was stepped on by several people in the multitude. Jesus slipped off the donkey, picked up the screaming child, kissed the blemished skin and said a brief prayer while he embraced the child. The screams from the wounded child stopped abruptly. Jesus handed the child back to his mother and climbed back on the donkey. By that time, there was an enormous knot of people which made it difficult for Jesus and the disciples to continue on their way.

Again, it was Julian who used his stature very gently yet firmly to make a path. Peter and several of the others disciples joined Julian to lead the way. Julian then moved behind Jesus to become the protector of Aunt Mary who was stumbling over the branches and thrown garments. Martha and Mary were very busy taking care of Mama and themselves.

What a wonderful day

When we arrived in the inner city people were calling:

Who is this? And there were
those who called back,
This is Jesus the prophet,
the man from Nazareth in Galilee!

I was scanning the crowd all the way to the Temple steps trying to see if Rabbi Levi might be watching this unusual scene. I did not see him anywhere, but at the top of the steps leaning against one of the stone pillars was Judas, the disciple, with several of the priests and scribes, and I thought to myself how that was an interesting combination. John was very close to me and I asked him to check what I thought I saw. He verified that I was right, and we moved on with the crowd.

Judas must have seen John looking his way, and he quickly disappeared. It wasn't long before Judas surprised us when he quietly appeared behind us and said, "This is quite a reception. I have never seen anything like it. Do you think Jesus will bring in his kingdom today?"

John looked at Judas and quietly said, "Judas you are not in control; it is Jesus's day, and the people are simply expressing their joyous appreciation for him as a prophet and showering him with their love and hope for tomorrow."

When Jesus arrived at the Temple, he went up the few steps and then inside. He stopped and surveyed all of the activity going on around and before him. His face suddenly changed from the joyful expression of the celebration to one of intense shame and anger at what spread before him. The outer court was filled with money changers and those selling doves, lambs, and other exotic animals for sacrifices in the temple. The merchants were loudly hawking their services and the people were just as loudly bargaining for a better price.

I have never seen Jesus's face take on such a look of anger. He despised what he was seeing, and he froze. Suddenly he bellowed:

"What are you doing? What is the meaning of this indiscretion? Why are you acting like heathen that know not the God of Creation who calls us to prayer and commitment?"

With that he caught the corner of the table nearest to him and he flipped it, money flew everywhere. He then grabbed another and when he overturned it, doves escaped their cages. Some of the disciples began turning over tables and benches and even throwing cages. Jesus yelled, "What are you teaching and observing here in this holy place?"

Even strangers were getting into the melee. People were running and screaming. The money changers were down on their knees trying to collect their spilled coins and others were trying to gather the doves and lambs.

Jesus mounted a table and his voice thundered out over the multitude:

> It is written, my house shall be called a house of prayer,
> but you have turned it into a pagan shop filled with disgrace
> and shame.

He jumped down from the table and pushed Julian in front of him to lead the way to another part of the Temple. He walked in a side entrance to the sanctuary and stood in the door gathering his composure. When he turned around, he went to a small alcove and there he stopped and prayed.

Almost immediately:

> the blind and the lame came to him, and he healed them.
> But, when the chief priests and scribes saw the wonderful
> things he was doing, and that children were shouting in
> the
> Temple the words, God save the son of David,
> the priests were highly indignant.
> Can't you hear what these children are saying,
> they asked Jesus.
> Yes, he replied, and haven't you ever read the words,
> Out of the mouths of babes and sucklings
> thou hast perfected praise?
> And, Jesus turned on his heels and went out
> of the city to Bethany, where he would spend the night.

When we returned to Bethany, Jesus told the disciples that they could do as they wished, but he would like them either here at Bethany or at the Gate Beautiful in Jerusalem the next morning. He then turned, went in the house, and waited for the area outside to hopefully clear of people. Mama prepared Jesus and Aunt Mary some cheese and bread, and we sat there and visited. Jesus had not recovered from his outburst at the Temple, and he remained restless and disturbed.

Martha and Mary went to the camp of the Galileans to visit with the twins and their families. They had asked Mama if they could bring Amos home with them when they returned. Mama agreed and that thrilled her daughters.

Julian remained close to give some protection from the people who might decide that they could barge into the house in search of Jesus. It was not terribly long before Julian came in and told us that for the most part everyone had gone. Jesus jumped up, patted his mother's shoulder, looked at me, and said, "Come on, let's go to the Garden of Gethsemane. Julian whispered to me that he would not be far away. He would be close enough that we could call for him if we needed him.

Jesus carefully looked outside and then set a quick pace for the Garden. When we got inside the Garden area, he slowed down and slipped off on a little side path that I had never taken. We came to a very private area entirely surrounded by low shrubs. It was beautiful and totally private. He sat down and began to pray. I sat a little ways away and joined him in meditation and prayer. I was suddenly surprised to hear Jesus start chanting some of the Psalms. I had only heard him do that once, and again I was impressed by the beauty of his voice. I quietly joined him on several of the Psalms and that was a very special experience to be chanting with Jesus.

He became very quiet and then laid back on the ground and closed his eyes. In a little while he said, "Lazarus this will be a hard week." There was a long pause and he again spoke very quietly. "It is going to be very hard on Mother. The family will be there to support her, but I need you and John to be very attentive to her."

"I will do all that I can for her. May I talk with John and give him a warning?"

"Yes, but don't think you know what is going to happen. Take each day as it comes and stay very alert," Jesus said.

"Jesus is this the time you predicted when they will take you and crucify you?"

After a little while he responded, "Yes, but remember Lazarus there will be a day of resurrection, and you will need to keep reminding Mother about what is to come."

"I will need to keep reminding myself," I said.

"Lazarus, do you remember that time Mother got so upset with a crucifixion outside of Jericho on the road toward Jerusalem?"

"Yes, and you and your family went home by way of Sebaste after the Passover. And we had that frightening confrontation with the Roman soldiers at our campsite."

"That was upsetting," said Jesus, "but to think, I missed it all?"

"This coming week will be much harder on Mother than anything that she has ever experienced. The rest of the family is here except for James, and they will be dissolved in sorrow and fear. So I need you to be a stabilizing force in their midst until things begin to take on new life," Jesus told me.

"We have had some wonderful and interesting experiences together over the years. Lazarus, thank you, for being such a good friend. You have helped to make the rough places a little easier, and you are going to have to do the same for Mother during this week," Jesus said.

We had come to the place where I did not know what to say, so I remained very quiet and listened.

"Lazarus, I know that Jonathan has extended a sincere invitation for you to move your family to his farm, and he would build you a house there. Because of your friendship with me and your being raised from the dead, you may find it easier to move away from Bethany and establish your home on Jonathan's farm," Jesus said. "Then you can turn your business over to your partner, Judas, and become a partner with my brother, Juda," he added.

I sat there listening as Jesus planned my future.

"All you say seems very reasonable and for me most acceptable but there are three other people who need to be carefully consulted and listened to and included in the planning. Mama may even like to live closer to Aunt Mary," I told Jesus.

"Lazarus, let's take some time for prayer, and perhaps God, the Father, will give us direction."

Immediately Jesus was in a state of deep meditation. You could tell by looking at him that he was in a different world, and he was very comfortable there. He suddenly jumped to his feet and said, "Quick, Lazarus we must return to your house, something is very wrong."

Jesus knew the way. I did not know that he could run so fast, and he was jumping on large stones. I was soon worn out, but he was still going and urging me to follow quickly. When we were almost in sight of the house, Jesus stopped and walked slowly. Everything seemed very quiet and Mama told us that she was fine.

"Where is Julian?" asked Jesus.

"He took a large jar to bring me water from the well," she answered.

"The well," said Jesus as he looked for me to lead. We started running again and arrived in time to see a frightening sight. Julian was surrounded by Roman soldiers ready for a fight. There was one soldier on the ground and he was not moving. The others had swords drawn and had Julian surrounded and were closing the circle. It would appear that they had very malicious intentions.

I whispered, "What do we do now?"

Jesus raised his hands toward the heavens and just that quick there was a lightning storm that was blinding and terrifying, mixed with swirling wind and hailstones. Now, the amazing thing was that it did not affect us—only those around the well and that circle of Roman soldiers. Julian dropped the sword and bolted the area before anyone realized he was leaving. He quickly disappeared into the woods and still no one had seen him.

When Jesus turned to leave, everything stopped except the lightning, and it was over when we were well away from that well. We could hear a lot of yelling, and I realized those soldiers must be very confused and frustrated that their prisoner was gone

Jesus had not said a word. We were almost home and he turned toward the Garden of Gethsemane. All was quiet there. Jesus turned off the main path, walked down a very narrow almost hidden path, and there sitting on the ground was Julian. He was cut on one arm and out of breath.

He looked at Jesus with a shy smile and said, "I wondered if you might be there somewhere. Thank you for the confusion you caused with that storm. It allowed me to slip out of their control and for that I am deeply grateful."

Jesus took his arm in his hands and said, "Julian it is time for you to go home. Leave here by going to Jericho and up the river. Do you understand?"

"Yes, Lord. I will go at your command, but not because I am running from fear," said Julian.

"You will be in my prayers and care," said Jesus. "So go to your Bernice."

"Lord, how can I live with being a killer?" There were tears in his eyes. "One of those soldiers recognized me and there was immediate trouble. There must be an order for my arrest."

"Julian, are you listening? The soldier is alive and well. You are not a killer. Now, go home by way of Jericho and up the River."

"Yes, Lord, and thank you, Lord. Lazarus, I hope I will see you soon?'

"You will!" I said.

Julian did that automatic Roman military salute to Jesus, turned, and walked quickly away.

"Julian," Jesus spoke, "Slow down, you do not want to draw suspicion as though you are running from something."

"Wait just a moment, Julian." Jesus walked to where he was and took off his outer cloak. "Here. Give me your cloak and you wear mine. Lazarus, take off your head scarf and give it to Julian. Now, help him get it tucked around the side of his face."

Jesus watched. He made a few corrections to the scarf and then told Julian, "You look like a different person. Now, be on your way."

"Yes, Lord!"

And with that he was gone.

Jesus and I walked back to the house and told Mama that Julian needed to go home and we were sorry, but we did not know the whereabouts of her jar.

"Mama. There is another jar in the shed," I said. "I will find it and clean it for you and get it filled this evening."

Jesus walked back in our room, and I realized I was extremely tired and followed him. There were questions in Mama's eyes, and I did not want to be in the room when she could not hold them any longer. I could give her answers later.

Both Jesus and I fell asleep, and we were awakened later by Mama calling us to come for an evening meal. We had just started eating when Judas, my partner, appeared and sat with us. He kept watching Jesus with a very strange, questioning look. After the meal, I asked Judas for his help. We went outside and I said to him, "Judas, I need to find a jar that has been stored in the merchandise shed, which we put there for future use several years ago."

"I know exactly where it is," he said. He went in the shed, moved two small storage containers and there in a third container was the jar.

"Now, Lazarus, I will go and get water for Mama 2 while you rest from your excitement at the well."

"You were there," I asked.

"Yes, I saw the whole thing. Jesus is amazing. I wish I could lift my hands skyward and create as much excitement as he did. Those soldiers were so frightened that even their commander was not able to function efficiently. I am sure that Julian is far, far away from here."

"Judas, forget all that you saw and heard," I said.

"How did Jesus do all that he did?"

"Judas, he didn't do anything, and you don't know anyone named Julian. Don't tell your mother and especially don't tell Jonah; or, was he there also?" I asked.

"No, thank goodness, he was not there."

"If you need to talk with someone, come and talk with me. Agreed?" I told him.

"Agreed! What will Jesus be doing tomorrow?" Judas asked.

"I cannot tell you; but if I find out, I will let you know."

"See you in a few minutes. I am going to the well. It will be interesting to see if it has settled down." Off he went and I was somewhat worried about what he saw and how he would manage his information.

I went back into the house. Martha and Mary had just come from the Galilean's Camp and were excitedly telling Mama all about their day with family.

Jesus was in our room in a very deep time of prayer and meditation. I tried to be as quiet as I could and finally settled on the pillows in my corner of the room. I ended up going to sleep and did not awaken until the morning and by that time Jesus had gone for his morning prayers.

We were all gathered about the table eating our morning meal when Jesus came back to the house. He sat down, ate a little, got up, and left the house again. He hadn't said a word since last night.

Long Hard Days

Jesus just disappeared. Some of the disciples appeared at our house looking for him, and when we told them we did not know where he was or when he might be back, that threw things in confusion.

Mama did her best to keep a few things to eat out on the table, so that anyone who appeared at the house could find some refreshment to eat and drink. But all who came wanted to be with Jesus and not eat in our house.

It was a surprise when Judas, disciple, appeared and told us that Jesus was sitting outside one of the Gates into Jerusalem.

"Come, let us go to him where he is waiting," said Judas.

On the way, we met several others coming toward Bethany, who were looking for Jesus. They joined us and by the time we got to Jerusalem we had a considerable crowd. Jesus was waiting and talking with some people and he was surrounded by children.

He smiled a greeting to each of us as we took our places at various points surrounding where he was sitting.

Jesus got up and motioned for us to remain seated. He walked a little ways to a fig tree and looked for food. There were no figs on that tree. He came back to his seat and looked at the people around him and said,

> *No more fruit shall ever grow on that tree. All at once that*
> fig tree withered away.
> Someone asked, How did that fig tree wither away like
> that.
> Believe me, replied Jesus, if you have faith and have no
> doubts in your heart, you will not only do this to a fig tree,
> but if you should say to this hill,
> Get up and throw yourself into the sea, it will happen.
> Everything you ask for in prayer, if you have faith, you
> will receive.

Jesus went on talking with a few people. Nathaniel walked over to the tree and after examining it he picked one of the leaves and brought it back for the others to see. All were amazed but no one seemed willing to ask any questions.

Then Jesus rose and went into the Temple with a large crowd following him. He began to teach and almost immediately...

> *The chief priest and Jewish elders*
> came up to him and said,
> What authority have you for what you are doing,
> and who gave you that authority?
> Jesus said to them, I am going to ask you
> one question, and if you answer it
> I will tell you by what authority I have for
> what I am doing.
> John's baptism, now, did it come from heaven
> or was it purely human.
> At this they began arguing among themselves:
> If, we say, it came from, he will say to us,
> Then why didn't you believe in John?
> If on the other hand we should say,
> It was purely human—well, frankly,
> we are afraid of the people—for all

of them believed John was a prophet.
So, they answered Jesus,
We do not know.
Then I will not tell you
by what authority I do these things!
returned Jesus.
But what is your opinion about this?
There was a man with two sons.
He went to the first and said,
Go and work in my
vineyard today, my son.
His son said, All right sir but he never
went near the vineyard.
Then the father approached his second son
with the same request.
He said, I won't do it.
But afterward he changed
his mind and went.
Which of these two sons did
what their father wanted?
The second one, they replied.
Yes, and I tell you that tax collectors
and prostitutes are going
into the kingdom of God
in front of you! retorted Jesus.
For John came to you as a saint,
and you did not believe him—yet
the tax collectors and the prostitutes did!
And even after seeing that, you would not
change your minds and believe him.

There was hesitancy about challenging Jesus, so Jesus left that area of the Temple and walked outside with many people following him. He walked up to a street vendor and asked for a flask of water, which he was given in a routine fashion. Then the vendor realized who Jesus was and his eyes flew very wide open. He gasped as he knelt behind his work table. The vendor was talking to Jesus, but no one understood a word he was saying because he was hidden by the table where he knelt and his head was bent toward the ground.

Jesus walked around behind the table and took the man's arm and had him stand. He was very nervous, almost frightened, and finally Jesus was able to get him calmed down. The vendor turned and pulled a curtain back which revealed a young boy severely handicapped lying on a bare table and unable to do more than babble in his attempted speech.

Jesus walked behind the improvised bed upon which the boy lay. The boy's head bobbed from side to side and his arms and legs jerked in many directions. His father dropped to his knees and just then the man's wife appeared. At first, she thought something was wrong with her child, and Jesus took her hand and raised it with his as he began to pray.

She caught her breath and pulled her hand away as she draped herself over the top of the bed on which her boy lay. Jesus continued to raise his hands and many of us joined him. He still held the flask of water in his right hand and suddenly he shook the flask and gathered some of the water in his left hand and sprinkled it over the boy. The boy giggled and squirmed and his mother was making motions like she was petting him. Jesus again scattered water over the boy and his mother and father.

That warm glow moved from Jesus to the family. The son became very quiet and Jesus took his hand and told him to sit up and embrace his mother. That was absolutely the happiest scene I have watched. The boy and his mother embraced for the first time in their life. A brother and sister burst through a curtain at the back of the vendor's stall and they became very confused with the scene before them. Their father quickly explained and then began thanking Jesus. It was quietly suggested that they take their son to the Temple for a blessing and that they make this Passover the best one in many years. The mother jumped up and embraced Jesus and gave him a kiss. There was a warm, happy smile on Jesus face. Jesus withdrew from that area and walked just out of town where the people and children could find a place to sit without being in the way of pedestrians moving around the commercial district in Jerusalem. It was very warm and many were feeling extremely hot, and some were sharing their water.

Jesus in his usual manner was directing where the children should sit around him. They sounded like a giggling hive of bees, and Jesus was enjoying every minute of it.

Some of the Pharisees that day were discussing how they might trap him and bring embarrassment to him. They eventually got the courage to send a small delegation to question him:

> *"Master we know that you are an honest man who teaches*
> the way of God faithfully and that you are not swayed by
> men's opinion of you. Obviously you don't care for human
> approval. Now tell us—Is it right to pay taxes to Caesar
> or not?

All conversation ceased and everyone's attention was on Jesus. He was very quiet as he looked around the crowd. A slight smile spread across his face.

> *But Jesus knowing their evil intention; said, why are you*
> playing this trick on me? Show me the money you pay the
> tax with. They handed him a Roman coin. He turned it
> over in his hand.
> Whose face is on this coin and whose name is in the
> inscription? Caesar's they said with glee.
> Then are you listening?- give to Caesar what belongs
> to Caesar and give to God what belongs to him.
> This reply staggered them and they did not know how
> to answer; so, they slipped through the crowd and left
> him alone for a little while.

Judas was very quick to come to Jesus's side. He took the coin and dropped it in the common purse. Jesus whispered to Judas and then motioned for him to kneel down beside him with the children.

One little boy was unhappy that Judas was in his way, so he got up and pushed over to stand beside Jesus. Momentarily, Jesus sat with his arm around the child, and then he picked him up and put him on his lap. The child brightened with the joy of the attention he got from Jesus.

During this time the Pharisees had gathered their courage and they returned to stand just behind the seated children:

> *One of them an expert in the Law,*
> put this test question to Jesus.
> Master, what are we to consider
> the Law's greatest commandment?
> Jesus answered him in a very firm voice,
> Love theLord your God with all your heart,
> with all your soul and with all your mind.
> This is the first and great commandment.
> And there is a second like it: You shall
> love your neighbor as yourself.
> Everything in the Law and the prophets hangs on these
> two commandments.

Jesus stopped and looked at the children and said to them, "Are you listening children?" A few said "Yes," but most just nodded their heads.

"Always remember what has just been said, two commandments; the first is what?"

Some of the children called out "Love God," then they looked around for help.

"You are right," said Jesus, "but there is a little more to it—Love God with all your heart, and with all your soul, and with all your mind. Now say it with me, with all your heart," with that he pointed to his chest and so did the children. "Then with all your soul," Jesus embraced himself with his arms and swayed side to side...The children followed and giggled. "Then what...remember?...Love God with all your mind" and he tapped himself on the head with his forefinger, and so did the children.

"That is very good and you never want to forget it—love God—say it with me and do the actions, love God with all your heart, and with all your soul, and with all your mind. Good! Now, the second is like unto it, Love my neighbor as myself. Now say that one with me, are you ready?" They all nodded, "Love my neighbor as myself."

"It is very important—are you listening?—It is very important to love yourself. That is where you develop your self respect. And it is self-respect that allows you to stand tall and it is the root gift of your happiness. Plus, it is the way you learn to love others even your mother and father. Your self love is the limit of your love understanding. You cannot love your mother any more than you love yourself. You cannot love your friends anymore than you love yourself."

The children seemed to perfectly understand what Jesus was saying, but the adults were struggling.

"Why do you adults have such a puzzled look on your face? I am not talking about a sick pride that develops into a warped illness. That comes from a boastful, selfish, arrogant, distorted pride that invades you from the kingdom of darkness. It creeps in and destroys all your self-esteem. Are you listening? I am asking you to see yourself as God sees you. You are a child of the King, revered, cherished, and blessed by all the heavenly hosts. Love your neighbor as the angels see you.

Children, will you try to live that way?" There was a resounding "Yes."

"Adults, let me ask you, will you now work to see yourself in such a way and live as a blessed child of the King?" There was a feeble "Yes."

Jesus stood up again and looked at the mass of adults. "You, adults, will you work to see yourself as God sees you? That you will love yourself as he loves you? And that you will serve others in the light of that love to God's glory? Will you?"

The response was better but still rather weak.

A voice spoke up from the crowd, "Jesus, I want to see myself in that way, but I just cannot."

"Come here to me," said Jesus. A rather disheveled looking man stepped out of the crowd. He looked like he had been in a severe windstorm, and he had a terrible limp. He looked like he wanted to run but couldn't. Slowly he came face-to-face with Jesus who was quietly praying.

When he finally came face-to-face with Jesus, one of the children stood up and took his hand and ever so quietly said, "I love you."

The man almost dissolved in tears as with wide eyes he looked at the child. Jesus looked at both of them, smiled, and spoke to the child, "Thank you, now stay here with your new neighbor."

Jesus looked at the man and asked, "What is your name?"

"Micah," he answered.

Jesus again looked at the child and said, "Did you hear? His name is Micah."

The child had repeated the name before Jesus spoke it.

"Micah," Jesus said with a very forceful voice, "Look me straight in my eyes and don't take your eyes away from mine." Jesus was quietly praying as he stared into Micah's eyes. Suddenly, Jesus reached down and picked up the child. "Look into Micah's eyes and now Micah look into the child's eyes."

"Look into our eyes, Micah. Don't look away. Look deep into my eyes. Don't look away. Micah what do you see?" Jesus asked.

"In your eyes," Micah said, "I see myself as a new person, tall, handsome, laughing, and with hope in my eyes."

"Look into the little boy's eyes. Do you see anything?" asked Jesus. "Look deep and long."

Micah began to quietly cry, "I see myself as a young boy who...I was so excited to be alive and rose everyday to face the world with excitement, expectancy, and joy in my heart. God was with me everyday."

"He still is Micah," Jesus said as Micah slipped to his knees and began crying. The child struggled to get down and when Jesus put him down, the child walked up to Micah, raised his face in those small hands and looking into Micah's eyes, he said, "Micah, I love you. With that they both embraced as the little boy kept saying over and over, "Micah, God loves you...God loves you... Micah, God loves you, and I love you." He didn't stop saying that until Micah stopped crying.

Finally Micah got control of his emotions and asked, "Who are you, what is your name child?"

With his young head held high he said, "I am a child of the King and my royal name is Isaiah. God loves you Micah, and so do I."

Micah said, "Isaiah let me look into your eyes. Yes...Yes, I am still there."

Micah rose to his full height, straightened his clothes and hair, smiled, and then laughed a warm laugh filled with joy and hope. He and Jesus stood and kept looking at each other.

"God will be my guide and my King," Micah said.

Jesus responded by speaking to the crowd gathered around him, "Are you listening?...That is available to every one of you young and old. When you pray don't just speak hollow words that dissolve into the air around you. Look into the face and eyes of God and pray with praise and power. Be proud of who you are and share that pride by loving others, your neighbors, as you serve God."

A small young woman edged up to Jesus and introduced herself as the mother of Isaiah. Jesus took both of her hands and quietly said, "You have a remarkable son, and you will see the great things he will do in God's name and to God's glory."

It was beginning to get late in the day and the people were stirring around in every direction, some were leaving while others were still coming. A group of Pharisees were in a small huddle off to the side, and Jesus walked over to them. Several of the Pharisees saw Jesus coming toward them, and they became restless.

When Jesus got close enough he asked:

What is your opinion about Christ? Whose son is he?

They froze and turned toward each other. They got in a small huddle so that no one could hear them discuss the question. Jesus waited patiently and they turned toward him. One of the Pharisees spoke for the group:

> Christ is the Son of David!
> *Jesus responded, How then does David when he is inspired call*
> *him Lord? In Holy Writ, it is recorded*
> The Lord said unto my Lord,
> Sit thou on my right hand,
> Till I put your enemies underneath my feet.
> If David then calls him Lord, how can he be his son?

Jesus stood and waited while they gathered in their huddle again. After a considerable time the group broke and slowly left the area. It seems nobody wanted to answer that question and from that day on none of the Pharisees questioned Jesus.

Isaiah's mother returned and came to Jesus. "Thank you for being so kind to my son. I was afraid he was bothering you when you had to place him on your lap."

"No," said Jesus, "God brought him to me and he became God's answer to Micah who was struggling so hard with his life issues."

The fading light encouraged people to begin moving toward their homes'. Isaiah's mother took his hand and turned to leave just as Isaiah called, "I love you Jesus!" What a wonderful close for the day. Jesus spoke to a few of the disciples and then he came to me and asked, "Would it be too much to expect that your Mama and sisters would have something for us to eat at your house?"

"Let's go and see," I responded.

Jesus decided we would go to Bethany by way of the Gate Beautiful where the elders were always in session. When we arrived, they were in the midst of their discussions and arguments. Jesus tried to keep his identity hidden by tightening his head scarf around the side of his face. But as soon as we sat down one of the elders pointed his finger, and all he said was, "You..." Another elder pushed his arm down and invited him to leave with him. That started a procession of those who left until all were gone except for a few stragglers who probably had no place to go.

We left and made our way to Bethany.

Mama was glad to see us, and we were surprised to discover that Aunt Mary was there with them. The greeting between Jesus and his Mother was warm and filled with laughter. Soon, she said, "Jesus, Jonah has been looking for you."

"Am I supposed to go find him or will he return here?" Jesus asked.

"I really think he is close by."

"Then let me go outside and search for him. Lazarus, come, and let's try and find him," Jesus said.

Mary, my sister, jumped to her feet and said, "I will go with you, Jesus." Together Jesus and Mary went out the door, and I followed.

We had not gone far when Jesus stopped and asked, "Do you know where Jonah lives?"

"No I don't," said Mary, "but perhaps we can walk toward Judas's house and they..." Mary stopped, earnestly listened, and said, Jesus, listen. I can hear a baby crying very close from here."

Slowly we walked toward the shed behind our house and the crying grew louder.

Entering the shed we found Jonah, Judas, and another young couple. The woman was cradling a crying child in her arms. Jonah jumped to his feet and faced Jesus.

"Please, Jesus, can you help my brother, Esau and his wife, with their new baby girl?" Jesus walked toward them.

Jonah continued "The baby has not stopped crying since birth, and no one seems to know what must be done to help the child."

Jesus reached for the child, and when he touched that baby, it screamed. The mother tried to take the baby back, but Jesus walked to the side of the shed with the child. He sat down with that screaming, thrashing child in his arms, and began to remove the small blanket as he prayed. The child was covered with a bright red rash and several open sores.

My sister Mary came and sat down by Jesus and began talking to the child. Slowly it grew quiet and Jesus transferred the child to Mary who was absolutely delighted. She turned and walked in the house with the baby.

The mother of the child went right behind her. In just a few moments, it was the mother, who shrieked in the house and came running out to her husband.

"The rash and boils are gone," she cried out to her husband.

Together they ran back in the house and when they came back outside they were carrying a cooing child who was quiet and happy.

Jesus said, "That is a beautiful little girl. She should bring you much happiness in the years to come. You live close enough to the Temple. Go soon and praise God for her recovery from that rash and boils."

The mother looked at her husband and said, "Let's go now. I am so happy and relieved for the child and for us."

Jesus responded, "It is getting a little late in the day, so why don't you stay here with us and have some dinner, and I am sure that Martha and Mary would be delighted to care for your child and play with her. What is her name?"

"Esther," said her mother. I thought the husband started to say something but he stopped.

Martha came outside and asked if she could hold the child. She went back in the house happily cradling Esther in her arms. Mama soon called us to eat, and we all went inside. I looked at Martha holding the child and said, "Martha why don't you have some words of thanksgiving and praise."

Martha looked at Jesus, and he nodded for her to go on:

"Father God, the Lord of life and health. Enfold Esther in your arms in the years ahead. Sweep away health issues and keep her strong, unblemished, and happy. May she bring much joy to her home and others around her. Turn her cries into a song of praise for her gift of health. Make her heart sing with joy, and her soul bring happiness and pride to you and her parents. Now bless our food, our fellowship, our night's rest, and all of our tomorrows. Amen"

"Thank you, Martha," said Jesus as he walked to the table and looked at what had been prepared for the evening. He sat down in a corner and began to eat and I joined him. "Lazarus, I feel the need to go to the Garden for a time of meditation and prayer. Would you be willing to go with me?" Jesus asked.

"You must know that I am ready to go anywhere with you," I said.

We lingered with the family about our evening table, and soon everyone was relaxed, and laughter became the music of the hour.

Jesus got up and thanked Mama for the meal and excused himself after he embraced Aunt Mary. I followed him outside. The night air was perfect for a long time of meditation in the Garden.

We walked to a lonely place and each of us sat down and leaned against a tree. Jesus was very quiet, but I could hear him praying in the darkness. He shifted his position and lay on his back looking up at the glory of a clear night sky. He kept saying "Praise the Lord Almighty"…Hallelujah…Glory to God in the highest"…Let his wonder be seen in the sky above."

"Lazarus, I am glad that we have a chance to pull away from home and friends this evening. It will probably be the last earthly visit that we will have."

"What are you talking about, Jesus?"

"Lazarus, over the next few days it will be revealed who I truly am as God's son. It is going to leave you, the disciples, and all my family and friends extremely confused, some will be angry, others will run and hide, and a few will just disappear."

"I am not sure I understand," I said.

"You understand far more than you are willing to admit. For almost thirty years we have been the best of friends, companions, and shared in special events that have been crafted by God. We studied the prophet Jeremiah together under Rabbi Levi and God's servant promised a new covenant."

"Yes, I am fully aware of his words of promise," I said.

"Lazarus those words are going to be fulfilled during this week here in Jerusalem" Jesus said.

I became very quiet and began to consider the other prophecies about the Messiah. My mind jumped from one prophecy to the other, and I experienced radical joy and a torrent of fear and confusion. I began to pray and I realized at some point that Jesus was praying with me.

"Lazarus, tomorrow will be the last day of our being together in our earthly friendship," Jesus said.

"Then Jesus, why did you bring me back from the dead. I could have been waiting for you to receive you in God's Kingdom?" I asked.

"Your resurrection was the trumpet call for the week ahead."

"I am not sure I like being a trumpet," I said.

"God's will and the prophet's message will merge into one revelation of justice and mercy, divine truth and heavenly forgiveness. It will be a new day; and you, the disciples, and my many friends will become a new people. It is not going to be easy. There will be heavy loads to bear and painful crosses to carry."

He paused for a long time, lifted his arms toward the heavens, and prayed intensely. He was perspiring profusely. He was in a struggle that was tearing at his heart and impacting his mind. I was praying hard for him as I watched him carefully.

Tears came to his eyes and he looked directly at me. "Mother will have a heavy load to carry, and she is going to live a long life. Keep her in the circle of love with you, Martha, and Mary. She will need you and she does not realize how much she will need you. That is another reason it was important to call you from God's throne back to his footstool, this earth."

"When is all of this going to happen?" I asked.

"When I leave your house in the morning, I do not know if I will be back. I hope I will because it is a comforting home for me...My heart will be here, and we will talk in prayer, but there will be radical changes over the next few days. The circumstances will happen fast and explosively. You will be watching me and I will be watching you. The strength of our friendship will be alive within me to uphold and comfort me, and I will draw from the well of your spiritual strength what I need to face and endure the days ahead. Now, let's have a time of prayer," Jesus said.

We prayed all night. Sometimes, we knelt, at other times, we walked. We sometimes leaned against a tree; and then again, we would kneel down and at other times we would call out with a bold or timid voice. There were times that I wept and Jesus would embrace me. The night was long and very hard. At times, I would start shaking and Jesus would come and lay his hands upon me and sweep away my anxiety.

When dawn began to break, it was going to be a beautiful day. The breeze came from the west, and there was the salty smell of the sea that was refreshing. Both of us were startled by some movement in some bushes a short distance away from where we had spent that long night. I walked over to the spot and there was Mary shivering in the cool of the morning.

"How long have you been here?" I asked.

"I followed you when you left the house," she said.

"Mary, you are cold and shaking," I took off my outer cloak and put it around her and tied my belt around her waist.

Jesus walked over and embraced her as he prayed for the warmth of God's Spirit to protect and nurture her in her needs. "What were you doing during the night?" asked Jesus.

"Well, I couldn't see anything, but I could hear you. I listened, prayed, and cried," responded Mary. "I felt like you had already left us and the loneliness that filled my heart was almost unbearable."

"Mary, I have told my disciples and followers to always remember that I am always with them, awake or asleep, I am here. Mary will you embrace and believe that in your mind and heart?" Jesus asked.

"Yes, Jesus!" She almost yelled and then began to sob. "But I want you here with us and nowhere else."

Jesus again took her in his arms; and after a little while, she became quiet.

"I must go home," she said, and she broke away from Jesus to run toward our house.

I was about to run after her, but Jesus put out his arm to restrain me. He didn't say a word but stood there solemnly watching Mary run home. He was praying quietly as he watched her disappear, and then he turned, and said, "Come, Lazarus, it is time for us to go home also."

It was a long silent walk. It really wasn't long, just a short distance, but it seemed ten times longer with the weight I carried in my heart.

I kept expecting that dove to appear but, it never did which surprised me. I wondered if Jesus missed the bird's visit, but his mind was definitely on other things.

Mama had a morning breakfast laid out for us and laughter began to stir in our hearts again as Judas and Jonah joined us. It wasn't long before those two began to talk business, and my mind went in a totally different direction.

Jesus soon stood and said, "I need to go to the camp of the Galileans and speak to some of the family and friends that are there. Thank you, Aunt Sarah for your evening meal last night and for the morning treat today."

He turned to me and simply said, I will be watching for you later in this day. Mary ran up and hugged him as he went out the door.

I have never started a day with so many unanswered questions.

The Gathering Storm

I had a feeling it was going to be a long day, but I had no idea of the circumstances that would make it that way.

When I went back into the kitchen, Mama was taking care of some of her household duties. She was her cheerful self and blessed me with a big hug and a kiss. She was not often outwardly affectionate, so I was somewhat surprised.

Mary just stood around looking at me. She didn't say anything, she just stared at me and that was very awkward; plus, it was embarrassing. I went outside because I was afraid I was going to become angry, and such words did not need to be spoken to anyone especially on this day. So, I took a walk.

The cool air of the morning cleared my mind and made me feel a lot better; and when I returned to the house, I heard Mama's cheerful voice before I got to the door, and that gave me a boost, and a smile broke across my face.

"Lazarus, you really look tired. Why don't you go to your room and take a short nap, and I will waken you in a little while," Mama said.

"I really ought to go into Jerusalem very soon," I said.

"Just for a little while. It will freshen you and the day will go better for both you and Jesus," Mama said.

So I slipped off to my room and was asleep the moment I stretched out. I was more tired than I thought.

It was Mary who awakened me, and I felt like it was very late in the day. Mary assured me that there was plenty of time to go and see Jesus, and she announced that she planned to go with me.

I ate some cheese and bread with some fresh goat's milk and we were off to find Jesus. The closer we came to Jerusalem the more I was amazed at the number of people who were here for the celebration of the Passover this year.

We went directly to the Temple, but there was no sign of Jesus. I saw Rabbi Levi and asked him if he had seen Jesus or heard some say where he was teaching today and he said he had not.

Finally, I heard someone tell another person that they understood Jesus was teaching close to the Pool of Bethesda near to what was known as the Sheep Gate. So we started making our way in that direction. Mary was following along a little behind me and she called out.

"Lazarus, to your right, isn't that Peter's wife, Suzanne?"

"You are right." She seemed in a hurry, but we caught up with her. She told us that we were going in the right direction, but that Jesus kept changing places from time to time.

"So, by the time you get to where you expect him, he will probably be somewhere else, but there should be someone who knows where he went. Now, please, excuse me because Peter has sent me to the Temple to try and find several of the disciples that we have not yet seen today."

She turned and left, and we moved in the direction of the Pool of Bethesda. The closer we got to the Pool the larger the number of people were, and all seemed to be talking about Jesus. We arrived just as Jesus suggested that they take a break from his teaching session, and he would start again in just a few minutes at the same place.

He seemed glad to see us, but he also seemed distracted.

"Lazarus, I am in need of a personal meditation time to collect new strength, comfort, and insight. The crowds will not allow it. They keep pressing me for more teachings, and there are many sick and maimed here at the Pool of Bethesda. Lazarus, pray intensely for me like you have never prayed before," I nodded to him my agreement with his request.

With that he walked back to a little raised area and the crowd pushed in close around him. I was glad to see that there was no harassment or other distractions going on from people in the crowd. Those gathered were very intent on listening to Jesus, and I left that area to pray.

> *Jesus addressed the crowd and his disciples:*
> The scribes and the Pharisees speak with
> the authority of Moses. So, you must do
> what they tell you and follow their instructions.
> But, you must not imitate their lives!
> For they preach, but do not practice what they preach.
> They pile up backbreaking burdens and lay them
> on other men's shoulders, yet they themselves
> will not raise a finger to practice what they
> require from others.
> Whatever they do is for show.
> They like to have places of honor at feasts
> and the chief seats in the synagogues,
> to be greeted respectfully in the streets
> and to be addressed as rabbi.
> Don't you ever be called rabbi—you have only one teacher,
> and all of you are brothers.
> The greatest among you must be your servant.
> For whoever exalts himself will be humbled,
> and he who humbles himself will be exalted.
> But alas, you scribes and Pharisees, play
> actors that you are!
> You lock the doors of the kingdom
> of heaven in men's face,

but you will not go in yourselves
neither will you allow those at the door to go inside.
You scribes and Pharisees, play actors…
You scour sea and land to make a single convert.
Then you make him twice as ripe for destruction
as you are yourselves.
What miserable frauds you are,
you scribes and Pharisees!
You clean the outside of the cup and dish,
while the inside is full of greed and self-indulgence.
Can't you see and understand?
First wash the inside of the cup,
and then you can clean the outside.
What miserable frauds you are,
you build tombs to the prophets
and decorate monuments for good men
of the past and then say,
if we had lived in the times of our ancestors
we should never have joined in the killing
of prophets.— you are indeed
the sons of those who killed the prophets.
So, go ahead, finish off what you're
ancestors tried to do, you serpents, you vipers!
Listen to this: I am sending you prophets
and wise and learned men; and some of these
you will kill and crucify,
others you will flog in your synagogues,
So, on your hands is all the innocent blood
spilled on this earth, from
the blood of Abel, the good, to the blood
of Zechariah,Barachiah's son,
whom you murdered between the
sanctuary and the altar.
Yes, I tell you that all this and
more will be laid
at the door of this generation.

Jesus sagged from weariness. I thought Mary was going to run to him, but I restrained her, and she crumbled into my arms and wept. When she gathered her emotions, I suggested that she take to Jesus a flask of water and offer him a piece of bread. Jesus took both and seemed delighted to see Mary by his side.

The crowd was stirring around with some leaving and others coming. There were small clusters of people discussing what they had just heard. Some of the scribes and Pharisees had very sullen looks on their faces, but they remained aloof from Jesus because of the favorable comments they could easily hear expressed by the people. They restrained any comments or action on their part.

Jesus stood and started walking in the direction of the Temple. And as he walked he would talk a little from time to time, more to himself than to others.

> O Jerusalem, Jerusalem!
> You murder the prophets and
> stone the messengers
> that were sent to you…

He was walking more briskly now, and some began to drop by the wayside while others walked with a more leisurely gait and let the crowd pass them by.

> O Jerusalem, Jerusalem!
> How often have I longed to
> gather your children around me
> like a bird gathering her brood together
> under her wings—and you would
> never have it.

He stopped again for a drink of water that someone else provided. He then turned and looked for us, and when his eyes found us he smiled. In his eyes was that warm gift of recognition that bound our hearts together. He had said that he would be looking for my presence and I was so glad that I had come.

O Jerusalem, Jerusalem!
All you have left is your house
I tell you that you will never see me again
till the day when you cry out,
Blessed is he who comes in the name
of the Lord!

Jesus came to the Temple, mounted the steps, and entered the sanctuary to share in the service of worship that he loved so dearly. Most of the people dropped away and this allowed me to slip in beside him. Mary remained in the Women's Court and reminded me not to leave her.

I was surprised how long Jesus stayed. The disciples joined him one by one until all were there except for Judas. Several times, Jesus turned and whispered something to John. Once John turned to leave the sanctuary and he took the arm of Nathaniel. They left together. He was back within a brief moment, but Nathaniel was not with him.

Mary and I realized later after I had told her about what had happened in the sanctuary that Nathaniel had gone to purchase some bread and cheese to eat when they left the Temple.

After the service, Jesus came from the Temple and stood for a moment on the steps and looked at all the buildings. Some he had not seen since he was last in Jerusalem. The disciples came around him and were talking and pointing to those buildings that had been recently built. Jesus responded to them:

You see all these, but I tell you every stone
will be thrown down till there is not
a single stone left standing upon another.
Then Jesus walked out to the Mount of Olives
where his disciples gathered around
him for a private visit.
Theyhad escaped the crowd
and sat with Jesus.
James the Less asked him, "Tell us,

when will all these things happen
that you have been talking about?
What will be the signal for your coming?
When will the end of this world happen?
Be careful that no one misleads you,
answered Jesus, for many men will come
in my name saying I am the Christ,
And they will mislead many.
You will hear of wars and rumors
of wars—but don't be alarmed.
Such things must indeed happen,
but that is not the end.
For one nation will rise in arms
against another, and there will be famines
and earthquakes in different parts of the world.
But all that is only the beginning of the birth pangs.
For then comes the times when men will hand
you over to persecution, and kill you.
And all nations will hate you because you bear
my name.
Then comes the time when many will lose
their faith and will betray and hate one another.
Yes, and many prophets will arise,
and will mislead many people.
Because of the spread of wickedness
the love of most men will grow cold,
though the man who holds out
to the end will be saved.
This good news of the kingdom
will be proclaimed to many
all over the world as a witness to all nations,
and then the end will come.

Jesus stopped and took a deep breath and stood very still. Others thought he may be leaving, and they rose, but Jesus turned and took from his robe a small piece of bread. He looked at Mary and myself and gave us a broad smile. He made a motion to his lips and Mary rose, found some water, and brought it to me; and I gave it to Jesus.

He continued to stand and began anew to teach:

When the time comes, then, you will see
the abomination of desolation prophesied
by Daniel standing in the sacred place,
then is the time when all of you should
escape to the hills.
A man on his housetop must not waste
time going into the house to collect anything;
a man at work in the fields must
not go back home to fetch his clothes.
Alas for the pregnant and for those
with tiny babies it will be difficult!
Pray to God that you may not have
to make your escape in the winter or
on the Sabbath day,
for then there will be great misery,
such as has never happened
from the beginning of the world until now,
and will never happened again!
Yes, if those days had not been cut short
no human being would survive.
But for the sake of God's people
those days are to be shortened.
If anyone says to you then,
Look, here is Christ! or There he is!
Don't believe it! False christs
and false prophets are going to appear
and will produce great signs and wonders
to mislead even God's own people.
Listen, I am warning you.
So that if people say to you, There he is,
in the desert! You are not to go out there.
If they say, here he is, in the inner room!
Don't believe it.

> For as lightning flashes across
> from east to west so will the
> Son of Man's coming be.
> Wherever there is a dead body
> there vultures will flock.

Jesus stopped again for a few moments. He seemed very tired, and there were those who wanted to press him with questions. But when he heard a question, he would turn away, take a few steps, and then he would do the same thing again. Something seemed very different and I kept praying for my best friend as best I could in a hard hour. Eventually, Jesus stopped and raised his hands toward heaven and entered a time of prayer. This was the first time I had not seen him answer all questions raised from the people around him.

Mary wanted to go to him and see if she could help him in anyway, but I restrained her, feeling that Jesus did not want any interference. He seemed to be on a very intense mission that must be completed.

He lowered his hands, and his face to again looked at the crowd.

> Immediately after those days of hardship,
> the sun will bedarkened
> and the moon will fail to give any light,
> the stars will fall from the sky,
> and the powers of heaven will be shaken.
> Then the sign of the Son of Man
> will appear in the sky,
> and all the nations of the earth
> will wring their hands
> as they see the Son of Man
> coming on the clouds of the sky
> in power and great splendor.
> And he will send out his angels
> with a loud trumpet call
> and his chosen will gather together
> from the four winds— from one end

of the heavens to the other.
Learn what the fig tree can teach you.
As soon as its branches grow full of sap
and produce leaves you know
that summer is near.
So when you see all these things
happening you may know
that he is near, at your very door!
Believe me, this generation will not
disappear till all this has taken place.
Earth and sky will pass away
but my words will never pass away!
But about that actual day and time
no one knows—not even the angels
of heaven, nor the Son,
only the Father.
For just as life went
on in the days of Noah,
So will it be at the coming
of the Son of Man.
In those days before the flood,
people were eating, drinking,
marrying and being given in marriage
until the very day that Noah went into the ark,
and knew nothing about the flood
until it came and destroyed them all.
So will it be at the coming of the Son of Man.
Two men will be in the field;
one is taken and one is left behind.
Two women will be grinding at the hand mill;
one is taken and one is left behind.
You must be on the alert then,
for you Do not know when
your master is coming.
You can be sure of this,
however, that if the householder
had known what time of night

the burglar would arrive,
he would have bee ready for him
and would have not have
allowed his house to be broken into. T
hat is why you must always be ready,
for you do not know what time
the Son of Man will arrive.

Jesus stopped for a moment and looked up at the sky. I realized he was not praying, but it appeared as though a terrible storm might break. The angry dark clouds were rolling and suddenly there was lightning and thunder in the distance. The people began to scatter and children started crying when they did not immediately see their parents. It was a bit of a confusing time and Matthew spoke to Jesus; and the two of them moved away from the Temple and to a house where Matthew had some friends.

Mary and I moved back into the Temple, and there was Rabbi Levi. It almost seemed like he had been waiting for us.

"Rabbi," I said, "How good to see you. Have you been listening to Jesus teach out on the steps of the Temple?"

"No, but I could see the impact of his presence. The stalls here in the Temple closed their business and ran. I rather liked that, maybe he could pass by everyday. Also, there have been many little huddles of people discussing their faith and beliefs and that is both unusual and exciting. You tell him to stick around," the rabbi said.

"Well, Rabbi, I wish he would; but by the first of the week, he will be on his way back to Galilee."

"It has been good to see you, Lazarus; and sometimes we must spend some time talking about what Jesus is teaching."

"I will look forward to that time," I said.

The rabbi was off through the crowds in the Temple to some meeting or a teaching session with an excited young man working toward his Bar Mitzvah.

I dropped Mary off in the Women's Court, and I moved into the sanctuary. I could hear one of my favorite cantors, and he drew me into the Court of Praise to let my spirit lift upward to the heavens in quiet worship and be wrapped by God's spirit with his love and peace.

I am sure that I was there longer than I thought because when I returned to the Women's Court Mary was pacing the floor and was very angry with me for staying so long. We went outside and stood still again looking for Jesus. He was nowhere to be seen, and again there was no crowd to give evidence of his presence.

Mary and I kept listening, but there seemed to be no clear direction that we should go to find Jesus. So we continued to wander the streets. Finally, someone said they had just come from the Pool of Siloam where Jesus was teaching. That was in the lower part of the city that in recent years had been included in the walled city.

We immediately picked up our speed, and soon we began to hear people talking about Jesus. We were going in the right direction unless he had moved.

The crowds began to grow. It seemed to me that there were more children than ever before.

Coming within sight of the Pool, there was Jesus talking with Peter and Andrew. Mary called my attention to Peter and John's wives, Suzanne and Priscilla, who were off to the side with some children. Mary went to them and they had a happy reunion.

Nathaniel brought Jesus some water, and it looked like cheese that he gave him to eat. Then Jesus sat down and there was a race by the children to sit at his feet. Jesus was delighted and showed some of them where he wanted them to sit.

He began to pray. His quietness brought a hush to the crowd. He folded his hands in his lap and so did the children. All of a sudden there was a shriek, some of the children started to get up and run. Mary did run to my side as the shrieking continued and the wildest man I have ever seen came running toward Jesus.

"Imposter, devil…You son of evil…Why are you in Jerusalem? You belong in the slime of desert mud." He started running at Jesus flaying his arms and screaming and yelling. Peter and Andrew put themselves between Jesus and the wild man. I was going to help, but Mary dug in her heels to stay where we were.

Jesus was very quiet, watching, and waiting.

The man lunged at Peter and Andrew and several of the other disciples ran to help. All of them had a hard time restraining him. Some in the crowd were laughing and others were trying to decide if they should leave. The children had run to their parents. Jesus's eyes became very intense and quietly he said to that man, "Look at me."

"Why should I look at the son of the devil."

"Look at me!"

The man started laughing hysterically and flaying his arms even faster and harder. The disciples were taking a real beating. I have never heard such hysterical screaming and the words of indignity and profanity were not for children to hear.

Then I saw something I had never seem from Jesus. He clapped his hands and raised them toward the heavens. He clapped again and placed them on the man's head and it was like a bolt of lightening striking a tree. The man dropped to the ground out of the grip of the disciples and Jesus knelt beside him. There was not a sound from the man or the crowd. The disciples were looking at each other and I don't think Mary nor I were breathing.

Jesus asked for a flask of water and he put it to the man's lips, he sipped very little. Then Jesus asked for several of his disciples to assist him and he tried to help the man sit up. Jesus handed the water flask to Matthew and then he raised his hands in prayer. There was that glow. He raised one hand toward the heavens and the other he rested on the man's head. Jesus waited and continued to pray quietly.

The man took a deep breath and turned to look around him. At first he seemed confused and then he began to make a sound that sounded like whimpering. Jesus was very quietly whispering to him.

Jesus asked, "Can you tell us your name?"

With a brash voice he almost yelled, "No, I will not, you son of…" He suddenly became weak and quiet, almost falling back to the ground, but the disciples held him, he continued to look at Jesus.

Someone gave him the flask of water and he drank considerable.

Jesus asked again in a very quiet voice, "Can you tell us your name?"

"Why do you want to know my name?"

Jesus was quietly persistent, "I would just like to know the name by which your mother and God know you."

The man suddenly stood up and looked around him. He was one of the dirtiest human beings I had ever seen. And the odor that spread from him was overwhelming.

He looked at Jesus, and then one at a time he looked at the people surrounding him. I thought he might strike out at some of the disciples, but he remained quiet.

Mary whispered in my ear, "Lazarus, I want to go home."

"Just stay here for a few more minutes," I said.

Jesus said very quietly, "Your name? I am sure your mother gave you one."

The man looked at him long and intently, "Josiah."

"Josiah, child of God, son of the king of life, I greet and bless you with peace and the forgiveness of God our Father and Creator."

Josiah just stood looking at Jesus with a very puzzled expression on his face and then he looked around at the crowd and seemed more confused. He seemed to have no idea where he was.

Jesus very quietly said, "Josiah, child of the King of Life… Celebrate this day your gift of life and love. Sit here beside me and children come now and sit around us."

Very slowly the children began to come and Jesus motioned where he would have Josiah sit. What an amazing mixture of people.

Jesus began to pray and he raised his face and hands heavenward. The children joined him and Josiah was almost overwhelmed by the worship setting that surrounded him. Ever so slowly he began raising his hands toward the heavens as he watched the children and Jesus. His face took on just a little of the glow from Jesus and then a smile briefly spread over his face and mellowed those hard lines that made him so frightening.

When Jesus lowered his hands he rested one on Josiah's left shoulder.

One of the little boys came toward Jesus but he stopped and hugged Josiah and you could read the child's lips as he said, "I love you, Josiah."

Josiah's eyes became as wide as a large olive, and they filled with those pure tears of amazement and discovery. He was discovering, who he was, a child of the King.

Jesus spread his arms out for quiet and he began teaching again:

> When the Son of Man comes in all his splendor
> with all his angels with him,
> then he will take his seat on his glorious throne.
> All the nations will be assembled before him
> and he will separate men from each other
> like a shepherd separating sheep from goats...
> He will place the sheep on his right hand
> and the goats on his left.
> Then the king will say to those on his right:
> Come, you who have won my Father's blessing!
> Take your inheritance—the kingdom reserved
> for you since the foundation of the world!
> For I was hungry and you gave me food.
> I was thirsty and you gave me a drink.
> I was lonely and you visited me.

I was naked and you clothed me.
I was ill and you came and looked after me.
I was in prison and you came to see me there.
Then the true men will answer him:
Lord, when did we see you hungry
and give you food?
When did we see you thirsty
and give you something to drink?
When did we see you lonely
and make you welcome,
or see you naked and clothe you,
or see you ill or in prison and go to see you?
And the king will reply,
I assure you that whatsoever you did
for the humblest of my brothers and sisters,
you did for me.
Then he will say to those on his left:
Out of my presence,
cursed as you are, into the eternal fire
prepared for the devil and his angels!
For I was hungry and you
gave me nothing to eat.
I was thirsty and you gave
me nothing to drink.
I was lonely and you never
made me welcome.
When I was naked you did
nothing to clothe me;
when I was sick and in prison
you never cared about me.
Then they to will answer him:
Lord, when did we ever see
you hungry, or thirsty, or lonely,
or naked, or sick, or in
prison, and fail to look after you?
Then the king will answer them
with these words,

I assure you that whatever you failed
to do to the humblest of my brothers
you failed to do to me.
And these will go off to eternal punishment,
but the true men to eternal life.
When Jesus had finished all this teachings,
he spoke very quietly to his disciples: Do
you realize that the Passover is about to begin,
and the Son of Man is going to be
betrayed and crucified.

The disciples froze and looked very perplexed. Several started to say something, but the words seemed locked in their mouth. Little did anyone know that at that very hour:

The chief priests and elders of the people had assembled
in the court of Caiaphas, the High Priest, and were
discussing together how they might get hold of Jesus
by some trick and kill him.

Jesus was invited to Bethany to the home of Simon the leper, whom he had healed earlier in his ministry. Simon was a dedicated follower and a big supporter whom Judas cultivated heavily for the necessary funds to support the disciples and the needs of those who followed Jesus around the country side.

Simon was a man of wonderful humor and the joy of his heart and the strength of his spirit always brought to Jesus a personal ministry of warmth and special blessings. His house always seemed to be filled with people that we never saw unless we were in his home. There were fewer people in his house on this day than usual. People were slipping in and out of the house and there at Jesus's feet appeared a woman whom I had never seen before:

She came to Jesus with an alabaster flask
of the most expensive perfume,
and poured it on his head as he was at the table.
The disciples were indignant when they saw this,

and said: What is the point of such wicked waste?
Couldn't this perfume have been sold
for a lot of money which could be given to the poor?
Jesus knew what they were saying and spoke to them,
Why must you make this woman feel uncomfortable?
She has done a beautiful thing for me.
You have the poor with you always,
but you will not always have me.
When she poured this perfume on my body,
she was preparing it for my burial.
I assure you that wherever the gospel is preached
throughout the whole world,
this deed of hers will also be recounted,
as her memorial to me.

The woman had become very nervous being criticized by the disciples, and now she became restless. Jesus took her hand and suggested that she sit on the floor beside him. He then offered her some grape juice, cheese, and bread. She was somewhat embarrassed and kept looking at Jesus for reassurance.

Jesus continued talking with those around him and there was a lot of laughter.

Aunt Mary came over and knelt by the young woman and offered her another piece of cheese. It was Aunt Mary's way of striking up a conversation with the young woman, and when she finished, she would know everything about her and then she would share it with Jesus.

Suddenly, everyone realized that Jesus had gotten very quiet and was praying. All conversation stopped immediately, and we joined him in a time of prayer.

In one of those quick moves by Jesus, he was suddenly gone from the room and disappeared outside. No one knew when he might return so the group began to break up and go their separate ways for the night.

Before they left Mama had invited the disciples to our house for breakfast the next morning because she said, "I am sure Jesus will be here to share the morning meal with us."

Marching Toward Heartbreak Hill

I rose and dressed before anyone else in the house because I wanted to go in search of Jesus. I didn't have to go far because when I went out the front doorway Jesus was sitting there.

Our greeting to each other was interrupted by a greeting from two of the disciples, John and Peter. They had stayed close by with a friend of Peter's. Slowly the other disciples and several other friends began appearing and all were there, even Judas, by the time Mama and Aunt Mary were ready to serve a light morning meal.

Jesus called on John to have our morning prayer: "Father and King of our life and the Author of our faith. We accept responsibility for this new day you have given to us. Thank you for the quiet night you gave to us to equip us to better serve you in this day. We have gathered to praise you in Word and Deed throughout this day. May it present to us exceptional opportunities to know you better and to grow in our love for each other. If we face a problem may you guide us; if we meet an opportunity, strengthen us. Enable us to grow in grace and peace together. To the glory of your name we pray. Amen.

The meal was exceptional and the fellowship was warm and happy.

There was a lull in the conversation and laughter when John asked Jesus:

> Where do you want us to make
> preparations for you to eat the Passover?
> Go into the city, Jesus replied,
> to a certain man there and say to him:
> The Master says, My time is near.
> I am going to keep the Passover
> with my disciples at your house.
> The disciples did as Jesus instructed them
> and the Passover meal was prepared.

Jesus instructed John to have the man of the house where the meal would be served to use Martha, Mary, and myself as a part of the team to serve the meal. He could not include us in that inner circle but he wanted us near. The three of us arrived early at the house and were given very specific instructions about what we were and were not to do during that evening.

> Late in the evening Jesus took his place
> at the table with the twelve
> and during the meal he said,
> I tell you plainly that one
> of you will betray me.
> They were deeply distressed at this
> and each began to say to
> him in turn.
> Surely, Lord, I am not the one?
> And his answer was:
> The man who has dipped his hand into
> the dish with me is the man who will betray me.
> It is true that the Son of Man

will follow the road foretold by
the scriptures but alas for the man
through whom he is betrayed!
It would be better for that man
if he had never been born.
Judas, who actually betrayed him,
said, Master, am I the one?
As you say! replied Jesus.

All in the room were stunned! Jesus paused, and Judas got up from his place at the table, picked up a small bag, and quickly left the room. All eyes followed him and when he had gone all those eyes came back to Jesus. We saw Jesus sitting quietly in prayer with a tear on his cheek. Jesus loved Judas just as he loved all of his disciples. These moments must have been hard for Judas; but, for Jesus it was a time of personal agony. His eyes dropped to the table and it seemed he wasn't breathing. Mary started crying and I made her leave the room to gather in her emotions.

Conversation around the table was very subdued as the meal continued. Jesus did not join in any of the conversations or discussions. I watched him carefully. Mary was still insistent on going to him to offer comfort and strength but I told her "No." The happiness and joy of a usual Passover Meal dissolved. In the middle of the meal without any warning, Jesus motioned to Mary suggesting that she come to him.

He whispered to her and she turned to leave the room and motioned for me to follow her. She went into the service area of the house; and without speaking a word, she picked up a wash bowl, wiped it clean, filled it half way with water and handed it to me. She poured water into a tall pitcher and picked up three towels and put them across her arm then motioned for me to follow her. We went to Jesus and he stood and kneeled down before John. He motioned for me to set the bowl on the floor and he began washing John's feet and then he took a towel and ever so gently he dried his feet. He then went from one disciple to the other in like manner. He never looked at them, but he was constantly praying. After every third disciple, Mary would take the bowl out of the room, empty it, and quickly return.

Each time he came to another disciple, they would turn and face him and accepted his outreach of servanthood. But when he came to Peter, he did not move, nor did he allow him to touch his feet.

Jesus looked up at him and reached for a foot.

Peter pulled his foot away and with rebellion in his voice said, "No, Lord, I am not worthy for you to wash my feet."

"If I do not wash your feet, then you can have nothing…nothing to do with me."

Peter froze and thought about what Jesus had said. "Then Lord, wash me all over that I may be completely yours." He then presented to him his feet.

Jesus just looked at Peter with a mixture of love and sadness and drew Peter's feet into the water. Peter was praying very intensely. Several times Peter tried to find words to speak to Jesus, but he was stopped by the quiet humility of his Lord. Jesus washed and dried Peter's feet and moved on to the next until he had washed every disciples feet. He handed the bowl to me and the empty pitcher and towels to Mary. We momentarily left the room to return those items to the Master of the House.

Upon returning to the room, it was absolutely quiet. Everyone was focusing on Jesus. Mary brought Jesus a much smaller bowl with water and one towel. He slowly washed his hands and dried them. He stood at his place at the table and looked from one to the other in the room. Then, he slowly sat down and entered a short time of prayer.

Jesus took a loaf of bread and after blessing it he broke it in pieces and gave a piece to each disciple.

He moved with great deliberateness and he prayed over each piece of bread. He looked to see that everyone had a piece of bread, then with great deliberateness he said:

Take and eat this, it is my body to be broken for you.

There was a long pause. Some of the disciples ate the bread immediately but others held it in the palm of their hand and looked at it for a long time and then would look at Jesus before eating it. Jesus words must have been ringing in their ears.

Then Jesus took the cup and, after thanking God, he gave it to
them with these words, Drink this all of you, for it is my blood.
The blood of the new divine agreement shed to set many free
from their sins.
I tell you I will drink no more wine until I drink it fresh with you
in my father's kingdom.

Jesus stopped and looked all around the table and finally he said, "Are you listening to me? It is most important to me that you continue to do this act of celebration as a special remembrance of me." He paused and looked with great hope at each disciple. "Let me confess to you before God, my Father, I have one fear in my life." Again, he paused and looked at each disciple with a sadness I had never seen in his eyes before. No one seemed to be breathing. I am afraid…that when I am gone…you will too soon forget me? So…I am asking you…please, do this in remembrance of me as often as you choose."

Jesus went into a time of prayer and everyone joined him, each in his our own way:

Then the disciples sang a hymn together and went out to the

Mount of Olives. There Jesus said to them, tonight every one of you will lose your faith in me. For the scripture says, I will smite the shepherd, and the sheep of the flock shall be scattered abroad.
But after I have risen I shall go before you into Galilee.
At this Peter exclaimed, Even if everyone should lose their faith in you, I never will.
I tell you, Peter, replied Jesus, that tonight before the cock crows, you will disown me three times.
Even if it means dying with you I will never disown you, said Peter. And all the disciples made the same protest.

Martha and Mary stayed to help the Master of the House clean up after the meal. I slipped out and followed along behind Jesus and the disciples. There was almost constant argument among them about what Jesus meant about Peter disowning him. And on top of it all, where did Judas go? There were many affirmations of loyalty on the part of each disciple to each other. They would never consider abandoning Jesus and would always remember him.

Jesus walked at a fast pace. He was a man with a purpose and no one was going to distract him or slow him down.

Then Jesus came to a place called Gethsemane and he said
to the disciples, Sit down while I go over there and pray.
Then he took with him Peter and the two sons of Zebedee
and began to be in terrible distress and misery. My heart
is nearly breaking, he told them, stay here and keep watch
with me. Then he walked a little way and fell on his face
and prayed, My Father, if it is possible let this cup pass
from me— yet it must not be what I want, but what you
want.

As I stood off to the side in the dark shadows, hidden by heavy shrubs I was filled with sorrow. The evening was almost over-whelming. Jesus was afraid of being forgotten. How could we ever forget. Why would we ever forget. His life and faith were imprinted deep within our mind and soul. And now in his prayer he kept saying over and over again, "not my will but yours be done." What did he mean? Jesus was perspiring so profusely I could see it in the dark with the help of a bright moon. Jesus got up and returned to where he left Peter and the sons of Zebedee and he found them fast asleep.

> He spoke to Peter: "Couldn't you
> three keep awake with me for a single hour?
> Watch and pray, that you may not
> have to face temptation.
> Your spirit is willing but human nature is weak.
> Then he went away a second time and prayed,
> My Father, if it is not possible for this cup
> to pass from me without drinking it,
> then your will must me done.
> He came and found them asleep again,
> for they could not keep their eyes open.
> So he left them and went away again
> and prayed for the third time, using the same words as
> before.
> Then he came back to his disciples and spoke to them.
> Are you still going to sleep and take your ease?
> In a moment you will see the Son of Man betrayed into
> the hands of evil men.
> Wake up, let us be going! Look, here comes my betrayer!

There was a growing rhythm of marching feet and clanking medal and loud whispering which was coming from a little deeper inside the Garden of Gethsemane. The disciples stirred and began standing up to see what was coming. They were sleeping so soundly that it was hard for them to get awake and several were still lying down when they found themselves surrounded by an armed guard.

Jesus words to them were still on his lips.

The wide-eyed disciples by this time were all standing and seemed very overwhelmed by the sight of an armed guard who appeared to be on a very definite mission. Why were these armed guards here in the early hours of the morning?

> Judas was at the head of the crowd armed with swords and staves. The Temple guards were sent by the chief priests and Jewish elders.
> (The traitor himself had given them a sign, the one I kiss will be the man, Get him!)
> Without any hesitation, Judas walked up to Jesus, Greetings, Master! he cried
> and then kissed him affectionately.
> Judas my friend, replied Jesus, why are you here?
> Then the others who came with Judas,
> seized Jesus and heldhim.
> Suddenly, Peter one of Jesus' disciples drew his hidden short sword and slashed at the High Priest's servant and cut off his ear.

Jesus caught that ear in mid-air and before anyone could counter that vicious act by Peter, Jesus put the ear back on the servant's head and his quick, short blessing arrested any fight that might have broken out.

Jesus held up his hand as a sign of restraint. The soldier felt his ear and another looked at it. There was no mark or blood. It was healed. Then Jesus said to the group:

> Put your swords back into their proper place.
> All those who take the sword die by the sword...
> Do you imagine that I could not appeal to my Father,
> and he at once would send more than
> twelve legions of angels to defend me?
> But then how would the scriptures be fulfilled
> which say that all this must take place.
> And then Jesus spoke to all those around him:
> So you have come out with your swords and staves to capture me like a bandit, have you?

Day after day I set teaching in the Temple and you never laid a finger on me. But all this is happening as the prophets said *it would*.

And at this point all the disciples deserted him and made their escape.

Light was barely breaking in the sky as the disciples ran in several directions and Judas, poor Judas, ran with them. Jesus stood alone. Even I his best friend was hunkered down hidden in the thick bushes so as not to be discovered by the Temple guard.

One of the guards came to Jesus and bound his hands together in front of him. When the guard turned to the Priest who was leading them for his directions, there was a sudden flapping of wings. Jesus raised his bound arms and a dove landed on his bound hand, sang a quick song and flew away before any of the soldiers could try to harm him.

The solders were so startled that they backed away from Jesus and became somewhat afraid of these strange phenomena by a wild bird. Jesus smiled as he watched the bird. The disciples abandoned him, but his friend from the sky stayed close and flew over him as they marched Jesus away.

I sagged to the ground as they left and wept many tears for Jesus. I fell asleep while grieving and suddenly I became aware that someone was quietly calling my name and seemed very close by. I opened my eyes and waited until that voice was no more than a few feet away from me when I realized it was Mary, my sister.

When I stirred and the leaves rustled under me, she almost ran until I spoke her name, "Mary?"

"Lazarus, why are you hiding here? Where is Jesus?"

The very question brought torrents of tears from me again, and I was too tired and weak to even stand up. Mary came and kneeled down beside me and embraced me as if I were her child I was shaking violently and the tears would not stop. I began choking along with the crying, that frightened Mary. It was a long time before I could tell her about the rest of the evening after the Passover meal. I would talk and cry and she would cry with me.

She finally said, "Lazarus, it is time to go home, Mama is waiting."

When I stood and we had walked only a few feet the dove returned and when I raised my arms and it landed on my eagerly outstretched hands. That bird looked at both of us with the most sad expression and then flew without singing a note. It flew away and disappeared among the branches of the trees. I thought to myself, that is what I would like to do.

I went home and again had to repeat the story of the night for Mama and Martha. After that very long and hard presentation I had to endure a lot of questions from all three of the family members and eventually my partner, Judas, joined us and there were additional questions.

"Where would they take him," I asked. "Where do I go to find him?"

My partner jumped and said, "Let me go with you and together we will find him."

Mama quickly said, "Lazarus, you are not going anywhere until you have some rest. You may find him, but you will not be able to make it back home."

"You are probably right Mama, so let me lie down for a little while; and Judas don't go anywhere. When I wake up, I will need you to help me."

With that I turned toward my room and said, "Mary, I know you will want to go too and you need some rest as well." So we both walked toward our rooms as Judas sat down at the kitchen table and Mama turned to her stove. She would try again to see if she could prepare enough food to fill Judas's hunger—that was one of her life goals.

I had a very restless sleep; and when I awoke, I was more tired than when I had laid down. I washed my face and called Mary and after a small meal which Mama insisted we eat, we were off to Jerusalem. As we left I turned to Mama and Martha and said, "Pray, please, pray. We need it and I am sure Jesus needs it."

We walked so fast that when we arrived at Jerusalem I had to sit down. Judas went to a vendor and bought us two pastries and some goat's milk. There was excitement in the air and it was all about Jesus.

There were a lot of young men running, and the people would stop them and simply say, "Jesus." The young man would tell you what he knew and then if you thought it was somewhat authentic, you would pay him a simple fee. There were dozens of these young men and you had to be careful as some of them knew nothing but had only made up their news.

One of the news bearers told us that Jesus had first been taken to the house of the High Priest, Caiaphas. He was briefly questioned by certain elders and through it all Jesus remained completely silent.

Caiaphas asked him,
Have you no answer? What about the evidence of these
young men against you?
Jesus remained silent.
"I command you by the, living God," said Caiaphas,
to tell us on your oath if you are Christ, the Son of God?
Jesus said to him, I am. Yes, and I tell you that in the
future you will see the Son of Man sitting on the right
hand of power and coming on the clouds of heaven,
The High Priest tore his robes and cried, This is
blasphemy. He deserves to die.

That was terrible news, if it was correct. But, it seemed to be the best we could get. Jerusalem was full and people were restless to hear any news and there seemed to be a lot of wild gossip making its rounds. Another young runner told us:

The chief priests and elders of the people met in a called council to decide how they could get Jesus executed. Then they marched him off with his hands tied, and handed him over to Pilate the governor.

We raced over to the Governor's Palace and after paying a priest a bribe we were allowed to enter the Governor's Courtyard. There stood Jesus with his hands bound. He looked exhausted, and Mary began to weep quietly.

It seems they had sent a petition to Pilate, the governor. They were waiting for his response. The governor finally appeared and sat in his Seat of Judgment, a large throne like a chair, which was a symbol of his power as an administrator in the Roman Empire. Several of the Priests approached Pilate, and they talked quietly so no one could hear. Pilate kept looking at Jesus.

He waved the Priests away and stood and walked to the top of the steps that led down into the Courtyard. He was surrounded by armed guards with only a slight opening before him.

> Jesus stood at the bottom of the steps facing
> Pilate who asked him, well, you—are you the King of the
> Jews?
> Yes I am, replied Jesus.
> While the chief priests and elders were making their
> accusations, Jesus made no reply at all.
> So Pilate said to him. Can you not hear the evidence
> they're bringing against you?
> And to the governor's amazement Jesus
> did not answer a single one of their accusations.

Jesus' refusal to answer any of the accusations created great consternation among the scribes and High Priests, and Pilate was frustrated with the Jewish leaders. Pilate left and returned to his quarters. When he returned, several High Priests came before him.

> There was a custom at festival time for the Governor
> to release any prisoner whom the people chose.
> And it happened that at that time

they had a notorious prisoner called Barabbas.
So when they assembled to make their
usual request, Pilate said to them,
Which one do you want me to set free, Barabbas or Jesus
called Christ?
For Pilate knew very well that Jesus had been handed
over to him through sheer malice.
And while Pilate was actually sitting on the Bench
his wife sent a message to him.
Don't have anything to do with that good man!
But the Chief Priests and Elders persuaded the mob
To ask for Barabbas and demand Jesus's execution.
Then the governor spoke to them, which of these two are
you asking me to release?
Barabbas! They all cried.
Then what am I to do with Jesus who is called Christ?
asked Pilate.
Have him crucified they all cried. At this Pilate said, Why,
what is his crime?
But their voices rose to a roar, Have him crucified!

Mary collapsed on the ground at my feet. She was sobbing
and neither Judas nor I were successful in quieting her. She only
responded to me when I said that we would need to leave this
place. She choked back her sobs and struggled to her feet. She
looked a wreck, I had never seen her look that way. She wiped
her face with the sleeve of her robe and tried to smile at me. I
embraced her, and we turned again to listen and watch.

When Pilate realized that nothing more could be done,
but that there would soon be a riot,
he took a bowl of water and washed his hands
before the crowd, saying…
I take no responsibility for the death of this man.
You must see to that yourselves.
To this the whole crowd replied,
Let his blood be on us and

on our children!
Whereupon Pilate released Barabbas,
but he had Jesus flogged
and handed over for crucifixion.

It was evident that Mary could not manage any more of this cruel trial, and I told her we were going home. She did not rebel. We had to stop many times on the way home and when we arrived Mary collapsed in Mama's arms. She put Mary to bed with Martha's help and then prepared some nourishment for me.

I told Mama, "I cannot tell all that happened. I would not be able to stand the torture of repeating it, but I will tell you a little."

Soon I went to my room in tears and Mama did not bother me for any more details. But I understand, Judas was very helpful to her in learning what had happened.

When I rested for just a brief time, I came out of the house and told Mama that I was returning to see what else was happening.

Martha said that she was going with me and I did not object. We hurried to Jerusalem. We were met by a parade of sorts and realized that it was Jesus and two others being driven by the soldiers for crucifixion.

Jesus was so weak he was stumbling under the weight of the cross.

Martha was so shocked that she covered her mouth with her hands, and all anyone could see was the wild expression in her eyes. When Jesus fell under the weight of the cross, Martha screamed. I had never heard such a sound come out of her.

The Temple guards pulled a man out
of the crowd to carry the cross for Jesus.
He was Simon, a Cyrenean from
northern Africa.
They compelled him to carry
the cross for Jesus.
Then when they came to a place
called Golgotha (which means the Skull Hill)

> they offered Jesus a drink of wine
> mixed with some bitter drug,
> but when he had tasted it he
> refused to drink.
> And when they had nailed him to the
> cross they shared out his clothes by drawing lots.

The scene was terrible and the crowds were even worse. It was noisy and confusing. They battered the bodies of the three men being crucified in getting them on the crosses. The other two were profane and nasty all the time. Jesus was quietly enduring the indignity and pain of those spikes being pounded into his hands and feet. And when they were nailed to those crosses they were raised and dropped into the holds. The pain must have been excruciating. The two criminals screamed, but Jesus grimaced and bore the agony.

Aunt Mary was right there and the pain her son was enduring was carving a deep valley of sadness in her heart. The twins surrounded her with their love and tried to protect her from the agony that Jesus was enduring. She wept silently. When she looked up into the eyes of Jesus, and he was looking down from that cross there was a bond of love that cried out and reached upward to God for strength and comfort.

> Over Jesus head they had put a placard with the charge against him: THIS IS JESUS, THE KING OF THE JEWS.

Aunt Mary cried out from the scalding pain in her inner being as she prayed aloud: Father; God; King of all Creation; hear me, let the full glory of your spirit fill my son, your Son, our son. Lord, just a few years ago he was my baby and now he is dying. As I took him in my arms to nurse and nurture him; take him into the bosom of eternal life and let your glory nurture and strengthen him. Her voice faded off, overwhelmed by the brutal inhumanity that was roaring all around her.

Two bandits were crucified with Jesus, one on either side
of him. The passers-by nodded their heads knowingly and
called out to Jesus in mockery,
Hey, you who could pull down the Temple and build it up
in three days—why don't you save yourself?
If you are the Son of God, step down from the cross.
The chief priests also joined the scribes and elders
in jeering at him, saying: He saved others,
but he cannot save himself! If this is the king of Israel,
why doesn't he come down from the cross now,
and we will believe him!
He trusted in God…For he said, I am God's Son.
Even the bandits who were crucified with him hurled
abuse at him.

Mama and sister Mary suddenly appeared. Mama looked at
the scene and was overwhelmed with inner pain and Mary would
not look at all. Mary came to be with Martha and me, and she
turned her back to the whole thing. Mama quickly moved to
Aunt Mary, knelt down beside her, and embraced her. Both cried
tears of anguish. Mama stood her full height, raised her arms
toward the heavens, and prayed. I really think I saw a slight smile
on Jesus's face as he recognized her.

John, the disciple, slipped in beside Mama and embraced her
and then knelt down with Aunt Mary. In that moment Jesus
spoke with a tenderness and love that was a miracle in such a situation. His voice was firm yet loving as he said, "Mother, behold
your son beside you."

Jesus closed his eyes for a moment, that brief effort took an
enormous amount of energy. But he opened his eyes and looked
at John, the disciple, with a pleading look and a strong voice, he
said, "John behold your mother!"

His eyes embraced both of them for a moment before pain
swept over him and he closed his eyes.

John knelt down and embraced Aunt Mary as Mama and I
knelt with them and gathered both of them in our arms.

Someone suddenly startled us when a totally different voice called my name, "Lazarus."

I stood up and found myself looking into the eyes of Samson. When I greeted him by name, Aunt Mary quickly stood and pulled him into a warm embrace. She drew back and looked at him to say, "Littlest shepherd, we again share the same moments together. You were there at the time of Jesus' birth and now at the end of his life."

"Oh mother Mary, he came with the angels singing Glory to God in the highest and peace on earth among all people of good will, and some of us will continue to sing his song and share his message of peace and hope."

We were all startled when a voice above us said, "Glory to God...peace on earth." It was Jesus' response to Samson's presence.

Mary, I cannot keep this coin any longer. It is yours. Take it and when you gaze upon it always hear his proclamation for peace and joy for all people," Samson said.

Aunt Mary took the coin, gazed at it for a long time; then she again embraced Samson. Aunt Mary looked around us on that hill and said, "this world is so far from peace but yes, Jesus will always be the 'proclaimer' of the Good News of God's righteousness. Oh, my son...my son."

> Then from midday until three o'clock darkness spread over the whole countryside, and then Jesus cried with a loud voice, My God, My God, why hast thou forsaken me? Some
> of those standing there heard these words which Jesus spoke in Aramic (Eli, Eli lama sabachthani?), and said, This man is calling for Elijah!
> And one of them ran off and fetched a sponge, soaked with vinegar and put it on a long stick and held it up for him to drink.
> But the others said: Let him alone!
> Let's see if Elijah will come and save him.

I began to realize as I watched around me that a crucifixion is a tragic curiosity show for all kinds of people. Some come out to jeer, mock, and even laugh at those being tortured. The soldiers make fun of those suffering an agonizing death. Family members are there with sorrow and distress that is beyond imagination. There are those who come to gawk at the victim, watch the agony of family, and play games with many other play actors. It is a horrible and sickening scene. Even the victims get into the act.

> One of the criminals hanging there covered Jesus with abuse,
> and said, Aren't you, Christ? Why don't you
> save yourself – and us?
> But the other criminal reprimanded him with the words:
> Aren't you afraid of God even when you're getting the
> same punishment as he is?
> And it's fair enough for us, for we've only got
> what we deserve, but this man never
> did anything wrong in his life.
> Then He said, Jesus, remember me when you come into
> your kingdom.
> And Jesus answered,
> I tell you truly, this very day you will be with me in
> paradise.
> Jesus gave one great cry,
> it is finished and he died.

There was an enormous flash of lightening that filled the sky and the thunder rolled on it seemed forever and forever. Then came the wind that swirled the dust of the mountain to hide us from one another. People were screaming and running down that mountain and when the dust cleared our little group of the family and friends of Jesus were pretty much alone with the Temple and Roman guards.

We all stood and looked into the face of the Son of God and the Son of Man. The world seemed to become very quiet. A warm gust of wind swirled around the area and swept away the stench on that hill. As we stood looking up at Jesus, his dove coasted to the top of the cross right over Jesus' head. That bird lifted his head and sang the most glorious song I believe I have ever heard. When he finished, he looked down at Jesus and flew back toward the Garden of Gethsemane. We all stood reverently wondering what were the words to the bird's song. We found new strength in that Bird's song and we began to smile again.

> When the centurion and his company
> who were keeping guard over Jesus felt the earthquake
> and saw all that was happening, they were terrified.
> Indeed he was a son of God! they said.
> There were also many women
> at the scene watching from a distance.
> They had followed Jesus from Galilee to
> minister to his needs. Among them were
> Mary of Magdala, Mary the mother of James and Joseph,
> and the mother of the Zebedee's sons.

The Roman Commander required us to wait until they were sure Jesus was dead and could not be revived. In the meantime John and I began to see who we could enlist to help us with taking the body down from that cross. That would not be an easy job. We sent Martha and Mary to find some grave clothes that we could use to wrap Jesus' body.

I looked around and none of the other disciples were there except for John, a few friends Samson, Judas, my partner, and me.

Nicodemus and Joseph of Arimathaea, two rulers of the Jews, who were friends of both Jesus and John quietly appeared, and Joseph offered a grave that was close by. He and Jesus had had several conversations about spiritual issues and both thought highly of the other. Joseph had also been to Pilate and been given a release for Jesus's body which he gave to the Roman Centurion.

We were in a difficult position because it was:

Now the day of preparation and the Sabbath was close
to starting.

If we did not get Jesus down from that cross and moved to a grave, we would have to leave the body on the cross for a whole night and the Sabbath Day.

The Roman Commander pulled a ladder from somewhere that allowed us to reach Jesus and loosen the grip of those nails that held both his hands and feet. We were trying to be very careful because all of us loved Jesus, and we did not want to desecrate his body anymore after what those soldiers had done.

Aunt Mary embraced her son ever so gently. Then Mama was able to convince her to go with her to our home where she could stay until the group that came from Galilee would return home.

Martha and Mary came running with adequate grave clothes to wrap Jesus's body. We quickly wrapped his body and followed Joseph to the grave he offered. We placed his body in the crypt and rolled a large stone in front of the cave entrance.

The women who had come with Jesus from Galilee
came to our house and began preparing spices and
perfumes
to use in anointing the body of Jesus after the Sabbath.

The Sabbath Day had begun and Jesus was sitting with his heavenly Father in the divine kingdom.

We quickly and quietly left the Garden to go to our separate homes, observe the Sabbath, and find comfort and strength for our spirits. It had been a long two days and perhaps that bird was singing "And on earth peace and goodwill to all people."

The Day of Glory

Early in the morning of the first day of the week the women were eager and ready to go to Jesus's tomb and anoint the body with *The aromatic spices they had prepared.*

Martha told me later it was a noisy group who chattered the whole time. Her comment was that the women of Galilee "talk too much and too loud and all at the same time. Tell me, how do they ever know what is being said?"

But they quit talking when they arrived at the tomb. The stone had been rolled away. No one wanted to be the first to go in the tomb, so Martha moved out in front, went in, and found the tomb empty.

She stood there looking at the empty crypt with the grave clothes folded neatly, laying upon the stone that had covered the place where his body had been laid. No sign of Jesus. She walked back to the opening into the tomb and stood looking at the knot of frightened women who stood away from the tomb.

"Jesus is not here."
While they were still puzzling over this,

two men suddenly stood at their elbow,
dressed in dazzling white.
The women were terribly frightened
and turned their eyes away and
looked at the ground,
but the two men spoke to them.
Why do you look for the living
among the dead?
He is not here: he is risen!
Remember that he said to you while he
was still in Galilee—that the Son of Man
must be betrayed into the hands of sinful men
and must be crucified, and
must rise again on the third day.
Then they did remember what he had said,
and they turned their backs on the tomb
and went and told all this to the
eleven and the others who were with them.
It was Mary of Magdala; Joanna; Mary, the mother of
James; and their companions who made this report to the
apostles.
But it struck the apostles as sheer imagination, and they
did not believe the women. Only Peter got up and ran
to the tomb. He stooped down and saw the linen clothes
lying
there all by themselves, and he went wondering what had
happened.

Martha and Mary raced home when they left the tomb. They
arrived at home totally out of breath and unable to talk. Martha
was babbling and Mary would only scream, so Mama made them
sit down until they began to calm down.

"Jesus is not in the tomb," said Martha.

I instantly turned to run to the Tomb in the Garden, but
Mama called for me to "stop and come back inside the house.
Let's talk about this before we start racing everywhere. All right,
Martha, tell Lazarus and I exactly what happened."

"We were going to the tomb with the other women to prepare Jesus's body before the heat of the day. And, oh Mama, how those women from Galilee talk."

"Martha, what about Jesus, not the women!"

"Sorry!"

Mary jumped in, "When we got there the stone at the entrance of the cave had been rolled from where it belonged. We had been talking about how to move that stone, but it was already moved. We stopped and didn't move and were very frightened."

"A little frightened?" said Martha, "Mama, the whole group froze. Eventually, I got up the nerve and went slowly toward the cave and very slowly went inside. Even the stone cap covering the grave had been removed. Jesus's grave clothes were neatly folded and placed to the side on the stone cover. They were folded just like Jesus always folded things when he was here with us."

Were any of the disciples there?" I asked.

"No," said Martha, "But I seem to remember that those women said something about finding them. Mary and I broke into a run to come home."

"Come, Lazarus," said Mama, "we are going to the tomb."

We walked at a very brisk pace and when we arrived no one was there. We stopped and looked at the surrounding area and then ventured inside. Jesus was not there!

We turned around when we heard something and my sisters were there behind us.

I went outside and looked all around for anything that would be a sign that someone had come and taken the body. There was nothing unusual or suspicious. I asked Martha to pick up each piece of the clothe and see what was there.

Martha counted the pieces and announced, "It is all here. All that Mary and I brought is here."

I said, "Let's pray." We gathered in a circle and put our arms around each other: "Lord of life. God of Creation. Your Son has conquered death as he told us he would. We did not listen, but all of us must now listen and proclaim the Good News, Christ is alive! Lo, he is with us always. As he himself said, he is as near as our breath. Fill us Lord! Make us messengers of his grace and love. God of all Ages, now we will truly live because he will live within us. May we be as willing to sacrifice ourselves for others as he sacrificed himself for us. Jesus, my brother, my best friend, my Savior, my King, thank you and lead the way and we will all follow. Amen"

We all stood there hugging each other and shedding tears of joy.

Mama said, "Lazarus, Jesus was here while you were praying. I could feel the warmth of his presence."

"Yes, Mama, you are right, he is here."

"Come," said Mama, "let's go home.

We were all quiet walking home. What an amazing day. Jesus has risen. We arrived at home and were beginning to settle down.

Martha with a gasp, suddenly spoke up and said, "We must go and find Aunt Mary and tell her the good news."

"You are right, Martha," said Mama, "Let's go, right now. Oh, I hope we get to her first and you two can share with her your experience."

"Mary, come, we must find Aunt Mary and her family," called Mama. There was no sound. Martha went to their room and she was not there. Lazarus looked in his room and there was no sign of her.

"Mama, we need to go. Mary can take care of herself and she will be here when we return after we see Aunt Mary," I said.

"You are right," said Mama, "let's hurry along."

We hurried down the path to go through the Garden of Gethsemane to the camp ground for the Galileans. We rounded the rock where years ago we saw Jesus with the dove I had knocked out of the tree. There was Mary sitting on that same rock where Jesus sat. She had a bird in her lap and she was weeping. I walked up beside her and sat down and after a few minutes I dared to speak.

"Are you all right?" I asked.

"No!" she screamed. I sat still for another few minutes. "Lazarus, I found this poor bird cold and dead lying on this very rock. Do you think it was the one that sang on top of the cross?"

I froze without knowing what to say or ask. Mama knelt beside Mary, "Are you all right, my dear?"

"How can I be when a beautiful creature has been taken from me and I know no reason whatever for it," Mary burst out crying. "Just like Jesus, why did they crucify such a beautiful, loving person. Why!"

"Mary, we need to go." interrupted Martha

"Just a minute Martha," I said. "Mary, perhaps that is the bird that sang on top of the cross and his song was to tell Jesus to come, "follow me." There was a special relationship between Jesus and that family of birds over the years. Just maybe this day they are sharing the glory of God's kingdom together. I tell you what, let's put the bird back over there behind that bush and when we return home this evening I will come with you and we will bury that very bird with a prayer before the sun sets.

Mary looked at me for a long time, kept sniffling and never spoke a word. Mama and Martha had slowly walked on.

Mary stood and went toward the bush I had mentioned. She knelt down and placed the bird very tenderly on the ground and covered it with some sticks, leaves, and fresh grass. "Jesus, take care of your bird, she said."

We turned and started to walk briskly toward the path to follow Mama and Martha and then broke into a slow trot. When we caught up, Mama started to say something, but I shook my head, and all of us continued in silence.

When we arrived at the Galilean camp, everything seemed to be in a stir. Mama looked at me and said, "They must know about Jesus?"

We suddenly recognized one of Jesus twin sisters, "Naomi," Mama called, "Naomi, where is the family?" She ran to us all wide-eyed and out of breathe.

"Have you heard the news?" she asked. "Jesus has risen; or, something at least has happened to him."

Martha answered, "Yes, we have been to the tomb and have come to see if Aunt Mary knows that Jesus's tomb is open and his body is not there."

"That's where they have gone," said Naomi, "I have stayed to take care of the children. Everyone was so excited that I knew they would walk so fast that the smaller children would never have kept up."

"Please," said Naomi, "tell me what you know about whatever has happened at the tomb. Mother was so excited that she couldn't talk. I have never seen my Mother that excited. Do you know if..."

Suddenly there was the sound of running feet and the clanking of metal. Everyone turned to look in the direction from which the noise was coming. A troop of fully armed Temple Guards ran into the camp and fanned out surrounding the whole camp. The Commander announced that no one was to leave. Children started to cry as they ran to their parents.

The officer who was in command began to slowly move around the camp looking at everyone who was there, and then he began looking in every tent and if there was a pile of anything he would kick the pile apart himself or he would have one of the men disassemble it. The five of us sat down on the ground and attempted to make light talk with Naomi while at the same time nervously watching what was going on.

A young boy came running from the direction of the tomb and when he crossed the line of soldiers surrounding the camp he was grabbed, slammed to the ground, and two spears were driven into the ground on either side of him and there was a big boot planted in his stomach. He could not move. His mother came to him, but she was told to get back and away.

The Commander walked over to where that boy was pinned to the ground. The officer motioned for them to stand him up. "Where have you been?"

"To the tomb in the Garden," the boy answered. He was so terrified that he was about to cry and he kept looking at his mother.

"Look at me," barked the Commander. But the young boy could not take his eyes from his mother who was close by.

"Put him down," shouted the Commander and again they slammed him on his back and the spears went in the ground and a foot on his stomach. "What were you doing at that tomb?

"Trying to find Jesus," said the boy.

"Find him? Come on, tell me, you helped steal his body. Where did you put him," shouted the officer.

The youngster just lay there and kept shaking his head with his eyes as big as a plate, "No."

"Tell us where you have taken him or we will kill you." The young boy couldn't speak but his mother jumped forward and knelt.

"Please, sir, please," she cried, "Please let him up and let me talk with him."

The officer looked at the woman and finally said, "Talk with him where he is and make it quick."

She scrambled over to her son. "Son, tell him that you had just gone to the tomb because you had heard from others that Jesus was not there."

The boy screamed, "That's right."

"Right, what's right," yelled the Commander. "That you stole the body of Jesus of Nazareth.

"No, no, I was just going along to watch and see what was happening," said the youngster who was now crying hysterically.

"To watch them steal the body and run with it?"

"No! No! Please"

"Where did you take his body?" Yelled the commander as he kicked the youngster in the ribs with his boot.

Both the mother and son were crying hysterically.

The officer was talking and yelling to all those who were in the area, "Who wants to save this boy's life by telling me where you took the son of Nazareth who is called Jesus? Tell me, right now before this boy dies and his blood is on you."

He circled around the camp area and walked back to the boy, put his foot on his chest, drew his broad sword while mother and son were screaming "Please, no," Please!"

The officer raised the sword over his head and with a huge grunting sound he swung it toward the ground. The blade buried into the ground right next to the boy's neck leaving a slight cut. The mother screamed and the boy fainted.

"The next time I will not miss," shouted the officer. "Now, somebody tell me where is his body…Now, right this minute… Now!"

There was not a sound.

The officer turned around and spoke to his men. "Tear everything apart in this camp until you find what they have hidden. Now, do it! Then he shouted to all of us, "Stay where you are until we have found what we are looking for"

No one moved. Mama leaned over to the four of us and said, "Pray quietly that Mary doesn't come back now." We started praying. Martha started crying quietly but I knew she was also praying.

The soldiers completely wrecked the camp. Several times they set fire to small piles of goods. Their Commander suddenly decided he had had enough of this camp and he told his men "If you want anything you have seen, take it." For a few moments there was total confusion as the soldiers looted the camp. "Now, pick up your weapons and we will march back to Jerusalem." They moved efficiently and quickly and were gone but still no one moved in the camp area.

I finally told everyone, stay quiet, and don't move around until we know that they have actually gone. I moved very slowly down the path where the soldiers had marched. When I became convinced they had gone, I returned and told everyone they could move around, put out the fires and see what they could reclaim that had not been completely destroyed or looted. It was a sad evening. We were blessed that it was warm and it would not be too uncomfortable to try and sleep outside.

We looked up and there came Aunt Mary and her family. Naomi ran to them and started explaining what had happened. Mama joined them and quietly kept the family from becoming too distressed.

I told Martha that we needed to go home and find some things for those who had lost everything. She agreed and after I talked with several of the men we left for Bethany which was not far away. When we got to our house in Bethany Judas, my business partner, and Jason, his helper, were there wondering about us.

When I told them quickly about what had happened at the camp and what was needed by the families, they volunteered to return to their homes and friends and collect what they could. Judas told me they would not be long. By the time Mama, Martha and Mary went through what we could give away and then had something light to eat, the two boys were back. They had two donkeys loaded with blankets, clothes and food.

We immediately left for the camp of the Galileans. They were very grateful for all the things we brought, especially the blankets. Several of the women carefully sorted and divided the few clothes we brought. Everyone had something and seemed to barely have enough. The soldiers had not broken the water jars and that was a blessing.

I asked one of the men if they had any animals so that the older women could ride. They had rented a small field away from the camp and those animals were safe and healthy. Plus, the soldiers had completely missed their stash of food and several of the women were working to prepare an evening meal for everyone.

By the time the sun had gone down and darkness enveloped the camp they all settled in for a night's rest. It was greatly needed. The adults were quietly talking and deciding what needed to be done to allow them to leave early in the morning. They did not want any more Temple Guards in their camp. I told them that I would be responsible for cleaning up the area and they could just leave the mess the soldiers left. Judas, Jason, and my sisters would all pitch in and we could care for it quickly.

Aunt Mary decided she would like to stay with us for a little while and her youngest son Benjamin would stay with her. We collected a few things still recognizable that the solders had not destroyed that belonged to Aunt Mary and Benjamin, and we left to go home to Bethany and our safe little house.

It was too late to bury that bird, so sister Mary and I decided we would bury the bird when we came back to the Garden in the morning to clean up the camp. It was good to get home and have a place to lay my head down and allow sleep to wash over me.

We were all restless in our sleep. There were too many things on our mind which we could not put aside. It had been an amazing day filled with surprises. We could all say, "Jesus had risen indeed!"

The Afterglow

I awoke early, lay still, and let my mind wander over yesterday. It was not long before Benjamin was up, he laughed, and then startled me by saying, "Did you realize that you talked to Jesus most of the night?"

I stood there amazed before saying, "Did Jesus answer me?"

"No, but there were breaks in your conversation which would have allowed Jesus to speak his part."

I thought about that as we finished dressing and I would find myself lost in thought about Benjamin's comment many times during that day. We went to the kitchen area where Mama and Martha were already there preparing a full meal.

"Why are you preparing such a full meal," I asked?

Mama came over and hugged me as she said, "Good morning, my son. Now, stop and think. No one ate yesterday with all that excitement and we will undoubtedly have a very long day today."

I thought for a moment and said, "You are right. And the first thing I need to do is go and bury that bird for Mary."

"I think you are too late," said Mama. "Mary has already left the house and I would imagine that is exactly where she is."

"Oh no," I said as I ran out of the house. I went to the shed for the shovel and it was gone. So, I ran to that path in the Garden as light began to break in the sky. She was there but had not broken any ground for the bird which she was holding and crying.

"Good morning, Mary," I said as I reached for the shovel on the ground.

Mary didn't say a word.

"Now, where would you suggest we bury God's beautiful creature?" I asked.

"I would prefer to put it by the grave in the Garden where Jesus was buried, but I realize at this hour of the morning that is not wise. So, let's just bury it here by the rock where one of its ancestor's fell into Jesus's lap," Mary said.

So, I found a place where the soil would allow me to dig and I made an adequate hole. Mary had collected some soft mosses and beautiful leaves with which she lined the hole. Carefully she laid the bird in the hole and then covered it with nature's very best. Together we spread some dirt over the bird with our hands and put more moss and leaves on top of that. Our last task was to put a rock on top of the grave.

Mary said, "Lazarus, would you offer a prayer?"

I put the shovel down, turned and embraced Mary as I prayed, "God of heaven and earth, Creator of humankind and all creatures. Touch us in our grief and guide us in our joy. We thank you for the attentiveness of those birds to Jesus during his lifetime. Now, we pray that they will sing to him in heaven as they did on earth. God of heaven and Father of earth, bless, sustain, guide, and comfort us in this day. Amen"

After a few quiet moments of quietness, Mary turned and said, "Thank you." She kissed me on the cheek, took my hand, and slowly we began our walk home.

It is amazing, when I think about it, never did another dove fly to us after that day. We would see them high in the branches and hear them calling to one another, but they never came to us.

We would stop to watch them and ponder about their special relationship with Jesus. But, they would never again show any interest in landing on our hand. That family of birds must have gone with Jesus to his heavenly home.

When we arrived home we were surprised to find John and his wife, Priscilla. Aunt Mary had guided Priscilla off to a corner of the room where they were happily visiting with each other. John was just sitting down to eat before that huge spread of food Mama had put out. He was a lot like my partner, Judas, he enjoyed food and the more there was the better the meal. We all became very quiet.

Benjamin prayed, "God of mystery and Lord of life. You have drawn Jesus home, but please allow us to claim him for the needs of this life. You gave him to us and we claim him along with you. Teach us to continue to live with him that we may join him in eternal glory and peace. Bless our fellowship and the food we share. Glory to God, Amen."

We opened our eyes to another surprise. There in the doorway stood Peter and Nathaniel.

"Come in and share this early morning meal with us," said Mama.

"That is kind and it is also needed," responded Peter. "Oh, my goodness, I wish you would look at all this food."

"Peter, do you have any idea where the rest of the disciples may be?" asked John.

"No, I don't know where they might be. Nathaniel and I have been looking for and inquiring about them. It seems that perhaps most of them may be in hiding and totally frightened by the circumstances that have taken place over the last few days. We probably need to go in search of them, give them some reassurance, and then find a time for all of us to sit down to talk and pray."

"What are they afraid of?" asked John.

"Of being arrested, put on trial, and possibly crucified just like Jesus."

"But, only Pilate can sign an order for a crucifixion, and I do not believe he would allow himself to be placed in a position to grant another such sentence of any innocent man," responded John.

Peter thought a minute as we all watched him, "I think you are right, but fear does strange things to people. Lazarus, do you know that Judas was found hanged."

I was totally taken back as was Mama, Martha, and Mary.

Mary cried out, "Dear God in heaven, forgive him!"

"Do you know the circumstances around how that happened," I asked.

"No," said Peter, "even now there are many different stories floating around; but, it seems he tried to give back to the priests the money they had given him as payment to betray Jesus in the Garden. The priests absolutely refused to take that money back, so Judas threw those thirty pieces of silver back at them and fled. Joseph of Arimathea shared that with me, he was informed about this from his friends who have positions in very high places."

"You don't mean that do you?" inquired Martha.

Peter said, "Yes, Martha he was given a bribe to betray Jesus. Then Judas, when he came to the Garden where Jesus was praying pointed him out to the Temple Guard with a kiss to Jesus's cheek.""That is horrible and disgusting," said Martha as she began to cry."I would agree, but isn't that often the way crude and desperate things happen. We so often destroy our best friends, and then we are left devastated by our actions and guilt. John, let's take a few minutes and you pray for Judas."

There was a long silence as John sat at the table looking at Peter. He closed his eyes and slowly raised his hands toward heaven just as Jesus would have done. "God of forgiveness and healing. We would ask that your righteous judgment will be kind to Judas. Your Son, Jesus, called him to be a disciple and Jesus loved him. Those of us surrounding Judas worked at being a blessing to him even though he often rejected our expressions of love toward him. God of Justice and Mercy wash away Judas's misunderstanding of the ultimate meaning of Jesus's ministry to this world. Cleanse Judas, who thought he was right and allowed himself to become an instrument of desperation and evil. His actions and betrayal left our hearts broken. Jesus was crucified but we pray that the glory of the resurrection will conquer all evil. Let thy will be done on earth."

At that moment there was an explosive clap of thunder after a binding flash of lightning that had preceded it. The force of both seemed to split and burn the air. Mary screamed and ran to her room. The air was dancing with excitement or was it judgment. Finally, after a long delay John quietly said "Amen." No one spoke or even moved. Everyone put down the food they were eating and sat looking at one another.

"Good morning, everyone," said Andrew in a bright and cheerful voice as he stood in the doorway. "You all look like you are lost in darkness and despair. Haven't you heard, Jesus is risen and there is a tomorrow."

"Come in," said Mama. And as he did James followed him. "Goodness," said Mama, "you two must have been caught in a bad storm."

"Storm? Where's the storm?" asked James, "It is beautiful out-side today. Andrew and I were just talking about God's response to the resurrection. It must be the glory of this very special day after the resurrection."

Everyone got quiet again and looked at each other.

"Come you two," said Mama. "Sit here and I will fix you a plate of food."

"I am famished," said Andrew, "Peter you left early this morning."

"I was trying to find some of the other disciples and they seem to have vanished," responded Peter. "Perhaps we could all go separate ways from here back toward Jerusalem, and we could tell any of them or their friends that we will gather this evening at the room where we celebrated the Passover meal with Jesus."

"That sounds reasonable," said John. "Lazarus, would you have time to go and talk to the man who owns that house where we had our last meal together and tell him that we would like to be there today for about two hours just before dark? Hopefully he has not scheduled the room for anything this evening."

"I will leave right now," I said, "and perhaps I can get there before someone else comes to request the use of that room."

"Wait, Lazarus," said my sister Mary, "I am going with you." She ran to her room as I looked at Mama, and she nodded her agreement encouraging me to let Mary go with me.

We were both out the door, took about ten steps and stopped to look at the blue sky and feel the soft wind blowing in our faces. I looked at Mary and said, "I am so surprised at this beautiful day after that sharp clap of thunder."

"Lazarus, that thunder scared me half to death. I could hardly breathe when I ran into my room."

"Mary are you all right?" I asked her. "Perhaps you need to stay home and get some rest."

"I'm ready to go. Come on, we need to get there in a hurry," Mary said.

So, we picked up our pace and soon Jerusalem came into view. The wife of the man of that house was at home and agreed to hold the room. She promised to clean it and asked if they wanted any food."

"Just some water and perhaps some dates, that would be more than sufficient," I said.

She agreed to provide those things and we left and started walking to the Temple area. I was hoping to see Rabbi Levi, but he was not to be found in the Temple. All seemed very quiet and worship was being celebrated. It was calming to hear a cantor's voice ringing in the halls of the Temple.

"Come Mary, let's go to a little café where the rabbi often visits to get a hot drink," I said as I left the Temple and started to across the street. When we went past the curtained doorway into the café it was very dark and Mary grabbed my hand. We stood still to allow our eyes to adjust to the darkness. There sat Rabbi Levi in the back corner with a cup of something to drink. We walked up to the table: "Are we interrupting anything?" I asked.

"Oh, Lazarus, come and sit here with me," he suddenly saw Mary, jumped up, bowed to her, and sat back down. We found ourselves looking at a man who seemed very disturbed. I had never seen the Rabbi in that kind of a mood.

"Rabbi, are you all right?" I inquired.

"Yes…No…I'm not sure what I am right now. Lazarus, please, can you tell me what is happening. I have heard so many different stories, and it has me completely confused and disturbed. Yes, I am troubled, and I don't mind admitting it. What I am hearing just cannot be, but I don't know what I want to hear. The priests say one thing; the people are saying something else, and I am caught in the middle. Oh, why is it my lot to know Jesus so intimately as a young man; and, yet know him so little spiritually. Lazarus, do not go to any of the gates into Jerusalem to listen to the elders. You are known by many of those elders and quite honestly you may be attacked by some very hostile people."

"Rabbi, I can understand your troubled feelings and thoughts because that is where we are. The stories about these last few days, they are all confused, different, and

some are troubling while others are glorious. All of us, who know Jesus, are trying to sort through each piece of information to find the truth, even the disciples are struggling."

Rabbi Levi looked around the room with almost fear in his eyes and then whispered as he leaned forward, "Lazarus, tell me," he looked away and stopped, "Tell me," he stopped and looked around again and leaned closer to me and then whispered, "What happened to the body of Jesus?"

He suddenly nodded his head and very gently said, "No, don't answer that yet." He then spoke to Mary, "Your name is Mary, isn't it?"

Mary almost choked as she said, "Yes, rabbi, I am Lazarus's youngest sister and we have been very close. Today, he had to run an errand and I asked to go with him. He is always very kind to me."

"I am glad you are here." The rabbi finally gave Mary a very brief smile that looked more like a grimace of pain. He glanced around the room again before whispering, "I would like to hear from someone I trust about what happened to Jesus's body. Please, speak very quietly because there are many ears in this room."

I waited for a few minutes thinking about the best way that I could tell him about the resurrection of Jesus. "Rabbi, I will say again, there is a lot that we do not understand, but I can tell you what I have heard and beheld. Jesus's body was placed in a tomb provided by Joseph of Arimathea."

"Oh, wait did you say Joseph of Arimathea," he seemed almost shocked.

"Yes," I said as I also nodded.

"That is very interesting," he said as he became very quiet. So, again I waited while he was lost in thought...

I started again, "It was Joseph who went before Pilate and obtained a release order for us to take Jesus's body down from the cross before the Sabbath began. He led us to a tomb he owned in the Garden close by."

"Was he a friend of Jesus?" asked the Rabbi, "I know him quite well and if he is a believer in his teachings, I will listen to what he has to say."

"Yes," I said, "he and Jesus had met a number of times to talk about spiritual issues. He seemed to be a great admirer of Jesus and Jesus respected him just as much."

Rabbi Levi got very quiet and looked away. When he looked back to me he whispered again, "Where is his body?"

"I cannot tell you. I myself went to the grave and his body was not there. Martha, my older sister, counted the grave clothes that were folded on the rock slab in the tomb and everything the women had used was there. Rabbi, Jesus had told me he would be raised from the dead, and I thought of it as some spiritual awakening for him, and for all the rest of us. There is nothing more that I can say except, he has risen from the dead."

Rabbi Levi folded his arms across his chest, leaned back in his chair, closed his eyes, and raised his face slightly toward heaven. Finally, he spoke very quietly as he opened his eyes. "You say his body was gone from the grave. You believe that he is raised from the dead?"

"Yes, Rabbi, I cannot believe anything else," I said.

"Thank you, Lazarus. I will now wait and hope to see Jesus and look forward to a visit with Joseph. I must get back to the Temple, but I want to thank you for coming, you have been a great help to me."

"It was good to see you Rabbi, and I will look forward to another time." He scooted off in one direction and I took Mary's hand, and we left the café and started toward home."

We took an extra long time in our walk home. We talked about Jesus all the way: about his ministry, his healings, his love of all people, his devotion to his Father in heaven, his loyalty to his family on earth, how he told us what was going to happen and our unwillingness to believe it and on and on and on. Several times we stopped and would keep looking at each other while we talked and talked.

Once we were standing in the road talking and were nearly run down by two horses and their riders. They were flying down the road toward Bethany. I pulled Mary out of the way and yelled, "Slow down before you kill someone." One of the horses stopped so quickly it reared up on it's hind legs and turned. The rider walked the horse back toward us and swung off landing on the ground and faced us. Mary was hiding behind me, she was so frightened. He removed the covering over his face.

"Julian, what are you doing here?" I shouted. By that time the other horse came and the rider revealed his face and it was Jonathan.

"Friends of Jesus and children of the King of Heaven. Welcome to Bethany and what, may I ask, are you doing here?"

Jonathan spoke, "We heard that there was trouble in Jerusalem for Jesus and we rode like the wind to get here. You are not the only ones we nearly ran over trying to get here in time to help if we are needed."

"I am confused, help with what?" I asked.

"That is what we do not know. Except we have been told Jesus had been arrested," said Julian."

"News travels fast and you faster. Let's go to our house and we will fill you in on much more that has happened," I said and turned to go home. They followed leading their horses and we were soon at our house. Mama came out of the house and was startled to find two men with horses in our yard. Judas followed Mama out of the house and I told him, "Take these horses and tie them at the shed and give them some water."

"Mama, welcome Jonathan and Julian," I said.

She gasped and said, "I would never have recognized the two of you dressed as you are. Come in and let me serve you something to eat and drink." She walked back in the house and we followed as both Jonathan and Julian stripped off their head coverings and outer robes.

Mama immediately began giving orders, "The two of you take the basins with water that we will give you and go to the wash board outside and wash your face and hands and then bring the bowl back and we will wash your feet."

They did as they were ordered and Martha and Mary washed their feet and threw the water outside. By then Mama had some food on the table and we all sat down.

"Was Jesus really arrested?" Julian asked.

"Yes, he was," I said, "and much more. He was taken before Pilate, Herod and the Chief Priests. And he was sentenced to be crucified." Both men gasped.

Jonathan jumped in very quickly, "Surely, someone appealed that sentence and he was set free."

"No, Jonathan, he carried his own cross to a hill called Golgotha and there was crucified with two criminals." Both Jonathan and Julian began talking and shouting at each other at the same time. What they were saying made no sense. I held my hand up for silence and continued, "We were there and watched him die on that cross. It was agony! Being close to the Sabbath, a friend offered a grave and Jesus was buried in that borrowed grave. On the first day of the week, yesterday, some of the women returned to the grave to anoint his body but he was gone. He had risen from that grave and right now we do not know where he may be, but let me assure you that several have seen him."

Jonathan and Julian just sat there. Several times they started to speak, but it was as though they either forgot what they were going to say or they thought better about saying what was on their minds at that moment.

"The disciples are going to meet this evening to talk and pray about what they need to do. Let me assure you, these recent days have been hard and most of all for Aunt Mary, Jesus's mother."

"You did say he died," asked Julian.

"Yes, I helped take him down from that cross only after we got an order from Pilate that we could have his body for burial before the Sabbath."

Jonathan had been quietly crying but then spoke, "What makes you think that his body was not stolen?"

I continued, "The small tomb had a large stone rolled in front of the entrance and the Temple Priests had two of their most trusted Temple Guards there to watch for any mischief. I will say, they were found asleep, but it would have taken a lot of effort by a number of strong men to roll that stone away, and they would have awakened those guards. Jesus has risen; he is a victor over death."

At that moment two women appeared at the doorway. They seemed very nervous and I was searching in my mind for where I had seen them before. Mama went to them and one of them introduced herself as Mary from Magdala. She immediately asked, "Is Jesus's mother here?"

"Come in, she is right here."

Aunt Mary stepped around and embraced her and was introduced to her friend who was also a Mary. Mama had the two women sit down, and they kept looking at all the people in the room with a great deal of uneasiness.

Aunt Mary spoke, "You asked for me, so can I be of help to you?" she asked.

Mama brought them a warm drink, and they took it with definite appreciation.

"Mary," said Mary of Magdala. "we felt we needed to find you and bring you news about your son, Jesus."

"Please, please, if you have word from him or about him please share it with all of us. These are all friends of Jesus." She pointed to me and said, "This is Lazarus whom Jesus raised from the dead after he had died in this very house."

"Oh, how blessed you are," Mary of Magdala said.

"Yes," I said, "we had been best friends since we were young boys."

Mary of Magdala straightened her robes a little and then began to amaze us. "Mary and I were at the crucifixion and stayed at a distance with the other women for as long as we could stand it." She started to shed quiet tears. "We heard where he was buried and I asked Mary to go with me very early before light so that we would not be visible to pray at the tomb." She was very nervous and Aunt Mary reached out and took her hand to reassure her.

Mary of Magdala continued,

> *When we arrived at the tomb, suddenly:*
> There was a great earthquake, an angel of the Lord came
> down from Heaven, went forward and rolled back the
> stone, and took his seat upon it. His appearance was
> dazzling like lightning and his clothes were white as snow.

The guards shook with terror at the sight of him and
collapsed like dead men.

Do you think we are making up what we are telling you?"
"No, child, please continue. You are bearing to us good news,
and we are all eager to hear what you have to tell us," said Aunt
Mary. "Now, continue as we all pray while you talk."

> The angel spoke to us: do not be afraid. I know that you
> are looking for Jesus who was crucified. He is not here—
> he is risen, just as he said he would.
> Come and look at the place where he was lying. Then go
> quickly and tell his disciples that he is risen from the dead.

"We went in the tomb and were very frightened. We have
not been able to find the disciples. Someone told us that perhaps
some of them may be here at Lazarus's home."

Aunt Mary quietly said, "You were told right. There are five of
them here; so you have done well to come."

"Wait," said Mary of Magdala, "there is more."

Everyone froze and drew closer to her.

> "The angel continued, *Listen, he goes before you into Galilee!*
> You will see him there! Now I have told you my message.
> We left very quickly to be on our way to find the disciples:
> Our hearts
> were filled with awe and great joy.
> We ran to give the news to the disciples.
> But quiet suddenly, Jesus stood before us in our path, and
> said, Peace be with you!
> We went forward to meet him
> and clasping his feet we worshipped him.
> Then Jesus said to us, do not be afraid.
> Go now and tell my brothers
> to go to Galilee and they shall see me there.

So, we have delivered his word to you and we will now be
on our way and return to our homes by the Sea of Galilee. If it

is God's Will perhaps we will see you again sooner than any of us expect.

Peter was listening so intently that the two Marys were almost out the door when he said, "Wait, wait...First, thank you for coming and being the bearer of good news. We will share your message with the other disciples when we see them this evening. You said that Jesus told you to tell us to go to Galilee and he would see us there. Did he say where in Galilee?"

"I have told you exactly what he said to us:

Go into Galilee and they shall see me there.

"Thank you again. Have a safe journey home and we will also hope to see you in Galilee," said Peter.

"That is very specific," said John, "it seems to me that we should leave for home as soon as possible."

Priscilla, John's wife, said, "you should be close to the Sea of Galilee to hopefully see your son if he is going to appear. I would like for you to come and stay with us."

"Let me talk with Benjamin and see what he suggests we do," said Aunt Mary.

"Mother Mary," said Julian, "Jonathan and I would like to go with you and Benjamin to be your security while you travel. We will be ready when you are ready."

"Things are happening a little too fast," said Peter, "first let's have our meeting tonight and then make plans about returning to Galilee."

Everyone agreed and suddenly we realized that it was really time to leave and see who would be in that upper room. Peter invited everyone there to be a part of the meeting and all agreed to go except Mama and Martha.

We scurried out the door and were on our way. When we arrived all the other disciples were already there except for Judas. The room was ready and everyone gathered and sat down. All got extremely quiet. We were all looking around as though we expected Jesus to walk into the room and be in command of our conversation.

John finally spoke up, "Let's have a time of prayer. Anyone here can speak a prayer as God leads you. So, let us pray."

It was very quiet for a long time. Nathaniel broke the silence as he lifted his hands toward heaven and prayed, "God of wisdom, please enable us to see the way and help us to divide your word of truth with faithfulness and devotion to Jesus. He called us to follow him. He challenged us to go out and serve him and you. We are ready to go and serve even if it demands from us more than we want to give. Here we are, take us, use us, fill us, empower us. All to your glory. Amen."

Andrew chimed in immediately: "God, Father of us all, I feel lost, alone and very frustrated. I need your Son, my Lord. He kept me going in the right direction and I need his guiding spirit to give me direction and purpose and to help me see a light of hope."

"Help Lord, my life is frayed and torn," cried out Matthew, "feed me Lord, feed me with your righteousness and love. Help me to be a light in the world to bring hope,

joy and peace. Make me a better follower of your Son. He has risen and we must help others discover him as the risen Christ and come with us to follow him. Amen."

Simon spoke and his voice broke, "God of heaven and earth… can you hear me? I am scared." Those words came out as desperation and several of the disciples got up and went to him and put their arms around him. "Can you hear me God? Can you hear me Jesus? I'm scared. I need the comfort of your voice and the strength of your words of victory! I don't want to be a coward. Help me! Help me! Help me be what you would have me be! Please! Please! Help me!"

Peter got up and walked over to where Simon was crying, "Dear God of everyday and every person. I'm scared too." He stopped briefly and started again. "Forgive me Lord. Forgive me Jesus! I denied you three times as you predicted at our Passover meal." There was a gasp that swept across the room. "My loud expressions of loyalty have been nothing more than whimpering words revealing my failure. Help me Lord! Forgive me Jesus! I am so weak. Help me do better! Please! Help me do better."

John stood and walked around the room. "Lord Jesus, you told us to come to you; so, here I am. Thank you for your trust in me. May my loyalty to you and your mother be a blessing to you and your mother in heaven and on earth. Let me be an instrument of your righteousness. When others hear and see me may they find the gift of your presence within me. May your love and quietness shine from me. Amen"

It was Thaddaeus who could not keep from crying but when he prayed his voice rang clear. "Thank you Jesus for calling me to be one of your disciples. Help me, strengthen me, empower me that I may not disappoint you. May I so serve you that others will be blessed and I will be known as a faithful and vocal disciple who is unashamed to speak your name."

There was a long silence before Thomas spoke: "Jesus, hear me, I said to the disciples, let's go with you to Jerusalem and die with you here but I would rather live and serve you. Yes, Jesus, I am scared. Cure my fear so that it will not cripple my witness. Fill me with the fire of your spirit. I am ready to be your servant. Yes, I am ready. Amen."

James, the son of Alpheus, was so quiet. His words were part grunt and muttering but his heart was as pure as gold. "God of the heavens and the earth. You brought our people out of Egypt and through the wilderness, Do it again Lord. We are ready to march where you would send us into a new Promised Land. Amen."

Philip had been standing by a very small window for some time. His voice filled the room with searching yet with strength. "Jesus hear all of us, now and in the hard days that will come. Make us strong enough to face those tumultuous hours of hardship and sustain us to win many victories in your Name. Amen".

Again, there was a long silence and eventually John spoke to James, his brother. "We are waiting James, you are the last one."

James replied, "I have been praying the whole time with each of you. So, Amen. Lord, Amen."

There was a lot of quiet stirring in the room. Peter said, "It is now time to go to Galilee and wait for Jesus to meet us there. You are welcome to come to our house at any time. I will see you there. Go in peace."

They all scattered with only a few lingering to talk. We walked home without saying a word to each other. It was confusing to Mama and Martha when we came to the house so soon after we left and then we sat down and there was not a word spoken. Mama kept looking at me.

Aunt Mary finally got up and told Jonathan and Julian that she would be ready to leave for home in the morning.

I suddenly spoke, "Wait a minute and let's all make some plans. Peter has asked everyone to go to Galilee to wait there for Jesus to meet us. So, I would suggest that we all leave tomorrow. Aunt Mary we will drop you off in Nazareth."

"Wait a minute," said Aunt Mary, "you are not going to drop me off. I want to be with the disciples when my Jesus meets with them in Galilee." Everyone laughed and that broke some of the tension that was there in the room. Aunt Mary got up and went to Mama and took her hand and they left the house for a visit and I am sure they made many plans.

Jonathan said, "Lazarus, you will move on to my house, you and your family can stay with us." We all got very busy making ready for tomorrow.

There was only one goal, to leave immediately for Galilee!

Life Is Good

I went immediately and brought Judas, my partner back to the house. I told him that we were planning to go to Galilee for an extended stay and asked if he could stay in our house for protection until our return.

"Lazarus, Jonah and I need to go on another buying trip, but I will see that your house will be protected and when we return my wife and I will move into your house."

"Thank you Judas, and I will probably make the rounds in Galilee to see what is available for me to bring back. I must get back to work with a family to support. Let me take two of the donkeys and if I need another I will purchase one or two.

The next morning came early but we were soon loaded and ready to go. Julian encouraged Aunt Mary to ride on one of the horses, but she would not even consider it and got on one of the donkeys. By the time we were on the other side of Jerusalem Aunt Mary and Mama were walking. We stopped to see Daniel. It was rather late in the afternoon and by the time a light meal was graciously provided by Rachael we settled in for the night. The women slept in the house and the men in the shed. Daniel joined us because he wanted to hear more about Jesus being cru-cified and his resurrection. He was so excited and Julian seemed to answer most of his questions with great enthusiasm. Very early the next morning we were on the road. Rachael had fixed us some light refreshments for which we were deeply grateful. Once on the road, there was virtually no conversation, we had a set pur-pose, to get to Galilee and wait for Jesus; that was all any of us wanted to do.

We stopped for a second night outside of Sebaste and camped. Julian was very careful to see that the men maintained a safety watch for everyone. The next day when we arrived in Nazareth, Jesus's family was thrilled to see us. There was a lot of explain-ing to the family that had not gone to Jerusalem and there were many, many tears.

Quietly James' wife and several women from the community prepared a wonderful evening meal. We gathered about the table and it was James who shared a blessing, "Father of heaven and earth; Father of the mysterious and what is known; Father of all that is seen and unseen, bless us in this moment. Open the windows of heaven that we may find our brother and shepherd Jesus. Enable us to become one as a family of earth that we may be strong to become a family of heaven. Bless all our needs and bless the food that has been so graciously prepared. Glory be to the name of Jesus. Amen.

Aunt Mary spoke up and said, "Let's have a relaxed and happy meal. Thank all of you who prepared these wonderful dishes so quickly. What a wonderful family be have. All of you have been a special support during some very hard times and some very joyful

moments as well. My mind carries many memories that sing with joy and a few that bring sorrow and pain to my soul. "I want you to always remember that all that has happened was in God's plan and we would never have wanted to put ourselves between Jesus and his heavenly Father. When he appears to us sometime in these next few days we will then know how to make any plans that will be important to our family."

Rest came quickly for all of us when we found our special place to lay down for the night.

The next morning Jonathan and Julian prepared my family to leave for his house. Martha and Mary had a hard time leaving the twins and their beautiful families. But soon we were on the road even though Mama appeared to be very tired.

Abigail welcomed us and was eager to hear all the news. So, we had to go through all of that with her and Abigail; plus, Samson and Tamar had come to the house just before we arrived. We were beginning to be able to share that wonderful and amazing story about Jesus without so many tears. Laughter was beginning to return to our circle as we sat down to share an evening meal.

Aunt Mary looked at Julian and asked him to have a blessing.

He froze but quietly raised his face and hands to the heavens and said, "Glorious Father in heaven hear our prayer. Jesus, friend and Son of that glorious Father, help us to stand tall and firm to face a new life. Bless what we share about this table, bless our conversation, bless our rest this night, bless our watching and waiting for these next days and bless Bernice who is carrying our child whose name will be either Joshua or Mary. Amen."

The table exploded with laugher, congratulations and blessings directed toward Bernice and Julian. The women were hugging Bernice and she properly shed some warm tears of gratitude and excitement.

The meal was soon over and all got very quiet. Aunt Mary got up and went to Bernice and sat down beside her. She looked directly into her eyes for a long time. "Blessings on you my child. As you move toward the day of birthing. My love, prayers and help will be with you. There is no more exciting time. It will be filled with mystery and joy, some pain and a lot of questions." People, especially the women were nodding with excitement and anticipation.

Aunt Mary raised her hand asking for silence. We began to realize that she wanted to talk.

She patted Bernice on her arm and tears suddenly flooded her eyes. Everyone became very quiet. "As Julian announced the birth of new life, my mind reached back to when I heard the news that I would bear a child whose name would be Jesus. My heart pounded with excitement but when I announced it to my family and a few friends, anger stirred deep and accusations were alarming. I found that my joy turned to fear and that quickly turned to terror.

Threats were made against Joseph by my family. They were considering stoning him. I was betrothed but we had not come together as man and wife.

I again explained to both families about Gabriel, but sneers and cruel laughter were the response to such a story. His family made threats toward me and a few stones were even thrown which never hit me. The pressure became so unbearable that one day I decided to run away and go to see my cousin Elizabeth whose husband was a Temple priest. They lived south of Jerusalem. I did not really know where they lived. My family had visited them years ago when I was about eleven years old. I did not tell Joseph or anyone. I just left early one morning with a few things hidden under my clothes."

Aunt Mary became very quiet and there were a lot of wide eyes watching her with some murmuring. Aunt Mary again raised her hand. She looked for a long time at Bernice and began speaking.

"It was a long journey. Most of the time I dressed as a man and carried one of their walking sticks and a small jar slung over my shoulder with water. In the late afternoon I would find a place to hide, change my clothes and then at a market find a little food to eat. I was tired, sore, lonely and very frightened. It took me two weeks to get to Elizabeth's.

When I arrived and spoke to her, identifying myself, outside her home she embraced me, and I collapsed into her arms."

Everyone gasped and some tears were being shed. James, her son moved to sit down beside her, and she laid her head on his shoulder for a few moments before continuing her story.

"Elizabeth took me into her house and prepared a warm bath and then put me to bed. I will never forget that she sat beside me and sang lullabies as I finally drifted off to sleep. I slept all that day, all night and late into the next morning When I awoke it was then that I found out that Elizabeth was in her sixth month of carrying her child who was to be called John. The story of her pregnancy was almost as exciting and disruptive as mine. We shared our stories and began to laugh and sing praises to God the Most High."

Elizabeth's husband had not come home from his work at the Temple where he would stay for weeks. That gave Elizabeth and me time for a long visit. I explained the reasons for my leaving home and coming to be with her. I talked about the threats made against both Joseph and me and explained that I had come to be with her because of fears for my safety.

She told me about her pregnancy and how God announced to Zechariah that regardless of their older age they would have a son. She told me how Zechariah laughed at God in disbelief and he was struck dumb and would remain so until their son is born.

Time flew by and I found myself still at Elizabeth's after almost three months. The time was getting close for her delivery.

One morning we were sitting in front of her house when I saw a man approaching us on the path to their house. My mind told me that the man sure did walk like Joseph. Suddenly my eyes assured me it was Joseph. I jumped up, squealed with delight as I ran to him and leapt into his arms. Tears were bathing our faces and kisses sprang from the joy of our hearts.

Finally we stood looking at each other with broad smiles on our faces and he said, "I have come to take you home. All is well there now, and they are ready to receive you."

"How did you know I was here?" I asked.

"I was pleading to God to know what had happened to you, and he told me to come here and bring you home."

Again, there were embraces which included Elizabeth. She fixed Joseph something to eat and he shared all the news from home. My mother, Elizabeth, has come to believe I am dead and had been sorely grieving for me. Such news brought tears to my eyes and I began to long to see my family in Nazareth.

Joseph rested two days and three nights and then we started home. We arrived in Nazareth under the cover of eventide and received a quiet welcome. My mother, Elizabeth, slept outside our room that night for fear that I would disappear again. Soon after that is when we received the news of the decree by Caesar Augustus that a census would be taken and we would need to travel to Bethlehem. That again would give us some rest from suspicious eyes and sharp words."

"Mother Mary," Bernice spoke up, "why didn't Joseph come for you earlier?"

"Bernice, don't be hard on Joseph," she said, "he was one of the most gentle and caring persons in this world, but I had not left any evidence or notes about where I was going. He did search a number of places, Cana was one of them."

James spoke up, "But, Mother why had you never told this story to the family. After all you had told a lot of other stories."

"You are right my son, but your father did not like me to speak of this part of our life experience. He became frightened if I ever spoke of it, and I did not want to bring him any more pain about that incident. That was a hard vigil for him.

So, the cycle of life continues and we are now called to a new time to possibly see Jesus. Life has been good because God is so good in his mercy and love. Come my children let's be busy to care for life that we will be ready when Jesus calls us."

Aunt Mary got up and everyone followed to clean and put things away. It was surprising how long that took.

After a light refreshment at noon the disciple Nathaniel appeared at the house. He was the bearer of good news. He was a very happy person, "several of the disciples have seen Jesus and he requested that you come to Capernaum and wait on his appearance again there."

It was good that we had straightened the house because everyone was standing outside ready to go. I had even brought two donkeys and they were loaded with personal things.

We were soon on our way and arrived at John's house by early evening. Priscilla, John's wife, had already planned where each of us might stay and she assigned us to families surrounding their house.

It was very difficult to sleep that night. In fact, I was up and outside most of the night. The night was warm and the moon was full, so some of us visited in that twilight just about all night long. Julian was like a military guard walking back and forth. When he spoke, it was crisp and to the point. From time to time, he would stop and pray and we could understand about half his words.

John came out of his house and looked around.

There was Julian right by his side. John asked him if he would mind taking Peter a message. Julian snapped to attention and John said, "Please ask Peter if he is planning on fishing today and where will he and the others gather? I am planning to go with them."

"Is that all, sir?" Julian quipped.

"Yes, thank you, Julian."

With that Julian turned and trotted off just like an official Roman courier. It was really exciting to see.

John stood there, watched him, and quietly chuckled before he turned and returned into the house.

Several of the group talked a little about Julian and the interesting addition he made to the followers of Jesus.

We had hardly finished that conversation when here came Julian trotting up the street. He went directly to John's house and called for John, who appeared immediately.

"You are back so soon," said John.

"Peter was outside his house with Andrew assembling some fishing nets. They are planning to go to Lake Tiberias to fish since there have been recent reports from there of excellent catches."

"Thank you, Julian. Now, we must notify any other disciples who would like to go along. I will leave immediately with James and Nathaniel," said John.

There was considerable activity as people began moving toward Peter's house. I decided I would go along even though I was not a fisherman. When we arrived at Peter's they were on the verge of leaving. It was explained to me that Peter's and Andrew's family fished on Lake Galilee but referred to the northern shore of Lake Galilee as Lake Tiberias. They kept a small boat available in that area for convenience when they received news about good catches being made in the inlets and lagoons.

These fishermen were strong walkers and I was working to keep up with them. Several of the disciples dropped by the wayside but Peter and Andrew kept leading the way to the north shore and the rest would catch up in time.

Light was beginning to appear in the east as we arrived at a small boat dock and preparations were quickly made to launch the boat. It was a small craft and I was not going to go with them. Since I was not a fisherman, I would only be in the way. But, I was fascinated in watching them sail a short distance out in the water.

Half light helped them to see enough to drop their nets several times and pull them up with no fish. Peter was barking orders and James was correcting him while John laughed at both of them. I was sitting on the shore watching a comedy show and from time to time I would laugh out loud.

There was some rustling in the grass behind me, and I jumped thinking I was disturbing some animal when a hand pressed down on my shoulder telling me to stay still. I looked up straight into the face of Jesus. My heart nearly stopped as I saw him mouth, "Good morning, best friend" and he motioned for me to remain quiet.

He called out to those in the boat, "Children, have you any food?"

They answered back with no thought that they were talking to Jesus.

"No," they called.

"Cast your nets on the opposite side of your boat, and you will find plenty." he called.

They did as he suggested and pulled in a huge catch.

Peter turned and looked to shore and called out, "It is the Lord!"

Peter grabbed his outer robe which he had removed and covered himself. He jumped into the sea to come ashore. The others came in the boat and got out to greet Jesus and I stood up. It was a quiet but heavenly kind of greeting. We saw a small bed of hot coals where we could cook our fish and there was bread there also.

"Come now and let us eat our morning meal." The disciples kept staring at Jesus but seemed afraid to call him by name. He looked the same but he didn't look the same. What the difference was I could not say.

When the fish had been cooked Jesus raised his face and hands heavenward and there was that subtle glow surrounding his face and head. How wonderful it was to see it again. Jesus was quiet and so were we but we felt surrounded by the power of eternity. Then he passed the fish and bread to us. I found out later that this was the third time the disciples had seen Jesus since he was raised from the dead.

The meal was shared with much quietness.

It was Jesus who broke the silence, "Simon, son of Jonah, let me ask you, do you love me with a divine love filled with the power of God and his righteousness? Do you love me more than these who have gathered here?"

Peter seemed taken back completely. When you think about it, any of us have been desperate for an answer. What did Jesus mean. We waited on Peter's answer.

"Jesus I love you like a brother who belongs in my life," responded Peter.

All eyes turned to Jesus and he seemed disappointed but responded, Then Peter go forth and feed my sheep who are waiting."

"Peter let me ask you again," Jesus remained quiet for a few minutes and then looked up into Peter's face, "is it possible for you to love me with a love that wells out of God's heart into your heart and then feeds my need for love and spiritual strength?"

"Jesus, I affirm before these here that I love you like my favorite brother," said Peter. Then Peter go forth and feed my lambs."

We were all struggling with Jesus' questioning as if he was questioning us.

Jesus looked at Peter with a tear in his eye, "Then Peter you can only love me as an earthly brother. With a love that will sometimes grow cold and forget me. But, you are saying that is where your love meets my love?"

"Yes, Lord, you know all things and that is my love toward you. I, Andrew, John, James, and the others. That is all I have to give. You know that I love you."

"Thank you, Peter, I ask that you and the others feed my sheep. Be diligent in your love for all people and search your love for me as you grow to understand the meaning and power of justice and mercy. Let your love for me be your guide. Feed my sheep. All of them."

Jesus turned and walked out on the sea and disappeared in the midst. We all sat there in silence with both our minds and hearts racing.

Would we ever see him again? Where did he come from? Where did he go? Why didn't he stay longer to teach and guide us?

That is the last time I would see him or hear him speak to me. No, that is not right because I often could think about Jesus and still hear him say with that quiet smile, "Hello, best friend." And then there was always that quiet chuckle.

"What a memory and what a best friend."

Hallelujah

Jonathan, Julian, and I spent most of our time in Capernaum with the eleven disciples waiting for another possible appearance of Jesus. We did not see him again, but we would keep telling our stories and experiences, the miracles and marvels of this divine Son of the Almighty.

The disciples told us about Jesus's final appearances and his Ascension into the heavens. It would have been wonderful to have been there, but we were blessed and we knew it.

Jonathan convinced us to stay in Galilee and visit our home in Bethany from time to time. He built us a beautiful house, and I still worked to buy merchandise and take it to Bethany. Judas and I would work together selling it and making other business contacts to continue supporting our families. Wherever possible we made our witness about Christ, "My best friend."

Julian and Bernice had a beautiful son who was called Joshua. That little boy reminded us often of Jesus; and Martha and Mary adopted him for their own; and they joyfully marched to his orders; and he soaked up their love and grew in "wisdom and stature before God and Man."

Judas and his wife moved into our home and had two beautiful children. It was always good to be in Bethany again, but my heart was not there, nor was it in that beautiful house Jonathan built for us.

My heart was always homesick for heaven where my "best friend" sat at the right hand of our heavenly Father. Praise be to God! Hallelujah! Amen!